3 Easy Ways to Order
Imani in Young Love & Deception

1.   Order Toll-Free 24 hours/day, 7 days/week:
        866-862-8626

2.   Order by E-mail:
        jackie.hardrick@enlightenpublications.com

3.   Order by Regular Mail: See the order form at the
        back of this book for more details.

*Special discount for an order of 10 books or more
(for more details, see the order form).*

- Also Available -

Discussion Guide for
Imani in Young Love & Deception

The <u>Discussion Guide</u> is a great supplement to the
novel.   The Guide was designed to provoke lively
conversations on the hot issues addressed in the novel,
Imani in Young Love & Deception.

The <u>Discussion Guide</u> is also an educational tool that is
perfect for use in the classrooms, book clubs, youth
organizations, youth mentoring programs, youth church
groups, etc. See the order form at the back of this book
for more details.

Imani

in

Young Love &
Deception

Jackie Hardrick

Enlighten Publications

Imani in Young Love & Deception

Published by Enlighten Publications

Copyright © 1999 by Jacqueline Hardrick
Library of Congress Card Number: 00-110333
ISBN: 0-9706226-0-0

Enlighten Publications
P.O. Box 525
Vauxhall, New Jersey 07088.

Cover design by Stephen Swinton

Printed in the U.S.A.

10 9 8 7 6 5 4 3 2 1

This novel is dedicated to

my dad,

Deacon Eddie B. Hardrick

You passed your storytelling gift on to me
and I'm gonna share it with the world.

Miss You...Love Always

Acknowledgments

I thank God for His partnership in this project and for all of His appointed Angels. I am not foolish enough to take all of the credit.

Thank you Mom, Melba Hardrick, for your unconditional love and support. It would take a book as thick as a bible to express my eternal thanks and gratitude for all you have done for me. Love ya so…

Much love to family & friends who didn't see much of me while I was engrossed in this novel but stuck right by me anyhow: Mom, Jeanette, Tyler, Tré, Dean, Gwen, Edward, Uncle Gene, Aunt Ruby, Aunt Bert, Cyndi, Angel, Wendy, Michelle, Bhriana, Timothy, Brandon, Ruth, and…

Kudos to my dynamic duo editors, Cornelia and Celeste Layton. You are one of those Angels I was referring to above. Your commitment & support is priceless.

Gratitude galore to Dr. Gayle Griffin, Dr. Yvette Bridges, Angela Kinamore, Lisa McFarlin, Larry Hall, Stephen Swinton, April Allridge, and every appointed Angel who has aided this project in some way. The list of new supporters continues to grow but to my old crew…

Mom, Gwen, Dean, Jeanette, Sharon, Wendy, Ruth, Cornelia, Celeste, Betsy, April…I cherish all of you, our years together, your words of encouragement and your prayers. Y'all knew that someday this would happen…

Regret

He was buggin' and beggin' that "Oh Baby, Baby,
if you loved me you would."

But he ain't mention the
      Blood
            Pain
                 And Regret.

While he was in a zone, I was all
      Alone
            Dirty
                 And Embarrassed.

Two months gone by and I'm pissed 'cause
I was dissed and I missed
      Oh
            No
                 Not this!

If you hear me Lord, please don't let me get
      Herpes
            Gonorrhea
                 Or Syphilis.

And AIDS - no way!
That's too high a price for a kid to pay.

                                    - Jackie Hardrick

IMANI

Swish.

Imani Jackson smiled as another jump shot caught all net. Practice had ended an hour ago for Westmoore High School's, girl's varsity basketball team, "The Jaguars." Yet, Imani stayed behind to try to perfect her already lethal jump shot. She dribbled against a phantom defender, pulled up and released the ball.

Swish.

"Hey, not bad for a girl," a guy's voice rang out.

Imani looked towards the doorway and there stood Tyler Powers. She felt the need to put that brother in line because nobody dissed Imani Jackson, not her game anyway. "What do you mean 'not bad for a girl'?" Imani asked as Tyler approached her.

When Tyler stood inches away from Imani, she realized that yeah, he was all that. Her eyes scaled his

11

6' something tall frame up to his smooth caramel gorgeous face. Chestnut hued eyes and wavy brown hair topped it all off. Tyler threw his megawatt smile at Imani and she caught sight of his white teeth.

"I was just messin' with you," he began. "I've been checking you out and I like your game." Tyler stroked his faint moustache and surveyed Imani's 5'8" athletic frame from the floor up. "On my worst day, you could probably beat me in a little one-on-one."

Imani recognized his skills too. Although it was his first season on the boy's varsity team, Tyler quickly made his way into the starting line up. His good looks coupled with his on court skills also made Tyler one of the most popular players. Yet, none of that mattered to Imani. She pounded the ball against the pine wood floor and then passed it to Tyler.

"Is today one of those worst days you're talkin' about?"

Tyler appeared surprised that Imani came at him that way but he didn't miss a beat and threw the ball back at her and said, "Ladies first, you take it out."

Imani couldn't help but stare as Tyler unsnapped his bulky Westmoore sky blue and white team jacket and tossed it aside. She checked out his well-developed physique and wondered how was she going to maneuver around all that body.

"All right, let's do this," Tyler said with a smile.

Imani was about to bust a move when the metal gym door slammed and grabbed her attention.

"I've been looking all over for you," Bhriana announced as she pranced onto the court. She wrapped her arms around Tyler's waist, and kissed him on the cheek as she kept one hazel eye on Imani.

Bhriana DuPree was "All dat," so the guys at Westmoore proclaimed, with her long sable colored hair, flawless café au lait complexion, and a size six figure. As far as Imani knew, Bhriana hadn't the chance to cast her magic on Tyler. Rumor had it that she still held Justin, her boyfriend at that moment, captive. Yet, she was all up in Tyler's face.

"Uh Bhriana, you and Tyler got something going on?" Imani asked.

Bhriana threw her shoulders back and her already voluptuous chest protruded even more beneath her gold cashmere sweater. "We go waaay back to grammar school. Right, Tyler?"

"Psst. It wasn't like we were tight," Tyler said then looked at Imani. "I was a straight up geek back then."

"That's not how I remember it at all, Tyler. Everybody looks a little nerdish in grammar school but most of us grow out of it." Bhriana cast her light eyes upon Imani then added, "And others... oh well." Bhriana took a deep breath and looked through Imani as she questioned, "And what's your connection to Tyler?"

"We play the same game at the same school. That's all."

"We were about to get into a little one-on-one. You wanna watch?" Tyler asked.

As Bhriana continued her steadfast glare upon Imani, she responded, "I'm quite sure that playing against what's her name-"

"Imani," Tyler interjected.

"Yeah, whatever," Bhriana replied, "I'm sure it will be quite interesting, but, I'll pass." Bhriana rolled

13

her eyes at Imani and turned to face Tyler. "I wanted to invite you over this weekend. We've been talking on the phone for a while now but I've never had you over." She patted Tyler's flat abs and continued, "We could work out in my new gym or watch videos or listen to CDs or..."

Imani couldn't stand the sound of Bhriana's syrupy high-pitched voice any longer. She turned to Tyler who had a big grin on his face and said, "Hey look Tyler, I'm tired and gonna head home. We can settle this at another time."

Tyler's smile faded. "Are you sure, Imani? I was really looking forward to-"

"Oh Tyler, you heard what she said," Bhriana interjected. "Don't she look tired?"

Imani rolled her eyes and walked away while Bhriana's laughter echoed off the walls.

* * * *

Imani stared out the cloudy window of the bus and thought about how she faced two different worlds since she became a student in that her junior year at Westmoore. Westmoore was a private school located in Hillsdale, an affluent suburb. Residents like Tyler and Bhriana lived there in expensive brick houses or mansions with beautiful green lawns and massive trees. Outsiders like Imani wondered if the owners of those gorgeous homes ever stepped outside. Besides the gardeners, no one ever seemed to be around.

As the bus rolled into Imani's neighborhood, where she'd lived all 16 years of her life, people in every shade of brown came into view. Groups of teenagers stood on the street corners as if they were waiting for something to happen. Imani watched them and recalled a story that her father told her of how the corners used to be a meeting ground to exchange tall tales or to harmonize a cappella. No harm, no foul, just a lot of laughs and camaraderie.

Imani heard similar accounts from senior citizens at her church. Now they were afraid to walk the streets at night or in broad daylight. The street corners and alleys had turned into gang war zones, pharmacies for illegal drugs, stores for stolen goods, and reception areas for bodies for sell.

The bus cruised down Clinton Place. Aside from the well-preserved churches and check cashing centers, several buildings were painful reminders of the 60's riots and plain old urban decay. A millennium later, charred frames of boarded up stores took up city space that could have been used for much needed housing. Most of the ancient high-rise projects were empty shells surrounded by trash filled lots. New one level dwellings replaced a few of them but the same old problems existed.

"Get out of the street!" the bus driver yelled as he honked his horn.

The four boys that he directed his orders to shuffled out of the driver's way.

"And, stay out!" he warned.

Imani shook her head. Why didn't he go down to City Hall and yell at the mayor or somebody? They had no where else to play. Parks and recreation centers were scarce so kids rode their bikes, roller bladed, played touch football and soccer in the street. The one game that wasn't played in the road was basketball. Basketball courts were plentiful.

The bus stopped at the one a few blocks away from Imani's apartment building. She fell in love with basketball on that weather-beaten cracked up court. The rusty net free rim tilted downward from past generations of slam-dunkers who hung onto them. Yet, that court was a little piece of heaven and a refuge that kept many black kids out of trouble. It gave them pride and assurance that if they possessed nothing else in this world, they had game and no one could take that away from them.

"You wanna sit here?" Imani asked a gray-haired elderly woman who entered the crowded bus filled with domestic workers.

"Thanks, Chile," the woman said as she eased on down in the seat. "I can hold that bag for ya."

Imani smiled. "That's all right, I'm getting off at the next stop."

Imani exited the bus and started out on the four-block walk home. On the second block along the route, a pulsating bass accompanied with peppered rap lyrics blasted from the doorway of a graffiti-marred abandoned building. Imani spotted a couple of boys on the crumpled cement steps with a boom box next to them. Each held a brown paper bag with the lip of a bottle in view.

"Party over here," one hollered and motioned Imani to come over.

Imani's eyes zoomed in on the joint between his fingers. She picked up her pace.

"Yo Baby, you gonna da-da-da-diss us like that?" the other asked.

Imani didn't answer. She felt like one of the elders in her church except that those guys looked to be her age. She hated that she was afraid of them. But, in a community where young crackheads replaced old winos and guns replaced fists, Imani's mother drilled it into her that "If it doesn't look right or sound right, keep on steppin'."

"Oh...so it's like that huh? Well go 'head with your stuck up self!" one of the guys yelled out.

Imani's long legs moved on at a brisk pace until she reached her final destination. She opened the door and to Imani's surprise, her best friend, Fatima, was in her living room.

The physical opposite of Imani, Fatima's what the brothers would call "thick." About 5'2" tall, in heels, the 17-year-old junior had hips, thighs, and back. Underneath layers of foundation and blush was a rich chocolate beautiful face. If the diamond stud in her nose or her doe shaped jet black eyes didn't grab a guy's attention, her outgoing personality did.

"Whassup!"

"Hey, Fatima, whatcha doing here?"

"Girrrl, it's one of them rare thangs when I ain't got no date so I decided to drop on by here," Fatima responded and cracked her chewing gum.

"Where's my mom?" Imani asked as she looked about the small room.

"She went out to play the lottery. If y'all hit that million somethin' dollar jackpot, don't be playin' like you don't know me."

Imani laughed.

"Did I say somethin' funny? You know how I get serious when it comes to money."

17

"Oh girl you know we won't forget you. Now come on." The girls hugged then headed to Imani's pint-sized room that she officially called hers since her sister, Roberta, went away to college.

Pictures of Roberta and a collection of her awards concealed many of the cracks and stains on the walls. Roberta's basketball and track trophies and letters also cluttered the top of Imani's wooden dresser. Imani plopped down on her twin-sized bed and sank into the lifeless mattress. She gave Fatima a suspicious look and asked, "So, where's Tyrone, Malcolm, and Money tonight?"

"If I knew that, would I be here with your lonely behind? Did I get all personal and ask you about what's his name?"

"Who?" Imani asked.

"You know who I'm talkin' 'bout. That new tall brotha on the b-ball team."

Fatima was Imani's sole confidante when it came to boys. Any conversation on that hot topic Fatima would never forget. Because of that, Imani knew that Fatima had not forgotten the name of "that new tall brotha."

"If you're talking about Tyler, Girrrl you know-"

Fatima put the palm of her right hand in Imani's face. "Hold up, I know whatcha gonna say. Ain't nothing happenin' or gonna happen with Tyler 'cause I ain't got no time for no serious stuff."

"Go on," Imani said, as she was impressed with Fatima's imitation of her.

"The only way that I'm gonna get to stay at Westmoore is if I get another b-ball scholarship next year so I gotta stay focused."

"And?"

"Oh yeah, and, with the fear of God and my daddy, I can't be messin' around and making no babies."

"And?" asked Imani again.

"And, uh...yeah...you would've said it all proper like my English teacher."

The twosome cracked up. Fatima paused and looked down at her long acrylic nails and then back up to Imani. She popped her gum in rapid succession and then told Imani, "Being for real girl, if I was you, I would go after that man. He's fine and ain't he rich too?"

"And so is Bhriana," Imani said. She laid down on her back and looked up at the dingy white paint chipped ceiling. "You should have seen Bhriana all over Tyler in the gym today. It's not that I'm interested in him but I would hate to see what seems to be a really cool guy get mauled by her claws." Imani sucked her teeth and added, "Shooot, even if I wanted too, I can't compete with Bhriana."

"Says who? I ain't never met that girl up close and personal and all. But from what I've seen of her out there cheering, she ain't all dat."

Fatima pulled her best friend up off the bed and directed her to the cracked mirror above the dresser. "Check you out, Girl. You're tall and lean but not sickly looking like them models. So what if you got some bumps on your face you still look good." Fatima stroked the contour of her own pear-shaped face. "Bhriana may be high yella but trust me, most brothas like their meat well done."

Imani blushed. Fatima could make her laugh ever since second grade when they first met. Fatima proceeded with her observations and continued to wear out that piece of gum.

"Them braids are tired but I know you sweat a lot and can't afford regular touch-ups. But, I know you can afford to pierce them ears."

Imani stroked her meaty ear lobes with her long slender fingers.

"And buy some nail polish, they cheap too," Fatima added.

Imani checked out her short raggedy nails and had to admit that they looked horrible. Ever since kindergarten, Imani bit her fingernails whenever she was nervous. "I thought you were supposed to talk about my good points...and ease up on that gum."

"It's better than eatin' up my nails. Look at 'em thangs of yours. Girrrl, I'm just keeping it real and tryin' to help a sistah out." Fatima pulled Imani's shoulders back, "And stop hunching over, you can stand up straighter than that. Didn't Roberta school you on this stuff?"

Imani looked around her walls and sat back down on the bed. "You know Roberta never had time for me. She was too busy winning all those awards. I hear more about her than actually talking to her and if one more teacher or coach tells me how great she is, Girrrl, I swear I'll lose it!" Imani exclaimed then took a deep breath and asked calmly, "Can we talk about something else?"

"Well dang. Do you hafta act all possessed every time I mention Roberta?" Fatima sat down next to a subdued Imani. "Well, forget her. Back to Tyler. If you wanna keep him away from that snooty you-know-what, you did call her snooty right?"

"That's how she acts," Imani replied.

"Then like I started to say, you could do it, but-"

"But what?"

"You may hafta give it up."

"Give what up, Fatima?"

Fatima rolled her eyes and sucked her teeth. "Oh come on little virgin you know what I'm talkin' about. I ain't sayin' he's gonna marry you or nothing but he can buy you stuff. Shoot, who do you think bought me this leather jacket? That's what boyfriends are for."

"You're just a little virgin too," Imani said and punched Fatima's arm. "And, I'm not puttin' out for any, Gucci, Mucci, or Smucci 'cause it ain't worth it. I can't believe your attitude and..."

"What's a Mucci and a Smucci?" Fatima asked with a confused look on her face.

"I just made those up but you know what I'm talking about. All that designer crap Weavin' Wanda, Big Butt Barbara, Tomika, Cassandra, and the rest of 'em be profiling in and ain't got a pot to piss in."

"Dang, you sound like my grandma."

Imani poked out her lips like she held snuff in her mouth and tried her best to imitate Fatima's grandmother. "And Baby, I worry 'bout you hanging around so many different boys. No decent girl would behave like that."

"Chill, Grandma, I'm just havin' a good time," Fatima replied as she played along with Imani.

"A good time, huh? What if one of 'em wanna carry that good time a little further and doesn't take no for an answer and rape you or even kills you or both?

21

Lord Jesus I don't know what I'd do if you came up dead."

"I ain't even sweatin' that. I got my own back." Fatima giggled and added, "How you like my rap?"

"I hope you can rap your way out of trouble if one of those big brothas you be hanging out with turns on you."

"How did this script flip to me? We were talkin' 'bout you and Tyler."

"Well let me tell you about me."

"Oh Lord," Fatima said with her eyes rolled up to the ceiling. "I done heard this a million times."

Imani stood back up and put her hands on her narrow hips. "Well too bad because I hear it from my parents everyday about how lucky I am to be going to Westmoore. How I have a chance to go to college and they didn't. How they have worked like dogs for years and look at where that's gotten us. Stuck here."

Fatima remained silent and stared at her friend as Imani looked around her tiny room. "Mom says college is my way out. I ain't Cinderella and this ain't no fairy tale. I can't depend on some rich boy to rescue me... I've got to rescue me."

"Hey, I hear ya but I worry about you too. Not the boy thing but you look beat down sometimes. You're in school all day, studyin' most of the night, and playin' b-ball everyday."

"Westmoore's no joke. I have to study more just to keep up. And, you've seen the competition on the court. I have to bust my butt if I'm gonna get another scholarship." Imani threw her hands up in despair, "Yeah, I'm tired but what else can I do?"

"Chill out sometimes."

"I do," Imani said in a meek tone.

"When?"

"Uh, like when I'm cooking or reading poetry, or reading mysteries."

Fatima turned up her pug nose and laughed. "That's the same old same old you been doing. I like watching mysteries and detective shows but clubbin' is my new thang. That's how I be chillin'."

Fatima's cell phone rang and startled them. Fatima retrieved the flip phone from inside her designer handbag and pulled up the antennae. She spit her chewing gum out into her hand. "You know who you called so speak."

"Yo Money, what's up?"

Imani watched Fatima out of the corner of her eye.

"You must be psychic. You know I'm down with that," Fatima said. "Pick me up at eight and we can hang until the club starts jumping at about 10 o' clock that way Grandma won't give me no flack about cuttin' out too late." After a few seconds of silence, Fatima said, "Later," and plopped the used gum back into her mouth.

Imani didn't know much about Money other than he was a 18-year-old high school drop out who always had money in his pockets. Fatima could never explain how he earned that money. She gave Fatima a "what were we just talking about," look.

"Oh come on Imani, you know that Money's cool. We've talked about him before and not that I'm sprung or nothing but I really like him and he's feelin' me. He ain't one of those fools you scared I'm gonna hook up with. Here, check this out."

"Um…hum…yeah sure, Fatima," Imani said as she stared at the latest photograph of Money. The brother sported a lot of gold, even a gold front tooth.

"Ain't he fine?" Fatima asked.

"Um…hum…yeah sure, Fatima. Money hasn't changed a bit."

"You wanna hang with us tonight at slammin' Club Paradise to get your freak on."

Imani laughed. "Girrrl, my daddy would beat whatever freak in me out of me if he found out I was in some club."

"Well, you know I ain't got no momz or pops to worry about catching me and grandma will be asleep by ten so I can lie and say I got back in the house by ten thirty."

"You got it all figured out, huh?" Imani asked.

"Yeah Girl, I want outta here too. You got your way and I got mine."

BHRIANA

Bhriana DuPree sat in drama class and day dreamed about how great life was when her parents were married. Since their divorce, Bhriana had not spent as much time as she wanted with her father. Tears welled up as she reminisced.

"Knock, knock."

"Who's there?"

"Surprise."

"Surprise who?"

Mr. Dupree handed seven-year-old Bhriana a small black velvet box. "Surprise for my baby girl."

Bhriana beamed with joy as she opened her gift. "Oh Daddy, diamond earrings. I love them!"

"Anything to make you happy. So is my baby girl happy?"

"Yes I am Daddy. Thank you." Bhriana fell into his arms and they hugged.

"Ms. Bhriana, is something the matter or are we boring you today?" her drama teacher asked.

"What?" Bhriana asked as she wiped her eyes and tried to focus.

Mrs. Gleason repeated herself as she approached Bhriana's desk.

"I'm fine and no you are not boring me. Why?"

"You seem to be someplace else. Have you heard a word that I've said?"

Bhriana never paid much attention in drama class, anyway. She felt that acting wasn't something she needed to learn because she was a natural born actress. Bhriana surveyed the room and found all eyes on her. She loved being the center of attention but not challenged. She certainly did not appreciate being the butt of anyone's joke. It annoyed Bhriana that her classmates had nothing better to do than to stare at her. "Why don't you people get a life!" she shouted.

"Ms. Bhriana, that comment and tone of voice was not necessary. Please stand up and redirect that anger towards reading your lines."

Bhriana made it through drama class and headed for her locker to get a change of clothes for cheerleading practice. It was her senior year and she took her position as captain of the squad seriously. Bhriana was anxious to show her group a new routine that she created and wanted to use at the next basketball game. She picked up her pace when she spotted Imani up ahead. Bhriana knew it was Imani because there were not many black female students at Westmoore and she was the only one who wore braids.

She pulled up along side of Imani and bumped into her left arm. Imani turned to her left and looked down at Bhriana.

"So, Imooni-"

"It's Imani."

"Imooni, Ipooni, whatever." Bhriana lowered her voice as she caught a glimpse of Mrs. Washington. "I just wanted to set some things straight since you're still kind of new around here."

Bhriana stopped talking because the pudgy old English teacher was within earshot.

"Hello ladies," Mrs. Washington said.

Neither girl spoke but both smiled.

"Imani, you rushed out of my class so fast that I didn't get a chance to ask you about Roberta. How is she doing?"

"Fine."

"I cannot tell you enough what a pleasure it was to have her in my class. I know your parents are so proud of their daughter. She is certainly destined to do great things."

"We're all so proud," Imani forced out between clenched teeth.

Mrs. Washington tapped Imani on her arm. "If you apply yourself, you will be a high achiever, too."

"I'll do my best."

"Glad to hear it. Now, tell my favorite student that I said hello and to come see me the next time that she is in town. Okay?"

"Sure."

"I'll let you two get back to your conversation," she said then moved on.

Bhriana huffed. "How rude of her to interrupt me in the first place."

"Bhriana, I don't know what this is all about but hurry up because I'm running late for practice."

They moved out of the middle of the hallway and stood closer to the lockers. The metal lockers were painted sky blue and lined the white walls on both sides of the hallway.

"Me too so listen up," Bhriana said as she maintained eye contact with Imani as she continued. "All of the girls here know that I can get whatever guy or guys I want. They would never think of competing with me. Understand?"

"So...what's that got to do with me?"

Bhriana put her hands on her slender hips and closed in on Imani. "You know I'm talking about Tyler so stop acting naïve. I've decided that I want Tyler so don't waste your time playing up to him."

Bhriana refused to give Imani much breathing room as Imani leaned back against the nearest locker.

"Uh look Bhriana, Tyler and I acknowledge each other's presence when we run into one another and I can tell he's probably a great guy however-"

"However, what?" Bhriana interrupted.

"However, I'm not interested in him in uh...in a boyfriend type way."

Bhriana could not leave well enough alone and kept the pressure on Imani. "Oh just say what you really mean, he would never want you."

"If you believe that, Bhriana, then, what's the problem?"

Bhriana looked about the hallway and no one was in sight. Bhriana turned back to Imani and it pleased her to see beads of perspiration formed on Imani's milk chocolate forehead.

"There won't be any problems if you stay away from him."

"If you want Tyler, he's all yours."

"Oh, like you're doing me a favor?" Bhriana asked. "I'm telling you, don't mess with me."

Imani didn't respond. She squirmed by Bhriana and walked away.

"Because I promise, you will get your feelings hurt," Bhriana mumbled as she stared at the back of Imani's head.

* * * *

Bhriana parked her new white convertible sports car in her circular driveway. Against her mother's wishes, Bhriana's father bought her the vehicle as an early graduation present. Her mother felt that her daughter was too young and inexperienced of a driver to possess such an expensive vehicle.

Ms. Austin, her maiden name that she reclaimed after the divorce, predicted that the powerful engine would entice Bhriana to drive like a speed demon. Bhriana's mother had the receipts for payment of the speeding tickets as proof that she was right. Yet, the fines were the least of her concerns for she feared Bhriana would crash into something or someone.

Bhriana headed towards the front door of the house that her parents had built. The DuPrees were the first blacks to move into the exclusive community and initially not accepted with open arms. All of their neighbor's fears or ignorance about "those people" diminished over time. The DuPrees did not fit the negative stereotypes they saw portrayed in the media of loud talking, slang using black people who threw wild parties and neglected their property.

Mr. Brandon DuPree gained more respect when the residents discovered who his father was. A few of the older residents frequented the elder DuPree's stores that were on the outskirts of town. They admired the way his son was able to maintain the high quality of service and merchandise in the stores he inherited from his deceased father.

Bhriana entered the house and marched up the spiral staircase. She reached the top of the landing and hurried past her mother's office.

"Hello, Bhriana."

Bhriana gave Ms. Austin a quick hello and proceeded to her spacious bedroom. She sat down on her canopy bed and stared at the 11x17 family portrait that held center position above a hand made dresser. A well-known artist painted the picture just one year before her parent's divorce. Bhriana wished she could relive that moment and remain frozen there forever, just like the happy teenager in the painting.

When Bhriana peeled her misty eyes away from the portrait, she noticed the red light flashing on her answering machine. She hit the play button and heard the voice of Tiffany Ellis, one of her friends from school.

"Hey Girl, I know it's a few months away but I'm thinking about running for Junior Prom Queen. Should I? Call me."

Beep...

"Hey Baby, I really need to be with you tonight," Justin Parker, her boyfriend of five months, announced.

"I drove by your house but I didn't see your car in the driveway so I kept going. Call me as soon as you get in. Love ya."

When the message ended, Bhriana glanced up and noticed her mother as she stood in the doorway and held a box of tampons. Ms. Vanessa Austin looked young enough to be her daughter's older sister. After her divorce, she exercised everyday to achieve her size eight figure. Bhriana had to admit that physically, her mother never looked better. Yet, Bhriana could not understand how her mother could be so happy when she was so miserable.

"Exactly what does Justin mean when he says he 'needs to be with you tonight'?"

"You're eavesdropping, Mother." Bhriana kicked off her suede light blue sneakers, stomped off to her bathroom, and ran water into the marble tub. She came back into the room and found her mother planted in the same spot.

"I'm waiting for an answer, Bhriana," her mother said and then tossed the pale blue box of tampons at her daughter.

Bhriana caught the box and placed it in her top dresser drawer where she kept them. Ms. Austin purchased tampons for her daughter because Bhriana refused to purchase such a personal item in public.

"Thanks. I'll need them some time this month."

"You're welcome, now answer my question."

Bhriana huffed and began to undress. She recognized the determined look on her mother's face and decided to answer so she would leave her alone. "All he means is that he needs to talk to me, something must be bugging him."

"That's all he wants, just to talk?"

"Yes," Bhriana responded dryly.

Ms. Austin came into the room and sat on the bed. Bhriana sensed that her mother followed her every move. "You asked me a question and I gave you an answer. Now what do you want from me?"

"Don't get fresh with me young lady," Ms. Austin responded then paused as if she wanted that last comment to sink in. Then she picked up where she left off. "Look, I like Justin and lately you've been talking about Tyler. From what I remember about Tyler, he was a nice kid. However-"

"Oh boy here we go," Bhriana interrupted then rolled her eyes.

"However, don't let Justin or Tyler or any boy for that matter interfere with your senior year and your chances to go to a good college. After your not so great junior year, you were supposed to focus on academics, not boys."

Bhriana pulled her fleece top over her head and tossed it onto the mauve plush carpet. "And why was my junior year not so great, Mother? It wasn't my fault that I was a head case after you broke up our family."

Ms. Austin stood and threw her hands up in the air. "Will you stop blaming me for that? It was a mutual decision between your father and me."

"Yeah, but you forced him into it, he couldn't live with you anymore. Everything was fine until you got all caught up in going to college and self-improvement seminars and whatever else. You had no time for Daddy and me."

"Everything wasn't fine, Bhriana. And, why is it every time I try to find out what's going on in your life, you get defensive and turn on me? I want to know if you're using protection so what happened to me won't happen to you. So you won't find yourself with a baby at 17-years-old and putting your life on hold and, yes, trying to catch up at 34 to get the degree you should have gotten at 22."

Ms. Austin's light cappuccino complexion turned crimson as she continued. "And, I'm not going to apologize for getting off my behind and taking responsibility for my life. A life that your father controlled for too doggoned long!" Ms. Austin took a deep breath and hazel eyes to hazel eyes, she asked her daughter, "Now, are you using birth control?"

That wasn't the first time that Bhriana's mother reminded her that she was an unplanned pregnancy. Although her parents told her repeatedly that they loved her, it did not alleviate the hurt. Tears cascaded down Bhriana's high cheekbones as she walked past her mother and sat on her bed.

"You are always accusing me of doing something that I'm not. For the last time, I have no need for birth control because I'm not having sex."

Ms. Austin sat next to Bhriana and stroked her back. "I just want you to learn from my mis-"

"Go ahead and say it again, Mother. I was a big mistake!" Bhriana shouted.

"Dating and lying down with your father for all of the wrong reasons was a mistake." Ms. Austin took a deep breath before she continued. "You know that I came from a poor family. I grew up dreaming of the day that I could live in a fine home and possess whatever material things I desired. Your father's family had more money than mine ever imagined."

Ms. Austin pointed to the family portrait. "And if you think your father is handsome now, he really had it going on then."

Bhriana was confused. "So why was marrying him a mistake?"

"Did you hear me say that I loved him? I liked him but I didn't love him. By the time I became pregnant with you, he was deeply in love with me and very possessive. He insisted that we marry right away and convinced my parents that his family could provide for us while he finished college. Of course, my going to college was out of the question. I became Mrs. DuPree the supportive wife with no mind of her own and a young mother with no clue."

Bhriana hunched her shoulders and said, "I still don't see what's wrong with marrying a rich good looking guy and having beautiful babies."

"Well other than landing that guy and having those babies, what do you want, Bhriana?"

"I don't know yet."

"I suggest you figure it out before someone or something decides for you," Ms. Austin said. "Look Baby, I've got to get to class." She kissed her daughter on the cheek and said, "We'll continue this discussion later."

"That's not necessary, Mother."

"Yes it is, Bhriana."

* * * *

"I can't talk long, Tiffany. Justin's on his way over and quite frankly this could be it."

"You're really serious about dumping him?"

"He's such a bore now, Tiff. All he talks about is family problems. It used to be all about me and hanging out and having fun." Bhriana paused and then added, "Shoot, what about my family problems? I have a father who the only way I see him nowadays is if he can pencil me into his busy schedule. I think we have a dinner date coming up but who knows if he'll keep it…"

Tiffany remained silent as Bhriana rambled on.

"Then I have a mother who expects me to admit that I'm having sex. Do you believe that? She is so worried that I'm gonna get pregnant but that's not going to happen to me. I know what I'm doing and so does Justin."

"Plus Bhri, that only happens to poor girls or the girls who sleep around with just old anybody." Tiffany said.

"Or everybody," Bhriana replied and the two girls laughed.

The doorbell rang. "Hey Tiff, I've gotta go."

"Wait! Should I run for Junior Prom Queen?"

"Go for it, Girl. I'll support you. Bye." Bhriana said then ran for the door.

The cold March night air greeted her and she in turn welcomed 18-year-old Justin in with a warm hug. As usual, he headed towards the staircase en route to Bhriana's room.

"Uh Justin, why don't we go into the living room and talk."

Justin turned around with a puzzled look on his golden honey face. He shrugged his shoulders, took Bhriana's hand in his, and led her to the white leather sofa in the living room. Bhriana sat and looked into Justin's greenish gray eyes and they were dull. Like a cloudy day, the gray seemed to overcast that usual sparkle. His old familiar smile was absent too but he was still gorgeous.

"Can I get you a glass of water?" Any other time she would have offered him a beer. However, that night, she wanted both of them to be clear-headed.

"I'll pass," he answered.

Bhriana stared at him and shook her head. What a waste if she had to turn loose a guy who had what it took to be a supermodel. The slanted eyes, straight nose, cleft chin, bronzed complexion, and those eyes made Justin look exotic.

Moments of silence crept by and it prompted Bhriana to break the ice. "O...ka...y. You said you had to talk to me. So, what's bothering you?"

Justin stood up and rubbed his hand over his soft glossy black hair. "Bhri, I don't know where to start. You know, I thought things were going to get better but I found out today that my father's bankrupt..."

Bhriana listened out of courtesy but felt there was nothing she could do.

"The worst part is that he has to sell everything … including the house."

Bhriana gasped, "You can't be serious?"

"This is serious, Bhri."

Bhriana cupped her hands over her mouth. He had to move out of their neighborhood and he was poor. She knew she had to let him go – for sure.

Justin sat back down next to Bhriana and he reached out and gave her a bear hug. "I don't want to lose you because of this," he whispered in her ear.

He would have to make a scene. How can I tell him it's over tonight? He might really lose it, ran through Bhriana's mind. She released herself from his grip and cleared her throat. "How's your family dealing with this?"

"They knew about this a long time before they told me. My folks said they were protecting me but I hate when people keep secrets that affect me."

Bhriana felt a lump in her throat.

Justin held her small hands and kissed her fingers, one by one. His dull eyes came back to life and their hypnotic powers reeled her in. A tingling sensation glided throughout her body.

"Bhri, you are my everything and I need to know that you'll hang in there with me," he said then pressed his satiny smooth lips against hers.

A soft moan slipped between her lips as the tips of their tongues touched. Bhriana closed her eyes and her mind as Justin's tongue explored every inch of her mouth. She didn't care how poor he was; he was still a master kisser.

"I need you tonight," he said as his hands roamed under her sweater.

A louder moan escaped from her mouth.

Suddenly, he pulled away and asked, "You got any condoms here?"

Bhriana opened her eyes and asked, "Why? I trust you. Plus, my period's coming soon – so we're safe," Bhriana said. She straddled her legs across Justin's lower torso and they gyrated in unison. Bhriana nibbled on his ear lobe and whispered, "Do you want me or what?"

"Yeah...I want you."

"Well then, finish what you've started before my mother gets home."

TYLER

Tyler poked at the tough chicken breast and mushy vegetables on his plate. The third cook his father hired since they moved back into town prepared the distasteful meal. Mr. Andrew Powers sat at the dining room table with his son and devoured the food as if it were grand gourmet cuisine. Tyler caught his father's eyes when he finally came up for air.

"What's the matter, son?"

Mr. Powers was Tyler's role model. He was a rags-to-riches intelligent business owner of Power Walk men's shoes and accessories stores. And, a dedicated father who raised Tyler alone ever since Tyler's mother died of cancer when he was 12-years-old.

"This food sucks," Tyler answered.

"Come on son, it's not so bad. Margaret's the best cook we've had thus far...or maybe I'm just hungry." Mr. Powers let out a hardy laugh and pushed back from the table. "Who am I kidding? This food s..."

"Sucks," Tyler chimed in.

Both father and son laughed. "You trash the food and I'll make the peanut butter and jelly sandwiches."

"You got it," Tyler said with a smile but then it soon faded. How he missed his mother. Especially, at the dinner table when he visualized her there with them. Peanut butter and jelly sandwiches would not be on the supper menu.

No other woman had spent a night in their home. Mr. Powers had women over for dinner, but no one serious enough to stay overnight. From the dinners that Tyler witnessed and the telephone conversations he overheard, his father treated his lady friends with much respect.

"Dad, will you ever get married again?"

Mr. Powers brought four sandwiches to the table and refilled their glasses with water. "Maybe, when you go off to college and I find 'The One'." Mr. Powers sighed and added, "No one will ever replace your mother but I can live with second best."

Tyler smacked on the sticky peanut butter and listened to his father. He always thought that his father had put that part of his life on hold. In a way, Tyler was glad.

"But, you know who I ran into the other day who's down right gorgeous?"

"Who?"

Mr. Powers' moustache raised as a smile crossed his handsome face. "Bhriana's mother, Vanessa. If she wasn't Brandon's ex-wife, boooy." He shook his head. "I can't get involved with a friend and possible business partner's ex. It's tricky mixing business with pleasure."

"Where did you see her?"

"Actually, I saw both Vanessa and Bhriana on the golf course yesterday. That Bhriana is something else, too. Now there's nothing wrong with you pursuing the daughter of a friend of mine. That could be good for business."

"Dad!"

"Oh...like you didn't have a thing for Bhriana when you were a kid. Your mother told me about it."

Tyler finished his sandwich and kind of ignored his father's last comment. He was close to his dad but girl conversations were off limits. Locker room talk or kickin' it with his homie, Steven, sure but not with Mr. Powers. "So you and Mr. DuPree want to hook up and start a business?"

"So you want to change the subject?"

"You mentioned it earlier so I um...you know, was just asking." Tyler said, but he didn't want to talk about business either.

Mr. Powers gave him a suspicious look before he proceeded. "We're working on a business plan to merge our existing stores or to create new ones. It makes sense for us to come together to give our clientele everything they need in one store." Mr. Powers reached over and slapped Tyler on his back. "And by the time you graduate from Harvard, Yale, or Princeton, we'll have an empire for you to help us run."

Tyler stared at the white ceramic plate in front of him and cleared his throat. He slouched down in his chair and tapped the plate with his fingernail. "I've been kickin' around the idea of going to a black college, like Howard."

"What? I couldn't hear you over that clunking sound."

Tyler stopped hitting the plate and sat up a little straighter. He still couldn't look into his father's dark brown eyes so he glanced down at the mahogany table and repeated himself in the same soft tone.

"That's not what your mother and I had planned for you. We agreed before she passed away that you would attend the finest schools that we could afford. And, that's what I've done and will continue to do."

"So are you sayin' that there's no great black colleges?"

"All of the schools you've attended thus far have been predominantly white so why all of a sudden you want to attend a black college?"

Tyler raised his eyes only to see his father's creased forehead. Tyler's eyes met the table, again. "That's part of the reason why I want to go. All my life I have lived with and gone to school with people unlike me. I'm black. But, I don't know that much about my people, our people."

"Don't you have black history at Westmoore?"

"Yeah one month, black history month, that's it."

"Well I'm sorry son, but if you want to learn more about black people, you can do that on your own. I'll even take you to the bookstore, library, black museum, wherever you want but I am not going to send you to a black college."

"Why not?" Tyler asked. His tone raised a notch.

"That's not what your mother and I envisioned for you."

"And?"

"And, you deserve the best."

41

Tyler searched his father's dark brown eyes and strained facial expression for another reason. He couldn't find one. "Dad, I don't buy into the hype that Ivy League schools are better."

"You don't have to buy anything. I'm paying for your education so I decide who'll get my hard earned money. Understand?"

Tyler understood that his dad was dead serious. Yet, he felt compelled to ask, "So that's it?"

"That's right. End of discussion."

"Some discussion," Tyler mumbled.

* * * *

"Thanks Man for giving me a lift," Tyler said to Steven.

"No problem, T-Man. Now tell me again why you're 16 and don't have your own ride."

Tyler fiddled with the CD player in his childhood partner's jeep until he hit the play button. "I told you that my dad promised my mom that he wouldn't get me a car until I turned 17. Evidently he promised her a lot of stuff that I didn't know about and now it's too late to do anything about them."

Tyler turned up the volume. Steven reached over and turned it down. "What do you think this is? A ghetto-mobile? I could get a ticket for driving around here with the volume pumped up."

Tyler knew that but he hoped that the loud music would wash away his nervousness. After all, it wasn't just any old girl he was going to visit. It was Bhriana. It occurred to Tyler that Steven hadn't asked for directions. He asked his short chunky partner, "Do you know where she lives?"

Steven raised his bushy brow and rubbed his hand across his reddish brown hair. He gave Tyler a sheepish grin then punched Tyler in his left arm. "You told me – remember?"

"No...I don't remember."

Steven appeared agitated. "Well...if it wasn't you, then she must have mentioned it to me."

Tyler smiled and told Steven to, "Chill Man, it was just a question." They rode down a few more blocks before either one spoke again. Tyler broke the silence. "I don't know what's up with my father, Man. As long as I give in to his demands, we're cool."

"Let me guess. The black college thing, right?"

"Yup."

"I told you he wouldn't go for it," Steven said with a grin on his face. But, you're lucky to have a father who's got your back."

"He's got more than my back – try my whole life. I wish he would cut me some slack."

"Oh like my father, the 'invisible dad'?"

"Mr. Clark's cool."

"Maybe. But, he would agree with your father and so do I," Steven said.

"So you don't think a black college is good enough for me either?"

"That's what I'm saying."

Tyler knew that Steven could be anti-black at times although he too was black. He could pass for white if it wasn't for his straight from Africa hair texture and wide nose. For his graduation present, he asked for a nose job and Tyler wondered if a perm was

43

next.   Steven's not an ugly brother but the girls gravitated to his charismatic personality and air of importance more than his average looks.   The young ladies who stood the best chance with him were fair-skinned with long straight hair, just like his mother.

"I still don't understand your attitude, either. Your parents are black and so are you."

"Man, I keep telling you that the only blacks I have a problem with are the poor ones just sitting back complaining and waiting for a hand out. As much as I hate rap music, at least they're doing something legal to earn a living. Otherwise, they would be out stealing cars or mugging people. Fortunately, you don't know what it's like living in the ghetto."

"And neither do you, Steven. So, how can you speak on it?"

"Hey, I watch the news and read the papers and we've seen a couple of those thugs-in-the-'hood movies."

"And that's what your opinion of all poor black people is based on?" Tyler asked.

"Isn't that enough? You expect me to go to the nearest slum and do research?"   Before Tyler could answer, Steven said, "Look, this conversation's too heavy for a Saturday."

Tyler shook his head from Steven's last comment on poor people. His mother always taught him that it was wrong to judge other people based on the color of their skin or economic status. Just because someone was less fortunate than him didn't make that person any less important.

"Hold up," Tyler said. "I see you eating in the cafeteria sometimes with Jazz Timmons and I know he's poor. So what's up with that?"

Steven sucked his teeth and waved his hand at Tyler. "Ah T, I've known him since ninth grade. I respect the brother because he hustles for money."

What would you know about hustling for money? You never worked a day in your life, Tyler thought. "Jazz should use some of that energy and hustle on defense instead of whining about me taking his starting position. All he wants to do is score."

"He would have scored with Bhriana by now."

"That was foul, Man."

Steven hunched his thick shoulders. "Hey, he's a player and the females at school think you're a player, too."

"Do you mean player as in p-l-a-y-e-r or p-l-a-y-a?" Tyler asked.

"You know which one I mean and your rep will be dust if Bhriana tells everybody that you haven't put a move on her."

Steven was his main homie but at times, he pissed Tyler off. "So being a playa is a good rep to have?"

Steven chuckled and said, "Yeah T, and that's a part of being a jock."

"Is that right?"

"T, would I lie to you?"

Tyler stared at Steven long and hard then asked, "Would you?"

"Lie to you? Oh come on, T-Man, you know me better than that. I feel like the older brother you never had."

"You only got a year and a half on me."

"I learned a lot in that year and a half that you wasn't here. And let me tell you something else little brother, don't start playin' around with that Imani chick 'cause that won't be good for your rep and by the way, where does she live?"

Tyler sighed before he responded. "Now what do you have against Imani? Too dark-skinned for you?"

Steven looked at Tyler briefly before he turned his attention back to the road. "Who needs to calm down now? And no, I'm not talking about her color. It's just that she's not fine enough for you. You can get whatever super fine tender babe you want so why settle for less?"

"I bet she's not a shallow airhead."

"So now I'm an airhead?" Steven fired back.

"Today, you're a *big* helium-filled nose up in the air - airhead. And if I want to get with Imani, which I don't, it's none of your damn business. Understand?"

"If you get some from Bhriana today, I guarantee you that you won't be so uptight," Steven said and then let out a gut-filled howl.

"That's it. Pull over."

Steven did exactly that. As Tyler opened the door Steven said, "I know you're not gonna walk."

"Just watch me," Tyler said and proceeded to Bhriana's house on foot.

* * * *

It was a clear and crisp March afternoon. However, Tyler's caramel smooth face glistened with perspiration from the brisk walk. His body temperature rose a few degrees when Bhriana answered the door in a pair of tight jeans and a cleavage filled white tank top. He commented on how great she looked and how beautiful the outside of her home was. Tyler then followed Bhriana into the living room and onto the white leather sofa.

"I'll take your jacket," Bhriana said as she helped Tyler out of it.

While Bhriana placed his jacket in a closet, Tyler swiped his forehead with the sleeve of his denim shirt.

"I'm so glad you could make it."

"Well, I'm a man of my word."

Tyler scratched his head. How corny did that sound? Why did he lose his cool when he was around her? He told himself that he wasn't in grammar school anymore and to act his age.

"Beer, champagne?" Bhriana asked.

"Ooh nooo, I can't drink during the basketball season. Water's cool." Truth was Tyler didn't drink alcohol at all but he wanted to sound suave.

Bhriana leaned towards him and asked in seductive tone, "Is there anything else you can't do during the season?"

Tyler tried not to look down at Bhriana's cleavage. But, it was difficult because her tank top hardly contained her voluptuous breasts. There was no bra for reinforcement. "Uh, I can't eat a lot of junk food but um... water...lots of ice."

"You're really thirsty, huh?" Bhriana asked as she circled her lips with her glistening tongue.

"Ye...yeah," Tyler managed to say as he fixed his eyes on her glossy coral hued lips.

Tyler loved the feel of her soft hand as it glided across his forehead.

"Why are you sweating so much? Am I making you nervous?"

Tyler denied it as he shook his head "no" but inside he screamed, "yes!" "Steven gave me a ride about halfway here and then I walked the rest."

"Walked? Why?"

"He's my boy but sometimes..." Tyler didn't complete the sentence he just exhaled.

"You don't have a car? Do you have a driver's license?"

Tyler was embarrassed to remind Bhriana that he was a year younger than she was. At sixteen, he was only old enough to have a permit.

"Ooh, you're just a baby," Bhriana cooed.

"I'm not a baby, Bhriana."

Bhriana slid over so close to Tyler that he felt the heat from her body penetrate through his clothes. He flinched when Bhriana placed her hand on his washboard abs and began to stroke in a circular motion. "Umm, I guess you're not a baby. I wouldn't mind if you used my car whenever you needed it. As a matter of fact, you can use-"

"That gla-gla-glass of water," Tyler stuttered as he fought the temptation to quench his thirst by sucking Bhriana's juicy looking lips.

"It is getting warm in here," Bhriana commented as she fanned her bosom with her hand then got up and sashayed into the kitchen.

"Yes it is," Tyler mumbled. While Bhriana was in the kitchen, Tyler tried to wipe away the new beads of sweat off his face. Bhriana returned with two glasses of water and a gorgeous smile. "Where's your mother?" he asked.

Bhriana handed a crystal tumbler to Tyler and eased down next to him. "She's at school in one of her many classes. I'm just glad she's not here. I can't stand being around her sometimes. No, most of the time... "

Tyler had never heard that side of Bhriana before. He was surprised at the way she spoke about her mother. She didn't sound like the same woman his father thought so highly of. "Bhriana, you really shouldn't talk about your mom like that."

"I really don't want to talk about her at all," Bhriana said. She brushed her hand back and forth over Tyler's thigh. "Sooo, you had a thing for me in grammar school, huh? Do you still have a crush on me?"

Tyler drank three-quarters of the glass of water before he stopped to take a breath. He glanced down at the delicate hand that still worked his muscular thigh. The heat from her hand seeped through his khakis and warmed his skin. Tyler knew then that Steven was right. He could take her at that moment, if he wanted to. "I'm too old for crushes but yeah, I'm attracted to you and so is every guy at school."

"But I'm not interested in any of them. It's Tyler Powers that I want."

"What about Justin?"

Bhriana waved her hand and a frown crossed her face. "Oh, plueeeze. Justin has too many problems to concentrate on a relationship right now. I never loved him or anything. We were just friends."

Tyler placed his glass on top of a crystal coaster on the center table. "I heard that you two had a serious thing going on."

"You heard wrong," Bhriana said with a straight face. She rubbed her bare arm against Tyler's sleeve. "Say the word and I'm all yours."

Tyler could not believe his ears. It all seemed too easy. He soaked up her beauty and wondered why he hesitated to take her. Tyler stroked across his cleft chin. He had an opening. Why didn't he take it to the hoop?

Tyler pried his eyes away from Bhriana and gazed about the spacious living room. He cleared his throat and asked, "Why don't you give me a tour of the place. You know, it being my first time and all."

"I am being such a rude hostess aren't I?" Bhriana giggled and grabbed a hold of Tyler's man-sized hands. "Let me show you my bedroom it's-"

"I um...was really looking forward to checking out that gym you were telling me about," Tyler interrupted. Bhriana appeared disappointed that he would be more interested in the gym than her boudoir. Just as they were about to go downstairs to the gym, Ms. Austin came through the door. She looked like a young college student in her denim jeans, ivory-colored fisherman sweater, and backpack. Her hair was slicked back into a ponytail. She gasped when she saw Tyler.

"If it isn't little Tyler all grown up. Come gimme a hug, handsome."

Tyler didn't hesitate to do what he was asked. He remembered what his father said about her and he smiled. His dad was right. She was all that! "Ma'am, I hope you don't mind my being here. I came over to check out your gym. An...d to visit Bhriana." Tyler added that last part after he saw the annoyed look on Bhriana's face.

"I can show you around if Bhriana hasn't done so already."

"That won't be necessary, Mother, I was just about to drive Tyler home." Bhriana tossed Tyler his jacket and threw on her brown leather coat. She looped her arm around Tyler's and led him to the door.

"You need on more than that skimpy tank top under there," her mother said.

Bhriana rolled her eyes and replied, "I know how to dress."

"Well go ahead, you never listen to me anyway."

"Good-bye, Mother."

"Tell your father I said hello," Ms. Austin yelled to Tyler before Bhriana slammed the door shut.

FATIMA

"Chile, this stuff gettin' hot up here in my head!" Fatima's grandmother exclaimed.

Fatima had permed Grandma Rose's hair so many times that it had become second nature to her. Yet, Fatima was so preoccupied with thoughts of her date with her boyfriend, Money, that she didn't base Grandma Rose's scalp as well as she should have. Fatima assumed as much because her grandmother never hollered "it's gettin' hot" so soon.

Fatima glanced up at the fruit and vegetable embossed clock on the beige kitchen wall. "Grandma, you hafta sit here a couple more minutes for me to work this stuff in real good," Fatima told her while she worked feverishly with her plastic glove covered hands.

Grandma Rose shut her eyes and gritted her teeth, make that dentures. She wanted her silver hair straight and shiny for that night's service at Holy Baptist Church. Grandma Rose sat close to the kitchen sink whenever she got a touch-up so she could get to the water. Quick. "I used to wash your mama's hair right here too. I would put two or three pillows on dis chair so she could reach the faucet when she was just a little thing."

Grandma Rose talked about Fatima's mother often. It was obvious that she missed the woman that her granddaughter had never known. Fatima was only five months old when her mother and father died in a car accident in which Fatima survived. Fatima was sick and her parents waited in vain for an ambulance to arrive. After a half an hour passed, they decided to take her themselves. En route to the hospital, a drunk driver ran a red light and crashed into their vehicle. It was said that Fatima's mother used her body as a shield to protect the infant.

"I would put the prettiest ribbons and bows in your mama's hair to match her Sunday dress. I had a time teachin' her to act like a little lady though. She was such a tomboy. Just down right wild sometimes, even in church." Grandma Rose wiped the perspiration off her round face and double rolled chin with a white handkerchief. She tucked the lace edged hankie back down in her ample bosom.

"I wish you'd change ya mind and come wid me tonight. I heard that the visitin's church's choir could make the devil shout, hallelujah!"

Fatima didn't address Grandma Rose's comment. Instead, she tapped her grandmother on her shoulder that signaled it was time to hit the water. Grandma Rose leaned her head back over the kitchen sink as far as she could go. The metal legs of the vinyl-padded chair squeaked under the weight of the full-figured woman. "Use cool water, Baby."

"I know, Grandma."

"And stop smacking that gum fo' I dig it outta your mouth."

"Sorry, Grandma."

Grandma Rose smiled as the cool water rinsed out the chemicals and provided long awaited relief. Fatima smiled too because in a couple of hours she was on her way to the mall on a shopping spree, courtesy of Money. As she continued to wash Grandma Rose's hair, Fatima replayed parts of her last conversation with Money in her mind.

"Thanks again for gettin' me into Club Paradise the other night. It was da bomb and the music was slammin'," Fatima said.

"Ain't no big thang. The brotha at the door is one of my boyz and he owed me one so I told him to let my girl in, you know."

"What's the big deal about being 21 to get in?" Fatima asked.

"You gotta understand Baby, it's a bizness and they gotta make money. Clubs be makin' mad money selling overpriced booze, Baby. And how old you s'pose to be to buy liquor?"

"21."

"There it is, Baby."

"So you said you had a surprise for me after we go shopping. Whassup?"

"Umm, yeah, well I'm gonna keep that a surprise for now. What time will granny be back from church?"

Fatima took time out of the conversation and looked down at her nails. A fresh coat of polish was needed. "Shooot, ain't no tellin'. Them choirs could be singing 'til daylight for all I know," Fatima said and they both laughed.

"That's them Baptists for ya. But seriously Baby, how long can you hang tonight?"

"Let's see...church will probably let out at about 11:00 or 11:30. By the time she gets home, it'll be about midnight."

"Perfect, Baby. Plenty of time for your surprise."

"Oh come on Money, tell me what it is."

"Naw Baby, you'll get it soon enough 'cause you know it's all about you right?"

"Better be," Fatima said.

Grandma Rose jerked her head and brought Fatima back to the matter at hand. "Chile, that water's runnin' down my neck. Where's your mind at?"

* * * *

Fatima and Money held hands as they walked through the suburban mall where they first met. Money sported more jewelry than Fatima owned. Three layers of gold rope chains hung from his thick neck. Gold hoop earrings decorated both ears. Gold rings lined three fingers on both hands. Even when he smiled, Money flashed a gold front tooth. He wore a black tee shirt tucked inside his baggy jeans that hung well below his waist.

Fatima's outfit color coordinated with Money's. She wore a short black lycra knit skirt with white racer stripes on both sides of her hips and a v-neck white tee shirt underneath her cropped denim jacket. The body hugging mini skirt showed off her "onion" and her thick and smooth rich brown legs. A gold anklet adorned her left ankle and a rose shaped fake tattoo decorated her right ankle. Her grandmother forbade her to get a real tattoo so Fatima compromised and wore fake ones.

One thing Grandma Rose never disapproved of was Fatima's creative hair dos. She spent so much time on her grandmother's hair that day that she settled for a ponytail and bangs for herself. Simple hairstyle or not, Fatima received and loved the attention that she got from the brothers in the mall.

In the first store that Fatima and Money entered, a security guard watched them too. The guard wasn't discreet about it either. "Ain't this a bleep?" Money asked Fatima.

"What?" Fatima asked as she browsed through the rack of clothes.

Money huffed loudly which got Fatima's full attention. "Every damn store I go into, they be watchin' me like I'm gonna steal something up in there. Like just 'cause I'm a young brotha, I ain't got no money to buy nothing," Money said in a volume for the guard to hear.

"Yeah, they do that to me too," Fatima said just as loud. Then she whispered to Money, "But, I ain't got no money." Then out loud again, "But I ain't no thief."

The guard seemed to have gotten the message, turned away from them, and scanned about the other customers. "You better be checkin' them other people 'cause they be rippin' y'all off while you stalkin' me," Money warned in a bitter tone.

"Let's get outta here and get something to eat. They ain't got nothing I wanna buy here anyway," Fatima said as she tugged on Money's chiseled arm.

Money led the way to the store's exit. When he reached the guard, he threw both of his hands up in the air. "Wanna pat me down before I roll up outta here so I can sue the sh…"

"Okaaay Money, let it go," Fatima interjected.

The couple marched out of that store and went to a fast food restaurant. Fatima watched Money barf down two sandwiches and a large order of fries. Had she been with Imani, her tray wouldn't have as much as a crumb on it. For some strange reason, she never had the same ravenous appetite when she was out on a date. So she sat and picked at her fries and chicken sandwich. "Do you want the rest of my fries?" she asked Money.

"Naw."

"Gum?" she asked and pulled out a couple of sticks.

"Naw. But, I do wanna buy you somethin' before we raise up outta here." Money stroked Fatima's bare wrists and asked, "What about some jewelry? How would my girl like that?"

Before Fatima could answer, a pretty sistah appeared at their table from out of the blue. The girl ignored Fatima and carried on a conversation with Money.

"When you gonna call me? Kevin told me that he gave you my digits."

Fatima turned her head away from the girl and her eyes caught Money's. He in turn looked at the girl. "Kevin's lyin'. He ain't give me no number."

Fatima rolled her eyes at Money and stared the girl dead in her mouth. That's when Fatima noticed the gold ball earring in her tongue.

"Oh really? Well if you want it, tell Kevin to give it to you."

Fatima sat in disbelief as the pierced-tongue sistah asked Money to call her while she was there with him. It bothered Fatima even more that Money hadn't introduced her as his girlfriend. He didn't introduce her at all. When the girl strutted away, Fatima asked Money, "So who was that?"

"Pssst, who her? She ain't nobody. We got a mutual friend and she's been tryin' to push up on me but I don't want her." He reached out and took hold of Fatima's hand. "It's all about you, Baby. I want you."

"Yeah right," Fatima responded in a sarcastic tone.

"What she got that your fine self ain't got. Baby, don't be sweatin' her." Money caressed then kissed her hands. "It's all about you, Boo."

Fatima was relieved to hear how he felt about her. He was a hot item and the sistahs knew he had money to spend. His good looks drew girls to him like a magnet. Normally it wouldn't bother Fatima that someone else was interested in her boyfriend. But, it was different with Money and Fatima wasn't about to share him with any gold digging skeezer.

"You know we have a lot of fun together and I like talkin' to you and stuff," Fatima said. She exhaled and then added, "I think I'm fallin' in love with you."

"And like I said, I care about you too, Boo."

Fatima wanted to hear him use the word "love." Yet, she was confident that's what he meant and didn't pursue it any further. Instead, she said, "Maybe we can get matching earrings or something and wear it at the same time to let people know we're tight."

"That ain't necessary. Let's just get you hooked up."

Once in the jewelry store, Fatima headed directly to the gold showcase. "Ooh! Come over here Money and check this bracelet out." Fatima glanced up and saw Money as he checked out a couple of security guards.

"Just chill," Fatima whispered to him.

Money huffed.

"May I help you?" a petite saleswoman with white hair asked Fatima.

Money reached into his back pocket and the woman froze. "Yeah, you can help her if you call off your watch dogs." He went into his wallet and threw a wad of bills on top of the counter. "Or, I'll take this and step on outta here."

The woman opened her mouth wide and Fatima gasped. She gave the guards a hand signal and turned to Fatima with a smile on her face. "What would you like to try on today?"

"Can you show me that gold bracelet and that chain and..."

When Fatima left the jewelry store, she sported a new gold bracelet, gold earrings and a tiny diamond stud earring in her nose. She tightened the back of her earrings to make sure that they didn't fall out of her lobes. As she ran her finger over the smooth gold, she wondered how she could have ever doubted Money's love for her. If he didn't care about her, why would he buy her expensive gifts?

Out of guilt and gratitude, she pulled Money's arm back and slowed his pace. She swallowed her chewing gum then leaned towards him and gave him a kiss. They smooched awhile before Fatima removed her lips from his. "Thanks."

Money smiled and said, "You can straight up thank me when we get outta here."

As they approached the exit, a group of teenaged boys surrounded them. Fatima assumed that the tall guy who stood directly in front of Money was the leader of the crew.

"Yo Money," he said, "we need to rap." The leader's presence intimidated Fatima but when she glanced at Money, he didn't seem phased by him at all.

"Later, I got my girl with me," Money responded and pulled Fatima closer to him.

The tall bald headed boy surveyed Fatima from the tiled floor up and nodded his head. Fatima felt self-conscience and tugged down on the hem of her miniskirt. The leader smiled at her and said, "Naw Baby, you can't cover all that stuff up." He continued to stare at Fatima as he told Money that, "I would hold on tight to that too, but I suggest you let go and take care of bizness 'cause me and my boyz need some answers, now."

"Man, get off my woman," Money retorted. "If you wanna rap, step outside." The four boys in the group turned around and walked out the door. Fatima attempted to follow them but Money held her back. "Stay here, I got this."

"Not by yourself. I've been known to kick a butt or two and I could probably take the short skinny punk."

Money laughed and put his hands on her shoulders. "Baby trust me, I got this. We ain't gonna do nothin' but talk and if talkin' ain't enough, well let's just say I never leave home without it." He kissed Fatima on the lips, turned and left.

"That fool's packin' a gun," Fatima mumbled. "Oh yeah, that's suppose to make me feel better. I'm gonna give them five minutes before I roll up on 'em." she mumbled. Fatima paced back and forth around the doorway and tried to decide if she should call mall security or just wait there a little longer.

"I can't take this. I gotta see what's goin' on," she spoke aloud. Fatima opened her handbag and rambled through it in search of anything that she could use as a weapon. "Oh great Girl, go runnin' out there and rescue Money with a comb and mascara but, ooh, this finger nail file is sharp."

With the nail file held firmly in her fist, Fatima pushed the door halfway open with her free hand, stopped, then turned around and walked back into the mall. "Shoot, I ain't heard no gun shots so everything should be alright. Uh come on girl and get out there, you ain't no punk. That's right, I ain't no punk!" She covered her mouth and looked around to see if anyone heard her and then she proceeded to the door again.

Fatima marched outside and the sunshine made her squint. She shielded her ebony eyes with her hand and searched for Money. "Yo Baby, let's go," she heard Money call out. Her heart rate almost returned to normal when she saw him a few feet from her. The other guys stood near Money but it looked like the conversation was over.

"Everything alright?" Fatima asked Money when she reached him.

"Everythang's cool," Money said as he kept one eye on the leader.

"For now," the leader said.

Fatima and Money turned and walked away.

Pop-pop-pop-pop ...

Fatima screamed and fell into Money's arms. The nail file dropped to the ground as she grabbed onto him with both hands. Money swung around swiftly and went for his piece and the gang laughed. The leader held both of his hands up in the air and waved firecrackers around. "This time man," he said, "this time."

* * * *

Fatima followed Money into an unfamiliar house that she assumed was his. She was still on edge by the firecracker incident at the mall. Fatima just knew that Money or she had been shot. Money tried to convince her over and over again that "everythang's cool." That's all he would say about the whole ordeal.

She held on tight to his hand as he led her downstairs to a damp and musty basement. A ray of sunshine streamed through the dusty white blinds and provided the only light in the room. Once in the center of the room, Money reached down, pulled up his left pant leg, and removed the gun that he strapped around his calf.

Fatima covered her ears as she fixed her eyes on the metal weapon. She hated the sounds of gunshots ever since she accidentally fired a gun. It was only a couple of months ago that Fatima dated a guy, Speed, who carried a gun everywhere. One day he visited her and she decided to snoop inside the pockets of his leather jacket while he was in the bathroom.

She pulled out a small silver gun.

"This bad boy is heavier than it looks," Fatima said. She supported the hand that held the gun with her free hand. She aimed and put her finger on the trigger just as she had seen it done on television.

"Hold it right there or I'll shoot," she said to an imaginary criminal.

Just then Speed entered the room and startled her. Fatima dropped the gun to the hardwood floor and it fired.

"What the hell is wrong with you?" Speed yelled as he grabbed onto his bleeding leg.

"Ohmagod!" Fatima screamed. She rushed to the phone to dial 9-1-1.

"Are you crazy? I can't go to no hospital and have cops questioning me. I ain't got no permit for that piece."

The bullet just grazed his leg but that was the last time she saw Speed. That was the last time she saw a gun up close and personal, too.

"Surprise," Money said and brought her back to the present. He wrapped his muscular arms around Fatima's waist and bent over to whisper in her ear. "We have this crib all to ourselves, just us Baby."

Fatima felt Money's hot breath on her ear then wet kisses on her neck. "Uh, can you get that gun out of my sight?"

"Anything for my Boo," Money said and placed the gun in a drawer.

"Whose house is this?" Fatima asked as she watched Money move around as if he was very familiar with the place.

"My boy, Darnel's. He let's me crash here whenever I want," Money whispered as he stroked her shapely hips. "So relax Baby, he ain't comin' home no time soon."

Fatima backed away and asked, "Where do you live?"

"Here and there, you know," he answered and caressed her arms. "Relax."

Fatima tried to but couldn't. She needed a piece of gum to calm her nerves but then she wouldn't be able to kiss with it in her mouth. As much as she had dated, Fatima had never been totally alone with a boy outside of her home. She felt in control at her apartment and if a guy got out of line, she told him to chill out or get to stepping. But here, she didn't feel that confident. She walked over to a sofa, which was covered by an old raggedy looking green throw cover. Her miniskirt inched up higher as she eased down on the couch. The springs came up through the seat cushion and poked her rear and the back of her thighs.

"I know what will get you in the mood," Money said as he walked over to the stereo system and popped a CD in the disc player. A slow mellow tune flowed through the speakers. Money glided over, slid next to Fatima, and embraced her.

She tried to back away from his tight hold but couldn't. "Are you sure it's okay for us to be here? I'm not so sure that-"

"Shhh..." Money said as he covered her purple painted lips with his fingers. From her lips, his hand traced the front of her body down to her thigh. Fatima grabbed his hand as it slid underneath her miniskirt and pushed it away.

"I ain't ready for this," she said then avoided his gaze and stared at the pendant on one of his chains. The pendant read "Money."

"You ain't a little girl no more and if I ain't think you were ready to be my wo-man, I wouldn't be with you and buyin' you clothes and jewelry and crap." He stroked her moist brown face and continued in a low sexy tone, "You are a fine chocolate covered sweet sweet woman and it's all about you, Baby."

Fatima blushed.

Nobody had ever broken it down to her like that before. How could she say "no" now? She imagined herself as a movie star or a video girl or even the sistah that pushed up on Money in the restaurant. She let that imagination overshadow visions of disgusted expressions on Imani and Grandma Rose faces. The slow and sensuous music drowned out their voices of disapproval of what she was about to do.

Fatima closed her eyes and swayed to the melody. Visions of Grandma Rose and Imani entered her mind again. She swayed harder to try to release them from her head. After all, what did they know? Grandma Rose didn't have a man and Imani never kissed a boy.

She felt her panties as they slid down her legs and it broke her private thoughts. Fatima tried to stop Money, again.

"Oh Boo, cut me a break. I know it's your first time but trust me, I ain't gonna hurt you."

"It ain't like I don't trust you or nothing but-"

"But what?"

"I'm scared that I'm gonna get pregnant."

"Trust me Boo, I ain't gonna let that happen," Money said.

"How? You got a condom?"

"You're really buggin' now. I know you're new to this but a man with my skillz don't need no rubber. I know when to pull back."

"I'm sorry Money but the only way I'm gonna do this is if you bag it up."

Fatima reached down and pulled up her panties.

"Okay, okay, daaag." Money said, "I got one." He took a small square red package out of his dollar bill packed wallet. He ripped open the foil type cover with his teeth and then reached in with his finger and pulled out the circular rubber. Fatima watched Money unzip his jeans and reached inside with his hand. He didn't appear to be the least bit embarrassed as he exposed his penis and rolled the vanilla colored condom down on it.

In what seemed like one motion, Fatima's skirt was above her waist and she was pinned down. She struggled to breathe under the weight of Money's body. Then, a sharp pain traveled up her back. Money had forced his way.

"Ouch, that hurts!" Fatima yelled but he ignored her. Fatima thought he was in pain too because he moaned. When she looked up at his sweaty brown face, he had a smile on it. A weird twisted kind of smile. No more sweet-talk. He grunted and panted.

"Stop Money!"

"Oh naw Baby. Not now," Money groaned and continued to maneuver on top of her. "Relax."

Fatima closed her eyes tight and gritted her teeth. She didn't feel glamorous or sexy like the actresses in those love scenes. She didn't feel loved at all. "Come on Money. Get off of me." Fatima tried to push him off but he bore down even more. His back and forth movements quickened and so did his breathing. He let out one long groan then seconds later his body collapsed.

"Where's the freakin' bathroom?"

Money didn't speak but pointed straight ahead. Fatima shoved him off her and snatched her panties from the couch. To her surprise, the condom that should have been on Money was beneath her panties. "You lied to me!" Fatima squealed as she pointed to the condom.

"Don't be buggin'. I started out with that thing on but it ain't big enough for me Baby. It slid off."

"Hold up," Fatima began with her palm right in Money's face. "That damn thing came off and you knew it but you just kept going knowing damn well I ain't on no birth control? Are you freakin' crazy?"

"Stop trippin' and trust me 'cause I'm the man. I pulled out in time, Baby. Everythang's cool now go on and clean yourself up."

"Everythang better be cool or you will be hearing from me, Money," Fatima warned before she turned and walked away. She took a couple of steps then did an about face. Fatima stuck her index finger in the center of Money's forehead. "And if I ever tell you to stop, damn it, I mean stop!"

Once in the bathroom, Fatima looked into the half-cracked cloudy mirror and a wild girl stared back at her. The ponytail holder that held her hair back must have fallen off because her hair was all over her head. Sweat slid down her temples. Lipstick smeared around her mouth. Her hands shook as she tried to wipe if off.

She felt something wet and sticky between her inner thighs. Fatima didn't want to wipe down there with her hands so she reached for tissue near the toilet. "What's this!" she exclaimed at the sight of a whitish gooey substance tinged with blood on the white tissue.

They don't show all of this clean up crap in the movies. Naaaw...those women just be layin' up all under their man lookin' freakin' perfect. Look at you! Fatima yelled to herself. She couldn't hold back the tears as she continued to vent inside. *Does he freakin' care? Hell no! I can't believe he didn't stop.*

Several minutes later, Fatima pulled herself together and exited the bathroom. She walked in on Money who was on the telephone. Their dark eyes met and he ended his conversation.

"What took you so long?" he asked her after he hung up the receiver.

"I'm in there bleeding and cleaning your icky sperm off of me and all you care about is what's taking me so long?"

"Pssst, I knew that," Money responded, "you left a spot on the couch but don't worry about it, I cleaned it up."

"I ain't worried about no dang couch," Fatima fired at him.

"Ain't no big thang, you know it happens like that the first time." Money looked down at his gold watch. "Look, I wish I had more time to rap with you but I gotta meet somebody in a few."

"So that's it? You hit it then run?"

"Hey, we both got our groove on," Money said.

"What we? Speak for yourself."

STEVEN

Steven telephoned most of his friends to invite them to his party on Saturday night. His parents were in Europe on business and left their only child in charge of the house. At 18-years-old, they thought Steven was old enough to be on his own for a couple of weeks. Although his parents traveled often, that was the longest period of time Steven was ever alone.

He figured his parents asked the maid to keep an eye on him while they were away. But, she wouldn't deter his party plans because she would be long gone by the time the party started.

Tyler was the first person Steven invited to his party. To his dismay, Tyler told Steven that he couldn't make it. The basketball team would be away for the weekend to prepare for the championship tournament. Steven tried to convince Tyler to sneak away the night of the party and he would help him get back to the hotel room before the coach missed him. Tyler didn't go for it because the tournament was too important to risk the wrath of the coach and a one game suspension if he got caught.

Steven didn't want to tell Tyler that he was his bait to lure girls to his party. Yet, Steven was confident that his charm would get them there. He also figured that without Tyler, there would be more girls for him. Steven was in between girlfriends and in search of his next conquest.

"Ooh...she was hot," Steven belched out.

He sat on the floor in the center of his bedroom surrounded by sketches of past girlfriends that he drew. The drawings took the place of a "little black book" that most guys used to keep track of their women. Instead of the star system to rate dates, Steven had his own unique method.

How far Steven got with the girl determined the degree of completeness of the portrait of the girl's face. If the girl went all the way with Steven, there was a complete sketch of her face. If she engaged in heavy petting, only half of her face was drawn. If all she did was kiss or hold hands, then that was only worth one quarter of a facial portrait. On the back of the portrait, Steven recorded the girl's initials. On the lower right corner of the front, he scribbled his signature and the date of the last time he was with the person.

"But this one..."

Steven picked up the drawing of KJ and traced the outline of her face with his finger. She was his last girlfriend and the only one to break up with him. KJ fell in love with someone else while she and Steven were together. His ego had not bounced back from that blow.

He continued to fix his eyes on the light eyes of the girl in the picture.

Steven hoped that the three bottles of beer that he guzzled down would help numb the pain of his lost love, KJ. They didn't. So he took a long swig off his fourth one and squinted at his guest list to see whom to call next. The letters were wavy, yet, Bhriana DuPree's name jumped out at him. He turned the bottle up again to his red lips and dialed Bhriana's number. She picked up after the fourth ring and Steven put her on speakerphone.

"Hello."

"Hi, may I speak with Bhrianaaa?"

"Speaking."

"Hey Bhriana, it's Steeeven."

"Hey, how you doing?"

"Faaafine." *But not as faaafine as you though,* Steven said to himself.

"I heard about your break-up with Kristy James. You sure you're okay?"

"Why? Don't I sound all...right," Steven slurred then let out a loud burp.

"Eeelll...what was that disgusting sound?" Bhriana asked. "And no, you don't sound alright."

Steven put the beer down as if Bhriana could see him through the telephone. "Eeenough about KJ. I'm throwing a party on Saturday. You wanna come? My parents are away-"

"Again?"

"Yeees againnn, sooo can you come? You can bring Justinn if yooou want tooo."

"Justin's history. I try to avoid his calls but occasionally I slip up and he catches me. Then, I have

71

to listen to him whine for hours. I even got my mother lying for me saying I'm not home or busy when he calls. I told her that I'm trying to concentrate on school work and she fell for it. Otherwise, she wouldn't lie for me. But I don't expect much help from her anyway..."

Steven let her ramble on about the problems that she's had with her mother. All he thought of in his groggy mind was, *Poor Justin, he must be a mess. They don't come much finer than Bhriana. I wish I had a shot at her.*

"Will Tyler be there?"

The name Tyler broke Steven out of his trance. "Uuuh, yeah sure."

"Ummm, that's funny because he told me he was going away with his team this weekend."

Steven tried his best to clear his head and control his speech. He wiped the sweat from his forehead with his shirtsleeve. "Pssst, that's my partner, he wouldn't miss my party. See, he's gonna sneak out and make it to the party then sneak back in."

"Oooh, well then count me in," Bhriana said in a higher more excited pitch. "But, will that lanky b-ball jock chick be there?"

"Whooo?"

"You know, that Imooni."

Steven searched his mind to try to figure out the girl she described. After a few seconds he laughed. "Oooh, Imani!" he blurted out and they both cracked up. Steven laughed so hard that the beer swished around in his stomach. He stopped as the beer traveled up in his throat. He covered his mouth with his hand so Bhriana wouldn't hear him gag.

"Well? Did you invite her?"

Steven swallowed back the beer. He took a deep breath and tried to respond. "No. Why?"

"Because she wants him, that's why."

"Tyler has mentioned her. Maybe I should-"

"Oh no you don't!" Bhriana exclaimed.

Steven chuckled then covered his mouth again as the bitter fluid crawled back up his throat.

"I don't know where that troll came from but she better back off."

"Oooh, I looove a feisty woman," Steven managed to say.

"Are you drunk Steven? I swear you sound real funny."

Steven's head ached. He rested it in his thick hands and answered, "Nooo... but, I will have booze at the party so what's your poison?"

"You know me Steven, nothing but champagne."

"Youuu got it," Steven said and then clutched his stomach. "I hafta make some more calls."

"I understand. I've thrown my share of parties so I know what you're going through," Bhriana insisted.

Steven shook his head. No she didn't. He tried to stand up but only made it to a squat position as he tried to wrap up the conversation. "Okaaay, so I'll see youuu Saturday."

"Youuu got it," Bhriana mimicked then chuckled.

Before Bhriana could say another word, Steven had crawled into his bathroom and bowed over the porcelain toilet bowl.

* * * *

73

Steven thought the maid would never leave. She must have sensed that he was up to something because she never worked overtime on a Saturday. Steven forbade the maid to enter his room so he was on his own to clean it up, which he seldom did. Any other day he wouldn't care but that night he thought he might get lucky with one of the females and he didn't want to give the impression that he was a slob.

Steven tossed the nudie magazines underneath the bed and placed law books on the nightstand. He picked up empty beer bottles and food wrappers. He dusted off his computer, printer, and the oak desk they sat on. En route to his closet, he tripped over a pair of khakis on the floor, which made him notice all the other clothes strewn about the room. They got scooped up and tossed onto the floor of his walk-in closet.

He stood back and surveyed the tidy room. He walked over to the entertainment center and loaded five mellow CDs into the CD player then put the remote control on his nightstand. He placed a finger to his temple and frowned.

Steven went back to the closet and retrieved his art portfolio. He pulled out the drawings that he was most proud of but none of the girls he had dated. Those were beautiful pictures of nature and animals. "Oooh yeah," Steven said out loud, "females love this kind of stuff." He spread them out over the queen-sized bed. That tactic had worked a couple of times before. It led the girls directly to where he wanted them and they would sit down, relax, and marvel at his talent.

Steven's artistic skills were extraordinary. He was accepted into a prestigious arts high school but he decided to use his mind, wit, and gift of persuasion to become a corporate lawyer. Westmoore High provided the education he needed to get accepted into an Ivy League school then a notable law school. He told his parents that he loved art but he loved money more. Steven loved the ladies too and as he glanced around the room, he was pleased with the seductive setting that he had created.

Steven showered but it didn't do much to cool him off. His body temperature was still high, from the beer that he drank, and sweat formed on his forehead as he awaited his guests. Steven gave Jazz money to pick up more beer and other alcohol because there was only one local liquor store in his town and the owner knew Steven was a minor and wouldn't sell to him.

"Jazz better come through," Steven said aloud as he surveyed the limited amount of beer and champagne that he had to offer. He had taken all of the beer and some bottles of champagne out of the wine cellar. Other than a select few, he didn't think his guests would drink wine, which his parents had plenty of in stock. For those few who didn't drink alcohol, he had soda and sparkling water.

The caterer delivered finger sandwiches, chips, dips, and other snacks so there was nothing left for him to do but wait for the doorbell to ring. There was a cool March breeze that came off the patio, which led to the in ground pool. It was dark as the full moon replaced the sun. Steven switched on the patio lights. The light reflections danced on top of the water in the pool and hypnotized him. His mind wondered back to the time when he was about six-years-old and his father first taught him how to swim.

Frightened to jump into the water, his entire skinny body quivered as he stood at the edge of the pool. Steven's father waited in the middle of the pool with outstretched arms.

"Trust me son, I'll catch you."

Steven did trust him and leaped off the edge towards the open arms of his father. Mr. Clark pulled his hands back and little Steven sank to the bottom. Somehow, the terrified boy fought his way to the top. His nostrils and throat burned from all of the chlorinated water that he inhaled and swallowed.

Mr. Clark finally grabbed hold of his son and told him, "My father did the same thing to me to kill that fear of the water. I've been a fine swimmer ever since." That confession didn't make little Steven feel any better. The words "trust me son" never meant the same to him since that frightful incident.

The doorbell sounded and brought Steven back to the present. He wiped his moist eyes and went to answer the door. He stopped at the entertainment center and turned up the volume. A rock tune blared through the speakers. "Let's get this party started," he announced. Steven opened the door and greeted a group of five. He left the door cracked so that the other guests could let themselves in.

Five grew into twenty-something. Teenagers of various races enjoyed the spread Steven had laid out. Most of the guys had a plate in one hand and a beer in the other. The young ladies help themselves to salad and champagne. The boys congregated to one side of the room and the girls the other. Although pleased with the turn out, Steven was anxious for the arrival of Jazz and Bhriana.

"Great party Steven," a couple of attractive young women said in unison. He zeroed in on the fairer skinned of the two, Porsche.

"Thanks," he replied and all the while gazed into Porsche's gray eyes. Steven wished her friend would get lost but she stood close to Porsche like a Siamese twin. He figured if he carried on a conversation with just Porsche, her sidekick would get the hint and move along. He was wrong. She didn't budge. In frustration he asked, "Porsche, can I call you tomorrow?"

Porsche recited her number as if she'd done it a million times. Steven insisted that he didn't have to write it down. He memorized it and repeated it back to her. Seconds later he spotted Jazz. "I'll be right back."

Jazz carried a keg of beer. Another brother that Steven didn't know followed behind him and toted a case of beer with brown bags on top. The crowd roared when Steven yelled, "Brews coming through." After Jazz placed the keg on the floor, Steven paid him fifty dollars as promised. "Uh, what about my partner here?"

"You never mentioned a partner."

"Did you think I was gonna come to your neighborhood at night by myself? Naw man, I wanted a witness just in case the cops around here pulled me over for no reason."

"The police officers around here wouldn't do such a thing," Steven insisted.

"I'm not gonna argue with you Man, just pay my partner."

Steven looked like a little bush sandwiched in between two towering trees. He didn't want Jazz to get indignant and embarrass him in front of his friends so he reached in his wallet and pulled out a ten dollar bill.

"You're kidding right?" Jazz asked.

"I'm not about to pay him fifty dollars," Steven responded in a loud whisper.

"Forty."

"Twenty-five."

"I'll take it," the partner said.

Steven and Jazz snickered as if each got the better of the other. Jazz turned his attention to the guests around the room and frowned. "Where are all the sistahs? And, what's up with that music? That's why nobody's dancing."

"You're not staying so what do you care?" Steven replied.

"Pssst, you're not dismissing me like some servant. My partner and I are hungry and we're gonna hang out here and throw down on some munchies."

Jazz, the tallest person in the room, continued to look over Steven's head and out into the crowd. "What, I'm not good enough to party with your friends? We're all Westmore Jaguars up in here."

Steven had long tuned Jazz out. As with most of his guests, Steven's eyes zoomed in on Bhriana. She stood in the foyer and soaked up all of the attention thrown her way. Bhriana looked like she stepped off a page of a chic fashion magazine. The black form fitted tank dress showed off her toned figure. A black cardigan draped around and accented her tiny waist. Her smooth and slender arms and legs were bare. Black sandals and a designer handbag complemented the outfit. Bhriana smiled and sashayed her way through the crowd and headed in Steven's direction.

Steven showed all of his white straight teeth, thanks to braces, as he grinned back at Bhriana. He took hold of Bhriana's delicate hands and gave her a peck on both cheeks. He looked around to see if Porsche had witnessed it. She didn't but her friend noticed and whispered into Porsche's ear. She looked at Bhriana and waved her hand as if to say, "She's ain't all dat."

Steven knew he would have to smooth things over with Porsche later because at that moment, Bhriana had his undivided attention. "The party's complete now that you're here," Steven told her.

"Oh brother," Jazz chimed in and laughed.

Bhriana gazed up at Jazz and rolled her hazel eyes. "Is Tyler here yet?" she asked Steven.

"Sorry, but, T-Man called me just before you graced us with your fineness and said he couldn't make it after all."

"I didn't know that Ty-"

"Uh Jazz, why don't you and what's his name go eat before the food's all gone," Steven said and gently pulled Bhriana away. Jazz must have gotten the hint because he winked at Steven and walked away without another word.

"I'm so bummed out that Tyler's not here. Maybe I should just leave."

"Oh, so our friendship means nothing? You're going to walk out on my party just because T-Man's not here? That hurts Bhriana."

"W-e-l-l-l," Bhriana responded and drew her shoulders up to her dangling sterling silver earrings.

"Well, how would it look if the finest female - I mean woman here leaves so soon? Don't make me look like a loser. Please."

"Since you said I'm the finest one here, how could I not help you out? I'll stay but I hope the champagne's on ice."

The corners of his mouth curled up. "Yes it is."

* * * *

It was well past midnight and only a few guests, the ones who had coupled off, remained. All night, Steven and Bhriana acted like a couple. They danced, talked, laughed, and drank a lot of champagne. Steven forgot all about Porsche. He thought that Bhriana had forgotten about Tyler until she brought him up again when they were alone out on the patio.

"...You know and he always asks me what I want to do or where I want to go and I tell him and we do it."

"Buuut, he hasn't done what yooou really want him to do... has he?" Steven asked and then laughed.

"Ladies don't kiss and tell."

"You don't have to t-tell. I know T-Man hasn't put a mooove on you yet. Maybe he wants somebody else?"

"Like who? I know you don't mean that jock chick?" Bhriana asked in a bitter tone. Bhriana and Steven were intoxicated and the words flowed. "I bet he would be here if Imooni was here," she continued.

"You're probably ri-right," Steven responded. He tried not to slur but he didn't want to talk anyway. He stroked Bhriana's silky smooth hair. She didn't resist. Steven wanted to kiss her so badly that his lips twitched. He zeroed in on the target. Just before contact, powerful hands gripped his shoulders.

Steven jumped and turned around and saw Jazz with a wide grin on his face. "What the heck are you still doing here?"

"Man, it's cold as a motha out here. What are you two? Eskimos?" Jazz asked.

"Why are you still here?" Steven asked again.

"My partner's in there trying to hook up with some wannabe. I told him not to waste his time but he's not hearing me." He stared at Bhriana and added, "I ain't seen nothing here worth sweatin' over. I got my hands full anyway."

"Is that right?" Bhriana asked in a sarcastic tone.

"That's right."

"I guess that means you can get any girl you want, huh?"

"That's right."

Bhriana eyes roamed up and down Jazz's tall muscular frame. He wasn't her type financially but physically, if it weren't for his prickly baby dreadlocks, she could be attracted to him. "Sooo, you're in the same league as Tyler, huh?"

"On and off the court."

"Shoot, my boy can take you anytime on the court. Come to think of it, he t-took your starting position," Steven said then let out a howl.

"Man, I do you a favor then you're gonna dog me out?"

"A favor? I paid you."

"Paid him for what?" Bhriana asked.

Steven told her the details then ended with, "But that's why I respect Jazz, he's a hustler."

"Respect this," Jazz said as he curled his long fingers into a big fist.

"Ummm."

"Ummm, what Bhriana?" Steven asked.

Her amber eyes captured him. The magnetic force was so great that he couldn't break away from the gaze even if he wanted to, and he didn't.

"Steven, you said we're friends right?"

"Right."

"And friends help each other, right?"

"Right."

She leaned over to Steven and he could smell her sweet perfume. So close that he felt her hot breath on his ear lobe. She whispered to him, "W-e-l-l-l, since Jazz thinks he can compete with Tyler and he's a hustler and all, why don't you pay him to keep that b-ball broad away from Tyler?"

Steven's eyes stung and he realized that he hadn't blinked. Not only were his eyes dry, but also his mouth which was held in an open get ready to kiss position. He swallowed a few times and batted his eyes before he answered. "I heard what you said but what do you mean?"

"You know, pay him to date her?"

"Nah..."

"Yes..."

Steven's eyes went from Bhriana to Jazz and back to Bhriana again. He leaned his head back and looked up into the star filled sky. He knew that Jazz would do it, but, what would he get out of the deal? What could Bhriana do for him? "I don't know, Bhriana. If my boy ever found out what I did-"

Bhriana stopped him in mid sentence with a kiss on his lips. She moved back just a little bit and then whispered, "He will never find out."

"What's up?" Jazz asked and broke Steven's daze.

Bhriana put her finger on Steven's lips. "Don't tell him while I'm here. I don't want to know the details. Just do it for me, plueeeze. "

"Yo Jazz let's roll. Everybody's gone man," his friend yelled.

"I'll call you Monday."

"Naw Steven, if my name's in it, we've got to talk now."

"Trust me, it can wait until Monday," Steven reassured Jazz.

"Yeah, I trust you alright," Jazz replied with a smirk on his face. "I trust you about as much as a hungry pit bull around raw meat."

"Later, Jazz," Steven said and escorted him and his partner to the door. As Steven closed the door behind them, he felt Bhriana's arms wrapped around his stomach. Then he felt the warmth from her body as she pressed against his back.

"Thanks for helping me out. It's an awesome idea getting Jazz and that girl together. Other than her, I don't understand why Tyler pulls away from me." Steven felt more of her body pressed in the hollow of his back. "Am I attractive?"

"Yeees," Steven responded.

"Sexy?"

Steven closed his eyes and said, "Oh, yeees." *Either I'm drunk or she's drunk or we're both drunk or I'm just imagining that she's coming on to me but who cares just take advantage of it...* Steven rambled on to himself. He turned around to face Bhriana and was surprised to see her head bowed. He gently lifted her chin up with his fingers and their eyes met.

"I can't speak for Tyler but to me, you are the most gorgeous girl on this planet." He drew Bhriana closer to him and kissed her. His tongue slid deeply into her smoldering mouth. It must have caught Bhriana off guard because he felt her body tense up and then she backed away.

"Thanks for pumping up my ego and keeping me company tonight."

"My pleasure."

"But...I've taken up too much of your time. Not that I'm anxious to go home to Mother, but, I should leave now."

"Why rush off?" Steven asked then kissed her velvety lips again and drew her back close to him. When their lips parted, he caressed her face. "I meant every word that I've said." He paused then continued, "Let me show you just how beautiful you are."

"How can you show me?"

Steven didn't respond in words. His lips, tongue, and hands spoke for him. Tired of the upright position and confident that she might go all the way, Steven took Bhriana by the hand and led her upstairs.

IMANI

Imani held her breath as Tyler launched the basketball from behind the three-point line in a game called "H-O-R-S-E." It was sort of like follow the leader. One person created a move and then shot the ball. If it went into the hoop, the next player had to make the exact same move and make the shot. If that player failed to do so, then he or she got the next letter in the word "horse." The first player who spelled that word completely lost the game.

Imani and Tyler were on the letter "R." If Tyler missed his next shot, he moved to "S." The ball arched high into the air and appeared on target to go through the hoop but it fell short and hit the front of the rim.

"Yeees!" exclaimed Imani as she jumped up and down and clapped her hands. She found a weakness in his game and decided to take advantage of it. "Give me the ball."

"It ain't over yet, Imani, so don't get too excited."

"It may be after this shot," Imani replied. She dribbled the ball back behind the three-point line and fired another one that caught all net. "Bam!" she yelled and the sound echoed off the gym walls.

"Not bad 'Hot Shot', I knew you had game," he said and threw Imani a movie star smile.

She perspired even more as her body heat rose up to her face. It wasn't the physical activity but his comment that made her feel flushed. If nothing else, he recognized her game. "If you quit now, I promise not to tell anybody that I beat you."

Tyler scanned the empty gym then looked back at Imani. "You talkin' to me?"

"Yeah you," Imani said with a straight face but couldn't hold it. They both cracked up.

"It's on now, Hot Shot."

"Go 'head with your bad self," Imani said.

Tyler did just that and made the basket. Imani didn't believe he could do it two times in a row so she took the same shot but missed it that time. "You went back to the well too many times," Tyler told her. He attempted the shot again and made it. "'S' for you too."

"It ain't over yet, Tyler, so don't get too excited," Imani said.

"Touché. But, it may be over after this shot. Sounds familiar?"

"Touché," Imani responded and giggled.

"How high can you fly, Hot Shot?"

Before Imani answered, Tyler took off into the air and slam-dunked the ball. "No fair!" she hollered.

In between deep breaths, Tyler laughed. Imani marched over to him, snatched the ball away, and then hit him on his rock hard arm. "I'll tell you what," Tyler said with a sympathetic look, "I'll lower the basket or give you two chances or…"

"I don't need charity thank you."

"I'm just trying to help a sistah out."

"Yeah right."

Imani stood at the free throw line and was about to make her move when Tyler interrupted. "You're gonna need more of a running start than that so you can stop and leap from where I'm standing."

"If I wanted advice, I'd call one of the Lakers, or Bulls, or Knicks, or…"

"Okay, Hot Shot, do it your way, but, I'm gonna stand here and catch you so you don't kill yourself."

Well that caught Imani off guard. It sounded as if Tyler cared. But, did he care about "Hot Shot" or Imani? That question weighed on her mind as she took Tyler's advice and moved back a couple of feet. Imani dribbled towards the basket, stopped and pushed off as hard as she could with her strong athletic legs. She stretched upward towards the rim with her long arms but didn't come close to it. Tyler caught Imani by her waist.

"Thank you," she huffed as she came face to face with him.

"You're welcome. Now try it again."

"For what? I got 'E', the game's over."

"Remember I said I'll give you two chances."

"Remember I said I don't want charity."

"It's just a game, Imani. Consider the first one a practice shot and this one will tie the game and that's how we'll end it. A tie."

"Since you put it that way then fine, I'll try it again."

Imani gave herself an even greater running start and forged ahead with determination. She gasped as Tyler's hands clamped onto her waist and his powerful arms guided her towards the basket. She slammed the ball through the rim and watched as Tyler ducked to protect his head.

"Tie game," Tyler said as he lowered Imani down.

"Why did you do that?" Imani asked.

Tyler ran off the court and up to the top row of the bleacher. She wanted to run after him but Imani feared that she would trip on the way up and truly embarrass herself. She wiped her sweaty brown face with her forearm and strolled off the court. *I hope he doesn't expect me to sit close to him with my stinky self. God, I must look a mess. I hope he can't see through this wet tee shirt. Where's Fatima when I need her? What do I say now?*

All of those thoughts raced through her mind as she stepped up the bleachers. She sat down a couple of feet away from Tyler and bit her fingernails.

"You know, our funk will cancel each other out," Tyler said.

Imani removed her fingers from her mouth then lifted up her arms and took a whiff of both armpits. "You're right, I don't smell anything."

"Told you."

They laughed and Imani slid over closer to Tyler and relaxed. It occurred to her that he never answered her question so she asked him again. He looked like he struggled for an answer. Tyler rubbed his hand across his shiny wavy hair then gazed into Imani's eyes.

"I guess you can say I was helping a friend."

Imani's brow raised. A friend? That was news she couldn't wait to tell Fatima. Imani smiled and said, "I really don't know much about you, friend, so tell me about yourself."

"Like what?"

"Like what else do you like to do other than play basketball and like what are some of your favorite things. You know, stuff."

Tyler stroked his square cleft chin and said, "Let me see what stuff can I tell you. Well yeah, basketball is my first love and I'm good at it but I'm not crazy enough to think that I'll be starting for the Knicks or Lakers one day. But, maybe a trainer for some professional team is a possibility."

Imani's eyes widened and she asked, "You wanna go into sports medicine?"

"Yeah, maybe."

"Me too," Imani replied. "I was also thinking about becoming a sportscaster or journalist and get this, if I wasn't afraid of being shot, a detective."

"A detective?" Tyler asked and then chuckled.

"Oh, you find that funny?"

"Not really. It's just that you don't fit the image of the fat, balding, cigar smoking detectives that you see on television."

"I'll take that as a compliment," Imani said. "But I'll play b-ball as long as I can. I'm busting my butt trying to earn a four year scholarship and hopefully make an Olympic team while in college. But, I have a back-up plan, too, especially after what happened to my father."

"What happened?"

"He probably would have been a pro football player but he got hurt in high school and that was the end of it. He works in a hospital now."

"Oh, he's a doctor, that's cool," Tyler said.

Imani was too ashamed to disclose his true profession and remained silent.

"I hear ya. My father told me not to put all of my hopes into basketball. He said that I've gotta have a plan 'b'. He thinks it's working with him but I'll probably go to med school or law school," Tyler said.

"Shooot, a player can fake it through college but it's not gonna get him into those schools or land him a decent j.o.b," Imani replied.

"Do you know what colleges you're gonna apply to?" Tyler asked.

Imani took a deep breath and thought long and hard about it. "I don't want to follow behind my sister and go to some Ivy League school. I want to go to one of the black colleges like Howard or Spelman or some other ones."

Imani watched as Tyler shook his head up and down in agreement with her. Yet, he looked dejected. "What's wrong?"

He leaned back against the cement wall and looked up towards the rafters. "It's funny you said that," he began, "because I had a disagreement with my father not too long ago about the type of college I wanted to go to. He doesn't think black colleges are good enough for me."

"You're kiddin'?"

"Nope."

Imani ran down a list of successful black people who attended black colleges. She mentioned Thurgood

Marshall, Booker T. Washington, George Washington Carver, Marion Wright Edelman, Zora Neale Hurston, W.E.B. DuBois, Toni Morrison...

"There are so many more that I could go on and on," Imani ended.

"Wow. See, my father just doesn't get it," Tyler said and went on and told Imani how his father had his life all planned for him. He talked about the promises his father made to his mother and how determined his father was to own up to them.

"If your mom was here, what college would she want you to go to?"

"I don't think she would care as long as I'm happy."

"You're only a junior. You've got some time to work on your dad."

Tyler chuckled and said, "That sounds like something my mother would say. I miss talking to her. I miss everything about my mom even down to something as silly as her sweet potato pies. I mean she could cook more than pies but she made those just for her and me. My dad called them poor southern folk's food and wouldn't eat them."

Tyler closed his eyes and took a deep breath as if he inhaled the sweet aroma of those pies. He shook his head side to side and said, "We have yet to find a good cook. Maybe your parents can refer one."

Oh, sure. You're talking to her now, Imani said to herself. Aloud she replied, "W-e-l-l-l actually my mom prefers to cook and I usually help her out. We like keeping it simple in our household."

Imani regretted that she used the word "household." She tilted her head up to the rafters and prayed to God that Tyler wouldn't ask her where she lived. She said a quick "amen" and then wiped the newly formed perspiration off her forehead with the back of her hand. Then she slid off the rubber band that held her ponytail, and unleashed her voluminous braids.

Oh no he's staring at my hair. If he asks me if it's all mine, I'll die. No I'll lie. No I'll die. Oooh get over it, Imani argued with herself. She folded her hands into her lap to keep her nails away from her mouth. Imani forced a smile and Tyler returned it with a wide smile of his own.

"You know," he said, "I love writing poetry."

"Speaking of left field."

"So what are you trying to say? B-ballers can't read or write?" Tyler asked.

"Nooo. It's just that I don't know many guys who like to write or read poetry. I'm a girl and I don't like writing it but I do love reading poetry."

"Do you like reading haiku?" Tyler asked.

"Hmmm, you mean the poems with three lines and the first and third lines are five syllables long and the second line is seven syllables?"

Tyler looked impressed. "That's it."

"Yeah, I like 'em because they're short and to the point."

"Well, when you let your braids loose and smiled, it inspired me to think of a haiku."

"Just like that?"

"Just like that," Tyler answered and snapped his fingers for emphasis.

"Bring it on. I wanna hear this."

Imani tried to maintain her composure as that gorgeous guy put his spell on her. Never had any boy said that she inspired anything in him. Then again, she never spent much time with boys unless it was on the basketball court. A couple of guys that Imani was interested in she avoided because they wouldn't understand the curfews and rules that her parents enforced.

She had to be in the house by 9:00 p.m., even on the weekends, and no telephone calls, male or female, after 10:00 p.m. Boys could not visit her at home, unless one of her parents was there to supervise. It seemed cruel to some of the teenagers she knew, especially Fatima, but Imani figured she could endure for another year. If she got a scholarship, she could enjoy her freedom at college.

Tyler cleared his throat and he began to speak.

"I call this one 'Gaze Into My Eyes'.

The reflection of
your beauty lies deep within
my chestnut brown eyes."

Dang! Imani screamed inside. "You must have written that for Bhriana."

"She's never heard that one."

"What's the deal with you two, anyway?"

Tyler had a sheepish grin on his smooth caramel-dipped face. He couldn't hide that gleam in his eyes when Imani mentioned her name. Imani came back down to earth at that instant.

"I'm attracted to her and we do spend time together. But I don't know, ummm, I'm just trying to take it slow." Imani held her breath as he reached over and took hold of her clammy hand. "We can still be friends, right?"

Not if Bhriana chokes me to death, is what she wanted to say. Instead, she settled for a weak, "We're cool."

* * * *

Imani sat on the number 70 bus and panted from the mad dash she made from the gym to the bus stop. Tyler offered to escort her home and Imani panicked. When he went into the locker room, she left him a note that said that her mother came by and insisted on driving her home. She turned heel and high-tailed it out of that building.

Imani transferred to the number 25 bus and stood all the way to her destination. She got off the bus and dragged her feet along her journey. Imani's mother taught her to be aware of her surroundings at all times. However, Imani was exhausted and focused on home, a call to Fatima, and then bed.

She trudged past dust covered children who played as if they didn't have a care in the world. Those apparently happy kids weren't aware that they were "disadvantaged." Neither did Imani until she saw how the students at Westmoore lived. She thought her environment was the norm.

When she discovered that it wasn't, it angered Imani. Not a hatred towards the rich kids like Bhriana and Tyler, but a driving force to make a better life for herself and her family. It drove Roberta, too. Imani knew that Roberta worked hard for everything that she'd achieved. Yet, Imani felt it only made her life more difficult as she tried to live up to the high standards that Roberta established.

"Yo sistah, two for ten."

Imani glanced at the gold watch collection that the man displayed along his ashy bony arm. A smile accompanied her "No thank-you" so not to tick him off.

He flashed a toothless smile. "Come on sistah, help a brotha out."

"Sorry," Imani said and lengthened her strides. She felt sorry for that man and it bothered her that she couldn't help him. But, money was tight in her family and if she had money to give away, it would go to her parents.

Imani appreciated how creative her parents were as they stretched a dollar and juggled bills. Yet, Imani remembered a couple of times when that led to dire consequences. Imani caught a chill with the thought of one of those incidents.

It was a snowy night in the dead of winter. The strong winds banged against the kitchen window. The flames from the candles cast shadows against the walls and gave the small living room an eerie aura. The then 8-year-old Imani and her 12-year-old sister were huddled beneath mounds of towels and sheets and the only two bedspreads that they owned. The curious girls uncovered their heads and listened as their mother pleaded with the gas and electric company.

"...I swear I'll be there first thing in the morning. Plueeeze, turn the gas back on so my babies don't freeze to death," Mrs. Jackson begged but it fell on deaf ears.

"I'm not cold," Imani said in an attempt to make her teary-eyed mother feel better.

"Me either," Roberta chimed in.

Mrs. Jackson tucked the girls in on the couch even tighter. Imani noticed that her hands shook which meant her mother was very cold or angry or both.

"Button up your coat, Ma," Imani suggested.

"Don't worry about me. You two stay put while I fix you something to eat."

Moments later, Imani saw the shadow of her father's figure on the wall. He looked like a giant to her. White flakes covered him from head to toe.

"What the hell's goin' on here?"

"You'd better get out of those wet clothes fo' you catch pneumonia," Mrs. Jackson told him.

Mr. Jackson looked at his two girls bundled up on the sofa. "I know damn well those dumb asses didn't turn off the damn heat and the lights and it's damn near zero degrees outside!"

Imani's body stiffened. She had never heard her father curse. That wasn't allowed in their home.

"I know you're upset-"

"No, Cora, I'm pissed off. Look at my girls!" he exclaimed and pointed to his daughters. "Did you call those stupid idiots down there?"

"I spoke to just about everybody down there and nobody cares."

"Did you tell them that we'll pay 'em tomorrow?"

"Yeah, but they ain't got the money today so we ain't got no heat or lights."

Mr. Jackson no longer looked like a giant to Imani. His broad shoulders slumped and his head dropped. "Let's pack these kids up and take 'em on over to Mrs. Wilson's."

It was then that Imani realized that her father wasn't superman. He was just a man who tried to do the best that he could for his family. Sometimes he won and sometimes he lost. But, he never ran away from the challenge and he never threw in the towel. Mr. Jackson swallowed his pride in the best interest of his family.

The smell of fried fish greeted Imani at her door and brought her back to the present. It was a family tradition to have fried fish, whiting, french fries and coleslaw or some other vegetable every Friday. Imani didn't mind because she loved seafood, especially shrimps. Occasionally her mother would surprise Imani with a fried shrimp dinner.

"Chile this fish's about to get cold," her mother said.

"You're a little late today ain't you, Imani?" her father, Robert, asked.

"And hello to both of you too," Imani responded.

"Oooh come here, Baby," Mrs. Jackson cooed and rubbed her soft chubby cheek against the side of her daughter's face.

Imani smiled and surveyed the dinner table. She surprised herself when she said, "I'd rather go straight to bed."

Mrs. Jackson touched her daughter's forehead and asked, "Chile are you sick? You never missed a fish meal."

"Baby Girl now come on and sit down and say grace so I can put this fish between my lips," Mr. Jackson said.

"Hey that kinda rhymed. Fish and lips," her mother said a broke into laughter along with her husband.

"Everybody wants to be a poet today," Imani replied and plopped down in a seat at the table.

"What you talkin' about?" her mother asked.

Imani thought about it but then decided not to bring Tyler's name up. She waved her hand, bowed her head and said grace. "Thank you God for this wonderful food that my mother's prepared. Thank you God for protecting us all day long so that we can have dinner together once again. Amen."

"Again. Amen. That rhymes too," Imani's father said and chuckled. "Baby Girl, pass me the bread."

Mr. Jackson's baritone voice and large stature only intimidated Imani when he'd reprimand her. He stood about 6'8" tall with broad shoulders, expansive chest and back. The only things that softened his athletic physique was a small pot belly and his warm smile. The full beard and moustache surrounded his dark chocolate face and made him look older than his mid forties.

Imani noticed the calluses on his large hands and the dirt under his fingernails as he put together his fish sandwich. He could have gone to college on a football scholarship if he hadn't gotten injured his senior year in high school. His parents couldn't afford to send him to college and his grades weren't good enough to earn a scholastic scholarship.

Mr. Jackson held two jobs ever since Imani could remember. He was a custodial worker at the local hospital and the superintendent in the complex that they lived in. The superintendent's job didn't pay but they resided there rent-free.

"I hope I don't have to remind you that it's your turn to cook Sunday's dinner," Mrs. Jackson said to her daughter.

Imani's mother never worked outside of the home. Her parent's couldn't afford a babysitter when Imani and Roberta were infants. When they began school, Mrs. Jackson felt it necessary to walk her children to and from school everyday for their protection. She was only available to work the few hours that the kids were in school. With that limited amount of time and only a high school diploma, her job opportunities were slim to none. She decided to use her talent as a seamstress and worked out of her home and she continued to do so.

"You don't have to remind me, Ma. We've been taking turns since forever."

"Did your mama tell you that Roberta called today?"

"Ummm I forgot to tell ya," Mrs. Jackson said and licked hot sauce off her thick fingers. She was a full figured woman with a hearty appetite. Her toasted almond colored face beamed as she told Imani that Roberta made the Dean's List again, ran track, and started on the basketball team. "She's gonna try out for the Olympic team for basketball when it rolls around."

"I don't know about that new boy though," Mr. Jackson said.

That brief remark caught Imani's attention. She turned to her father and watched him work on his second sandwich. Imani waited but her father didn't volunteer anymore information. "What new boy?"

"Ask your mama." Before Imani could ask her mother, Mr. Jackson added, "All I know is that he better not mess up that girl's program 'cause then he'll have to answer to me. Can't trust some of them college boys either. Do you know how many cases of date rape I see at that hospital everyday? That's somebody's daughter dog-gone-it!"

"Just watch out for them bones while you getting all worked up over there," Mrs. Jackson warned. Mr. Jackson mumbled something and then took a long swig of his iced tea. Mrs. Jackson tapped Imani on her hand and told her that, "He's a new boy that Roberta met but it's no big deal."

"Yeah, she better keep it that way. No big deal," Imani's father chimed in. He worked a wooden toothpick between his teeth and continued, "I ain't too worried though. Roberta's a smart girl and ain't never gave me a day's trouble. Lord knows I'm proud of her. I hope you're taking notes, Baby Girl."

"Yes Chile, you can learn a lot from Roberta," her mother added.

"Remember when you were pregnant with Roberta and we just knew she was gonna be a boy so we didn't have any girl's names ready," her father said and the couple cackled.

"I've heard this story a billion times," Imani mumbled and pushed back from the table with plate in hand. She offered what remained on her plate to her parents then scrapped off the rest. Imani tried to block out her parents' conversation. The telephone rang and her father frowned. Mr. Jackson hated to receive calls at dinnertime. Imani grabbed the telephone.

"Hello."

"May I speak to Imani?" an unfamiliar male voiced asked.

"Speaking."

"Hey, it's Jazz."

"Who?"

"Jazz Timmons...on the boy's basketball team..."

Imani glanced at her parents and their eyes zeroed in on her. In a loud tone she announced, "Oh hey, Fatima. Girrrl you got a cold or something 'cause I didn't recognize your voice. Hold on while I switch phones." Imani ran into her parents' bedroom and picked up the only other telephone in the apartment and then bolted into the kitchen and hung up that receiver.

"What happened to 'I'm sooo tired I can't eat I'm going straight to bed'?" her mother asked. Mrs. Jackson stacked more dirty dishes in the small white sink and motioned to them. "And when you stop running your mouth, you can run back to this sink and wash these dishes before you go to bed."

"I know. I know," Imani responded and hurried back to the bedroom. Questions spun about just as quickly through her mind. *How did he get my number? Why is he calling me? What does he want? How do I look? Look? What am I talkin' about?* She was out of breath when she reached the phone. "Hey... I'm back," she huffed.

"Who's Fatima?"

"Oh I'm sorry. I was trying to throw my folks off that's all."

"Did it work?"

"Seemed to."

"That's cool," Jazz said and then the line went silent.

Imani didn't want Jazz to hear her as she took deep breaths and bit what little nails remained. She pulled the receiver further away from her mouth and waited for Jazz to say something. A dot of bright red blood sprang up in the corner of her pinky. The silence was too much. She had to speak. "Sooo, how did you get my phone number?" Imani asked then licked off the blood.

"I got it from your teammate, Terry."

"Why?"

"W-e-l-l-l, I was too shy to approach you in person so I thought it would be easier to talk to you like this. I've had my eye on you for a long time but never had the nerve to speak to you."

"Why not?"

"I dunno. I tend to freeze up around beautiful sistahs. Your name's cool too. What does it mean?"

"Imani is 'faith' in Kiswahili and it's something I try to hold onto everyday."

"That's deep."

"Yeah it's deep but it ain't easy," Imani replied as she glanced about her meager surroundings. She thought about her parents and their unyielding faith. They had faith that the more they gave, the more they would one day receive. At least that was something that the preacher reminded them every Sunday right before the straw baskets traveled across the pews. The organist played an upbeat tune and the chorus and congregation sang about when they got over to the other side how grand it would be. Imani sang along but she was concerned about the present. She wanted life to be grand while here on earth.

"Your name's unique, too."

"Unique yeah but not as deep as yours. I still can't imagine my mother doing it but I was conceived in the bathroom of a jazz club."

"Get out!" Imani yelled and let out a genuine laugh.

"For real," Jazz began, "man, it's so cool to hear you laugh. You look so serious all the time at school. And on the court, forget it."

"You've seen me play?"

"I've been to a couple of games and you got skillz, Girl."

Imani smiled and thanked him for the great compliment. Her expression changed as she watched a bug crawl across the wood floor towards the bed where she sat. No matter how much she and her mother kept the house clean, bugs and mice tried to make it their home, too. She reached down, picked up one of her father's shoes, and squashed the roach.

"What was that?" Jazz asked.

Although Jazz was on the other end of the telephone and couldn't see what she had done, Imani felt ashamed. "A book fell."

"Oh. Well like I said before, I think you're a real beautiful sistah and no doubt got a lot going for yourself and I'd like to get to know you. Sooo, can we see a movie or something tomorrow or are you attached right now?"

Tyler's handsome face flashed before her eyes. She couldn't understand why she felt that if she went out with Jazz, she would be cheating on Tyler. After all, he said that they're friends. Not boyfriend and girlfriend but just plain old friends. "I dunno, Jazz. I really need to study for mid terms."

"Okay. Where do you live? I can come over and we can cram together. Unless you want to come over to my house."

"Where do you live?" Imani asked and took the heat off her.

"You're not familiar with my 'hood. On second thought, it's not a good idea for you to come here by yourself. I'd rather pick you up."

Imani shook her head from side to side. She knew that was out of the question. "Just tell me where you live," she said.

"I live in Bedford, a.k.a. Slum City in the projects on Green Street."

Dang! He lives right down the hill from me. How come I've never seen him around here before? Imani asked herself. Images of her neighbors roamed through her mind but she still couldn't spot Jazz. "Wow, you won't believe this but I live up the hill from you."

"You serious? I thought you lived near school."

"I wish I did. And if it wasn't for my b-ball scholarship, I'd never see that side of town."

"Hey, that's how I got into Westmoore, too" Jazz said.

"For real?"

"Yeah, but, I don't wish that I lived over there. What's wrong with our 'hood?" Jazz asked.

Both of them laughed at that question. Imani felt calm since she didn't have to hide where she lived from Jazz. She was elated that someone at her school came from her environment. "I don't like publicizing it, Jazz, so let's keep it on the down low."

"You really are ashamed of where you come from, huh?"

"Its nobody's business where I live. That's all," Imani responded in a defensive tone.

"Hey, if that's what you want, it'll be our secret."

The line went silent again. *I never should have told him but I've got to trust somebody. Don't I?* She pondered the answer to that question until Jazz spoke again.

"I don't care where you live. I still wanna hook up with you unless you have a problem with me. I mean if you prefer a rich brotha like Tyler, that's cool."

"Why did you bring Tyler into this?"

"I've heard him mention your name a few times so I figured he was feelin' you."

"He's a friend of mine but I don't see him as being better than you just because of where he comes from. Tyler's a good person and that's all that matters to me. Can you say the same thing?"

"Say what?"

"Say that you're a cool brotha and not some playa with a one track mind."

"Yeah, I can say that."

"Then you can take me to a matinee tomorrow. I hear that new mystery is good," Imani said.

"That's what I heard too. That's cool."

Imani told Jazz why it had to be a matinee instead of a late night movie then ran down all of the rules and curfews that she lived by under her parents' roof. Imani tried to envision Jazz's facial expressions as she spoke but nothing registered. He didn't express any objections to what she laid out so she assumed he was in agreement with them.

The call waiting tone sounded and Imani excused herself and clicked over. It was Fatima and for once, Imani could dominate their conversation with all of the events that had occurred since they last spoke. "Girrrl don't hang up. I'll get with you in a second," Imani told Fatima and clicked back over to Jazz.

"Jazz, it was nice talkin' to ya but I've gotta go. Can you call me tomorrow?"

"You know it."

"Great. Talk to you tomorrow," Imani said then clicked back over to Fatima.

"Girrrl!" Imani exclaimed, "you won't believe who I was on the phone with."

"Who?" Fatima asked in a flat tone.

"Jazz."

"Is that a guy?"

"Yup," Imani replied then grinned. She proceeded to run down the entire conversation that she had with Jazz, word for word. Imani blabbed on about Jazz and then told Fatima the details of her H-O-R-S-E game with Tyler. Then it occurred to Imani that Fatima had not said a word. "What's wrong with you? Why are you so quiet? You're not even smacking gum in my ears."

"Two men in one day? That's a record for you," Fatima said.

"Forget that, Fatima. What's up with you? I thought you'd be excited and proud of me?" There was more silence and then Imani heard Fatima sniffle.

"I am happy for you but it's just that I've been buggin' lately."

"What's wrong?"

"I haven't told anybody about this-"

"About what?" Imani interrupted.

"Swear you won't say a word," Fatima said.

"Iiimaniii. You've been on that telephone long enough. C'mon out here and get to these dishes," her mother yelled.

Imani looked at her watch. "Hurry up Fatima before my mother drag this phone out of my hand. You know you can trust me."

Fatima told Imani about her last date with Money. When she got to the part about sex and what happened to the condom, Imani shouted out, "You didn't. He didn't. It didn't. Ohmagod!" Imani covered her mouth when she realized just how loud she was.

Imani whispered, "I can't believe you did it. Why Girrrl?"

"Ain't that what the hype's all about? Wasn't I supposed to do it?"

"Says who, Fatima?"

"Where you been? Says the movies, and videos, and just about every sistah in school and need I go on?" Before Imani responded Fatima jumped in with, "And I'm pissed off at myself for buying into it 'cause it ain't like that or all that either."

"Did he hurt you?" Imani asked.

"Yeah but probably because it was my first time. But what hurts even more is that I haven't heard from Money since then." Fatima sighed then added, "I really liked him and I thought he cared about me too but now, I think I got played. Or as the old folks would say, 'wham bam thank you ma'am'."

"Did he thank you?"

"Naw. He ain't thank me."

"Maybe he thanked you in advance when he bought you that jewelry?"

"Uh-huh, maybe you're right." But, he still ain't care that I was in pain and ain't even care that I was bleeding. Nothing."

"Blood?"

"Just a little bit mixed up with his nasty sticky sperm."

"Yuck."

Imani tried to imagine her best friend down in that basement and she cringed. Fatima had come close a few times and talked about it all the time but Imani couldn't believe that she'd actually done it. "I knew something must have been up when I hadn't heard from you in a while. I've been so busy that I haven't had time to call you either. I'm sorry."

"Sorry for what? You ain't do nothing to me but try to talk some sense into me. If I had listened to you, I wouldn't be sweatin' this now and scared to death that I might be pregnant."

Imani gasped then covered her mouth again. "Or, one of those gross venereal diseases they talked about in health class," Imani whispered between her fingers.

"Eeelll, don't say that!" Fatima exclaimed.

"You gotta go down to the clinic and get checked out," Imani said.

"Eeelll, and have some stranger pokin' around down there?"

"As icky as it sounds, you've got to go. I heard that it's free and Grandma Rose won't ever have to know about it."

"I know..." Fatima answered then breathed into the receiver. And you know what else I know?"

"What?"

"Forget what I said about giving it up to get Tyler. 'F' it and him and Jazz if they can't deal with a virgin," Fatima said in a harsh tone.

"I know," Imani replied without hesitation.

BHRIANA

It was a gorgeous hot May afternoon filled with bright sunshine. Flowers showed off their brilliant hues of red, yellow, fuchsia and violet. Leaves in all shades of green adorned once bare, brown branches.

Those vibrant sights and the sweet aroma of nature surrounded Bhriana and her father, Brandon DuPree, as they dined out at Little Italy. The scent of fresh baked bread and roasted garlic intertwined with the slight breeze that swirled about the patio. The tail of the red tablecloth moved about and brushed against the shopping bags on the ground next to Bhriana and her father's chair.

The contents of all of those bags belonged to her. Although Bhriana felt that her father didn't spend enough time with her, he never held back on money.

The new designer sunglasses that she wore not only shielded her from the sunrays but also covered up the hurt in her hazel eyes.

"Sweetheart, is something wrong? I thought pasta was your favorite," Mr. DuPree asked as his daughter picked at her Fettuccine Alfredo.

The shopping spree was a temporary pain reliever but it had worn off and the pain returned. If a stranger looked at Bhriana, he would never think she had a worry in the world. She always wanted to look her best when she went out with her father. Bhriana adorned a pale blue sleeveless linen dress and sandals. Her sleek hair hung straight and landed below her shoulders. A bang slightly covered her left eye. The only jewelry that she wore was the diamond earrings her father gave her and a sterling silver bracelet.

She forced a smile but didn't answer. Mr. DuPree reached across the table and held her left hand. He touched her bangle and then asked Bhriana, "Do you need a watch? I haven't seen you wear one since-"

"Ever since you and Mother broke up," Bhriana interrupted. She sipped her sparkling water then placed the glass back onto the table. Bhriana looked at her father's hand in hers and continued. "I don't wear a watch when I'm with you because I hate being reminded of the time. It goes by too quickly."

"Do you not like the food?" their waiter asked Bhriana. "If not, you can order whatever else you'd like," he continued in a thick Italian accent.

"Oh no, I'm just taking my time. He had the same thing and obviously it's good," Bhriana said as she pointed to Mr. DuPree's empty plate.

"Well alright then, I shall leave you two alone."

"Daddy?"

"Yes, Sweetheart."

"I want to come live with you. Mother and I don't get along. I've always been closer to you and I miss you so much. Please Daddy say yes."

Bhriana took off her dark shades so that her father could see her eyes. She stared at her father who was a youthful and handsome 36-year-old. Even his neatly trimmed beard and moustache didn't age him. Mr. DuPree wore his dark brown hair cut low. His rich brown eyes, complete with long thick lashes that any girl would envy, complimented his chestnut brown complexion.

Mr. DuPree tugged on his left ear that he had pierced after the divorce. He wore a small diamond stud in it which Bhriana thought made him look even more attractive. "Sweetheart, Daddy misses you too but now is not a good time for you to stay with me."

"Why not?"

"Because it wouldn't be fair to you. I'm working 12 hour days, travelling quite a bit, and Mr. Powers and I are right in the middle of our business plans to merge our stores. We wouldn't have any more time together than we do now."

"So you're saying that you're too busy for me."

"What I'm saying is that you need at least one of your parents to spend as much time with you as possible and right now that parent is your mother."

Bhriana sucked her teeth and rolled her eyes. "She doesn't want me there. All I am to her is a mistake." Bhriana put her sunglasses back on and turned away from her father.

Mr. Dupree reached across the table, placed his hand under Bhriana's chin and gently guided her face in his direction. "That's not true, Baby. Your mother and I were talking about marriage before you came along. You were the result of our union. How can that be a mistake?"

"According to Mother, I was the reason she didn't go to college and I was the reason that she got married so young and it was my fault that she got a late start on her career and on and on and on," Bhriana spat out.

Mr. DuPree shook his head in disagreement. "Your mother loves you, Sweetheart." He paused for a moment and then continued, "When you were an infant she would rock you all night until you fell asleep. And there were countless times that she worked around the clock trying to break your fever. Then there were the endless conversations that she had with you in your baby language."

"But I'm not a baby anymore."

"Exactly. You and your mother must find a way to communicate from mother to young woman and vice versa. And might I add, what a beautiful young woman you have become. I'm glad you got your mother's great looks."

"Oh Daddy," Bhriana said and waved her hand. A genuine smile crossed her face. She picked up her fork and ate her pasta again. In between bites, she gazed up at her father and noticed his eyes fixed on a toddler at the table next to them.

"Look at that," Mr. DuPree said in reference to the child. "I wanted three or four kids but your mother had a couple of miscarriages and then we began having marital problems so it didn't happen." He continued to watch the little boy and laughed when he sucked a long string of spaghetti in his mouth. "I still want a son, not that I have anything against girls, but I want a Brandon Junior."

"You're still young, Daddy. It could happen."

"I hope so."

Bhriana sat back in her chair and imagined what it would have been like to have siblings. She spoke up and told her father what was on her mind. "I probably would not have liked sharing you with other children, but, brothers and sisters would have been nice to have around during the holidays."

"So those were lonely times for you?"

"I guess. But back then, I was too busy having fun with Mother and you. Bhriana pushed her plate aside and leaned towards her father. "Let's make a deal. I'll try to work things out with Mother if you spend more time with me."

"I want you to work things out with your mother because she is your mother. And as your father, I'll make sure that we spend quality time together." Mr. DuPree took hold of her hands and squeezed. "Call me anytime of day or night, if you need to talk and I mean talk about anything. Understand?"

"Yes sir," Bhriana responded and looked over her shades. "Even boys?"

Mr. DuPree cleared his throat and his deep voice got even deeper when he asked, "What about boys?"

"You'll never guess who I'm dating now."

"He must be someone special. So who's the no good bum?"

"Da-dddy."

"I'm sorry," Mr. DuPree replied with a smirk on his face. "So who is the young man?"

"Tyler Powers," Bhriana said with a wide grin on her face.

Mr. DuPree displayed a big smile of his own that showed off his pearly whites. "My soon to be partner's boy?"

"The one and only."

The two continued to smile at each other as the short and stocky waiter approached them. "You like, aye?" The waiter asked in reference to Bhriana's almost empty plate.

The waiter refilled their glasses, removed their plates, and offered them dessert, which they both turned down. After the waiter walked away, Bhriana asked, "So are you surprised, Daddy?"

"Not really. Andrew told me that Tyler's always had a crush on you but more importantly, he's a good kid from a decent family. If he's anything like his father, he is going to be a hellava man someday. His father has big plans for him, too." Mr. Dupree raised his glass and saluted his daughter. "You've got my blessing on this one."

* * * *

Bhriana and her father walked through the door with all smiles and locked arm in arm. She called out to her mother and Ms. Austin peeked over one of her self-help books. "Where on earth are you going to put all of that stuff?" Ms. Austin asked.

"And hello to you too, Vanessa," Mr. DuPree said to his ex-wife.

"Hello Brandon," she replied but didn't make eye contact with him.

"I'll find the space, Mother," Bhriana said then turned to her father and offered him a drink.

"Your father's a busy man, Bhriana. I'm sure he must be somewhere else by now."

"That sounds good, Sweetheart. Sparkling water if you have it," he said and ignored Ms. Austin's comment. Bhriana proceeded off to the kitchen and strained to hear if they talked while she was gone. There was complete silence. She hurried back into the living room with the tallest glass she could find filled with water. "I could stand in that glass and drown," her father said then shot a look at his ex-wife.

Ms. Austin gazed up. "I didn't say it. You stepped into that one."

"Oh Daddy, you know Mother doesn't wish you any harm."

Except for the sound Mr. DuPree made as he sipped his water, the room was quiet again. He continued to stand as if he waited for Ms. Austin to offer him a seat. Drops of water streaked down the outside of the glass. Bhriana handed her father a coaster, took a seat on the plush carpet and hummed an unrecognizable tune. Ms. Austin turned her attention back to her book.

"I'm pleased to hear that our daughter is dating Tyler Powers. He's a fine young man," Mr. DuPree announced.

Ms. Austin turned the page of her book then looked at Bhriana and smiled. "I'm pleased that our daughter is pulling her grades back up to where they should be." The smile disappeared when she turned to her ex-husband. "Would you like to comment on that or is who she's dating more important?"

"Mother, don't start," Bhriana pleaded.

"I just assumed that Bhriana was doing well in school," Mr. DuPree replied.

Ms. Austin closed her book and rested it on her lap. She fixed her eyes onto Mr. DuPree's eyes and asked, "After the poor grades she got last semester, how could you ass-summme such a thing?"

Bhriana sensed from her parents' tone of voice and facial expressions that they were one exchange away from an argument. "Uh Mother, let me show you these awesome shoes." Bhriana jumped up from the carpet and rushed over to one of the bags.

"Not now, Bhriana," her mother said.

"What's wrong with the girl being excited about her new shoes? You used to get excited and couldn't wait to tell your friends and family about the clothes and jewelry and whatever else I bought for you when we were married. And thanks to my alimony payments, you can still enjoy the good life."

Ms. Austin swung her feet off the white leather sofa onto the floor then sat straight up. A crimson tone seeped under her almond complexion and creases formed on her forehead. Her hazel eyes narrowed and zoomed even deeper into Mr. DuPree's eyes. She didn't blink when she told him," You're not *giving* me anything. I earned that money."

Bhriana rushed over to her father and took the glass out of his hand. She grabbed onto his arm and said, "Uh Daddy, I'll understand if you have to go now. Let me walk you to the door."

Mr. DuPree never took his eyes off his ex-wife. He gently pulled his arm away from Bhriana and folded his arms across his chest. "What do you mean?"

Ms. Austin rose and placed her hands on her hips. She shook her head from side to side. "Since you asked such an asinine question, it's clear to me that you didn't appreciate my services."

"You call your wifely duties, services?"

"You call keeping your books, opening and closing your store, managing your staff, and God knows whatever else I did to keep your business in business wifely duties? No Brandon, I call that being your employee. So consider my alimony as payment for services rendered."

"Come on guys, don't argue."

Ms. Austin took a deep breath and looked up at the high ceiling. She turned her attention back to her ex-husband and continued. "Think of it as your way of saying, 'thank-you for putting your life on hold while I pursued my degree. Thank you for helping me run my business. I appreciate all of your hard work and dedication. Now I'm going to support you until you earn your degree and begin your career'."

"Dad! Just walk away," Bhriana pleaded.

"Not now, Bhriana," he said then turned back to Ms. Austin. "I never thought of you as an employee. You were my wife-"

"And friend and lover and maid and sounding board and your baby's mother and nurse and..."

Bhriana felt like an ignored little girl as she stood in between the enraged adults. She placed her hands over her ears but the tone of their voices and content of their conversation seeped through her palms.

Bhriana removed her hands from her ears and placed them over her stomach. Tears streaked down her face as she yelled, "You two are making me sick!" She left the room, sped up the spiral staircase and ran to her bathroom. Her body shook as she bowed over the toilet and tasted her pasta meal again. But that time, it was bitter.

* * * *

Bhriana woke up late the next morning and wondered if it was all a bad dream. The putrid taste in her mouth, still queasy stomach, and tear stained silk pillowcase were evidence enough that her parents' ordeal was real. She heard a faint knock on her bedroom door and her mother's voice followed. Bhriana covered her head with her white hand embroidered bedspread.

"Are you awake?" Ms. Austin whispered.

Bhriana laid still.

Her mother tapped Bhriana on her shoulder but Bhriana didn't budge. "It's 11 o'clock and it's not like you to lie around on a Sunday morning. I know you're pretending to be asleep so I'm going to keep on talking."

Oh, great, Bhriana thought to herself.

"I apologize for arguing with your father in front of you. That was wrong and I'm sorry. Neither one of us meant to hurt you nor is any of this your fault. I am truly sorry that we upset you last night."

"It's not just last night," Bhriana said and uncovered her head but her back was still turned to her mother. "You and Daddy argue all the time and I'm sick of it. I don't get to see Daddy often so is it too much to ask that you two get along for my sake?"

Ms. Austin rubbed her daughter's back. It used to be a comfort to Bhriana when she was a little girl but no longer. "I promise you that I'll make an effort to be cordial with your father in your presence." She gently shook her daughter and said, "Now stop moping around and come along with me and play golf. Jeanette and Gwendolyn are meeting me there."

"You go ahead and hang out with your friends. I'm just gonna lay here for most of the day."

"Are you sure? We're going to make a day of it. After a few holes of golf, we're going to have a late lunch and then take in a movie. Come on. You would enjoy yourself," Ms. Austin said.

"Some other time, Mother. I'm not feeling so well today."

"Okay then, I'm going to cancel and stay right here with you."

"That's not necessary Mother, please go. I mean, go and enjoy yourself."

"Is this your way of paying me back?"

"Once again, Mother, you don't believe anything that I say."

"Okaaay. If you say you're not feeling well then I believe you." Ms. Austin stroked Bhriana's soft hair and told her, "I'll cook something for you before I leave."

"I'm not hungry," Bhriana replied.

Ms. Austin reached over and touched her daughter's forehead. "Are you sure there's nothing else bothering you?"

"I'm sure," Bhriana said, "just you and Daddy that's all."

"Well that was being straight forward and I surely deserved it," her mother said in a dejected tone. She leaned over and kissed her daughter's temple. "I'll see you tonight. Page me if you need me."

Bhriana laid still until her mother's car pulled out of the driveway. Then she turned over and drifted off to sleep. An old familiar dream came into view. Six-year-old Bhriana and her mother sat on the floor in Bhriana's bedroom. They played with baby dolls and rearranged toy furniture inside the three feet tall dollhouse.

"Let's pretend this pretty doll is me," little Bhriana began. "Now I need a boy doll for my boyfriend and he'll do everything I tell him cuz he loves me."

"Since this is just pretend, I'll go along with that," her mother said.

Bhriana rocked the blonde-haired doll in her arms. "Then, we'll play mommy and daddy."

"What about doctor, lawyer, teacher…?"

"Oh Mom, that's no fun," Bhriana replied and then giggled. Afterwards, her smile faded and she scooted over close to her mother. "Debbie doesn't have a daddy anymore. Her mom threw him out of the house and now Debbie's sad cuz nobody loves her anymore."

"Debbie's parents are divorced, Baby, but her daddy is still her daddy. I know that he loves Debbie very much."

Bhriana shook her head from side to side and then nestled into her mother's lap. "When I hear you and daddy hollering at each other, I get scared that you're gonna kick him out, too. Please don't ever do that to my daddy."

Tears streamed out of the corners of her eyes and disappeared into one of her long thick braids. Her mother stroked Bhriana's small back and kissed her damp cheek. "Listen Baby, no matter what happens between mommy and daddy, we will never stop loving you." She lifted Bhriana so that their faces met. "I don't want you worrying about grown folk's business. All I want you to do, Little Girl, is to do well in school, have fun and be happy. Understand?"

Before the child could answer, her mother's arms engulfed her and Bhriana lingered in her mother's warm and tight embrace.

The telephone rang and it woke Bhriana. She picked up the receiver before she checked the caller ID.

"How come you haven't returned my calls?" a male voice asked. "What did I do wrong?" What can I do or say to see you again?"

Bhriana realized after the second question who he was. She wiped her eyes as she responded, "No time, nothing, and nothing." It was her third answer that got a reaction from Justin.

"So you're trying to tell me there's nothing I can do or say to be with you?"

"I don't want to hurt your feelings Justin but that's what I'm saying. I mean you haven't done anything wrong it's just-"

"Just what?" he interjected.

Bhriana huffed and asked aloud, "How can I put this?" She let out another long sigh and said, "It's just that I don't love you anymore. I fell in love with someone else. I was hoping you would get the message since I haven't returned your calls but since you made me say it, there it is."

"So you were trying to spare my feelings by ignoring my calls and just hoped I would disappear and let you off the hook."

"Well yeah, basically that's it," Bhriana replied without hesitation.

"You knew I was going through a hard time and you go and turn on me like this? I can't believe that you..."

Bhriana felt no compassion whatsoever for Justin as she listened to him. As far as Bhriana was concerned, she had her own issues and didn't have the time or desire to deal with anyone else's. She studied her fingernails and decided it was time for a manicure. All the while Justin poured his heart out.

"Huh? I'm sorry, what did you say?"

"You're not even listening to me. I can't believe this?" Justin said and his voice cracked.

That got Bhriana's attention. She took control of the conversation. "Look. I didn't mean to hurt you nor is any of this your fault." Bhriana shook her head in disbelief. Her mother said those exact same words to her. They didn't make her feel any better so she knew they wouldn't make Justin feel better either. "What I mean, Justin, is that it's not your fault that I don't, you know, love you."

"So what was our last night together all about? Were you giving me one for the road? Or should I say some for the road?" Justin asked.

"Since you asked, I did it because I felt sorry for you," Bhriana replied.

"So that was charity, huh?"

"You're taking this the wrong way, Justin, and I can tell by your tone that you're getting angry."

"You weren't listening, Bhriana, because I've been angry since this conversation started. And tell me something because I am listening, did you fall out of love with me before or after my father went bankrupt?"

Bhriana's brows raised and eyes widen. She was too embarrassed to admit the truth. There was no way she would date someone beneath her socially and financially. Good looks and a great body wasn't enough. She didn't tell Justin that. Instead, she said, "I realized that I wasn't in love with you when I fell in love with someone else."

"Who?"

"What's it to you?"

"Who? Bhriana!"

"You don't have to shout, Justin."

"Forget it, Bhriana. I already know who and he'd better watch his back."

Bhriana's heart raced. "What are you gonna do?"

"It's not what I'm going to do to Tyler."

"How do you know it's Tyler?"

"I still have friends at Westmoore so I know the deal."

"You have people spying on me? Get a life Justin and stay away from Tyler and me."

"I'm supposed to forget about you just like that?" he asked. "You're cold, Girl. Yeah, Tyler better watch out."

"That's the second time you've said that. Is that suppose to scare me or something?"

"Tyler's the one who ought to be scared. Scared of you, not me."

"I would never hurt-"

"Tyler the way that you would never hurt me, Bhriana? Give me a break," Justin said then exhaled into the receiver. "My parents asked about you and they told me that a true friend would stick by me. I argued with them and made all kinds of excuses for you..."

Bhriana laid back and covered her eyes with one hand and held the receiver with the other. She popped back up when she heard the call waiting tone. "Justin, hold on I've got to click over."

"Go 'head," he responded.

"Hello."

"May I speak to Bhriana?"

"Hey Tyler it's me," Bhriana replied in a joyful tone. "Hold on."

Bhriana clicked back over to Justin. "It's a long distance call. I've got to go."

"When I told you to go ahead, I meant for good. Bye." Click.

Bhriana pulled the telephone away from her ear and stared at it. She couldn't believe the way Justin dismissed her. She snapped out of the trance once it occurred to her that Tyler was on hold. "Tyler, are you there?"

"Yeah I'm here."

"Sorry about that," Bhriana said. She heard the sound of traffic in the background. "Where are you?"

"In Steven's jeep."

Bhriana looked at her caller ID and Steven's cell phone number was on display. She started to panic. Did Steven tell Tyler what happened the night of his party? She hadn't thought about their night of drunken passion until that instant. She recalled Steven's promise that "Tyler will never find out about this."

"Bhriana, can you hear me?"

"I'm here," she said. Bhriana listened more closely and detected a girl's voice in the background. "Who's in the jeep with you and Steven?"

"Steven's girlfriend, Porsche. You probably met her at his party..."

Bhriana remembered Porsche because of the dirty look Porsche gave Bhriana while she partied with Steven. That "look" enticed Bhriana to play up to Steven and it elated Bhriana to know that the one guy Porsche had her eye on she couldn't have that night.

"...So what do you say, Bhriana?" Tyler asked.

"Say to what?"

"Did I catch you at a bad time or something? You seem preoccupied."

"I can barely hear you," Bhriana replied loudly.

"I can barely hear you, too. I think the battery's low so I'll talk fast. I wanna see you today so we can talk."

"Talk about what?" Bhriana asked. She didn't give him a chance to answer and suggested that he come over for a dip in the pool or something.

Tyler's reply came through the receiver in incomplete sentences. "I'll be there ... you...didn't... Steven's party."

Bhriana's heart raced again. "What about Steven's party?" she asked. But all she heard over the telephone was static. "Tyler!" she yelled, "what about Steven's party?" Click.

She hung up her phone and it rang. Bhriana snatched up the receiver. "Tyler!"

"No Baby, it's Daddy."

"Oh hi, Daddy. Can I call you back?"

"Well yes but I wanted to say I apologize for last night. I checked in on you before I left but you were asleep and I didn't want to wake you."

"Apology accepted, Daddy, but I really gotta go."

"Okay but call me later."

"Sure. Bye."

Bhriana slammed the receiver down then yanked it back up. She dialed Steven's cell number. A recorded message said, "The cellular customer you have just dialed is not available. Please try your call again later."

Bhriana hung up again and the phone rang once more. "Hello!"

"Bhriana, it's me. I'm just checking up on you. How are you feeling? I'll come home if you want me to," her mother said.

Bhriana huffed. "I'm fine so you can stay out all day with your friends as planned so see you later, bye."

Bhriana dialed Steven's number again. She got the same recorded message. She tried again. Same message. How much time she had to prepare her story and to make herself beautiful she did not know.

If Steven opened his big mouth, I'll kill him, Bhriana thought as she ran over and pulled on her bathing suit drawer. She yanked on it so hard that the drawer slid off its track. Colorful swimsuits and several boxes of tampons tumbled on top of the carpet. The tampons reminded Bhriana that her period was due soon. She hoped it wasn't that day.

After a quick shower, Bhriana slicked her hair back into a ponytail. She tried on four different bathing suits before she opted for the lime green two-piece. The push-up bra and skimpy French-cut briefs left little to the imagination. She tied the lime green floral cover-up skirt around her waist then checked herself out again in the full-length mirror. Bhriana practiced the face she would use when she flat out denied ever having sex with Tyler's best friend. *Look at that face, how could he not believe me?*

The doorbell rang. She smoothed down her cover-up skirt and ran her hand across her hair then answered the door. Bhriana wished she had a camera to capture the expression on Tyler's face as he surveyed her from head to toe. His eyes lingered around the bust area the longest and when their eyes met again, Bhriana motioned him to come inside. She felt the warmth of his body as he brushed against her ever so slightly as he strolled passed.

"You're workin' that bathing suit, Bhriana."

Bhriana smiled.

"Sorry we got disconnected on the phone but Steven's battery died on me."

Tyler took a seat on the sofa and Bhriana followed him. She knew he would pick up where he left off on the phone. She hoped that she could take his mind off it. On the other hand, she wanted to know what he knew. "I tried calling you back but I couldn't get through. I'm just glad you could figure out what I was saying." Bhriana crossed her legs, took a hold of Tyler's hand and rested it upon her exposed thigh.

"Wow...you look...wow."

Bhriana smiled again.

"I heard you looked all that at Steven's party."

Bhriana's smile dissolved.

"I didn't even know you were there until Porsche mentioned it today. She told me that she couldn't get near Steven because of you."

"I forgot all about it. That was way back in ummm...March sometime so obviously it was no big deal if I forgot about it." She rubbed his hand across her thigh. "Plus, I didn't have a good time because you weren't there. I was gonna leave but Steven asked me to stay."

"Steven knew that I wasn't gonna be there."

"He didn't tell me that when he invited me. Otherwise, I would not have gone either."

"Porsche made it sound like you had a great time, though. After they dropped me off, Steven got out of the jeep with me and we had a man-to-man talk. He told me what happened."

Bhriana began to perspire. It was a hot day in May but the central air conditioning was on and the room was cool. Yet, her body temperature rose. Her mouth felt dry. She moved Tyler's hand away and stood up. "I'm thirsty, how about you? Iced tea?"

"I'll pass," he answered then followed Bhriana into the kitchen.

She felt his eyes on her and it made her even more nervous. She tried to figure out what to say next so that she didn't sound too defensive. Bhriana decided to play it cool and not say anything.

"So Steven took good care of you, huh?"

Bhriana's glass of iced tea crashed to the floor. She screamed.

"You alright?" Tyler asked. He glanced down at Bhriana's bare feet surrounded by broken glass. He stepped around the puddle, scooped Bhriana up into his strong arms and placed her down on the other side of the kitchen. "Where's a broom and a mop?" he asked.

Bhriana had to think about it. "It should be in that utility closet over there." She watched as Tyler proceeded to clean up the mess that she made. Bhriana hated to ask but the suspense got the best of her. "What did Steven tell you?"

Tyler gazed up at Bhriana. "It's a guy thing."

With that comment, Bhriana's nervousness went away and she became annoyed. She was tired of the guessing game and insisted that Tyler tell her what Steven said.

"Steven told me that you came to the party looking all delicious and he knew all the fellas were hungry, so to speak. Being my boy and all, he stuck with you all night at the risk of pissing Porsche off just to keep the vultures away." Tyler shook his head and smiled. "That's my boy."

Bhriana stood with her mouth opened. She inhaled then exhaled a deep sigh of relief. She signaled Tyler to come to her and when he did she wrapped her arms around his neck. "Steven didn't have to do that. None of those guys had a chance of getting with me. I got what I want."

"Ummm...I got what I want too," Tyler replied and caressed Bhriana's shoulders. He outlined her face with his fingers then circled her lips. "I have a poem for you."

"You making love to me would be the best poem I've ever experienced," Bhriana said then pressed her body into Tyler's.

Tyler backed away with a coy expression on his face. "Uh, I wish I had my swim trunks with me." Beads of perspiration formed on his forehead.

"Why do you do that, Tyler?"

"Do what?"

"Back away from me every time I try to get close to you," she answered as she untied her cover-up and it slipped to the floor. Bhriana spun around so that Tyler could get a complete view of what she had to offer. "Are you as hungry as those 'vultures'?"

Tyler zoomed in on Bhriana's beautiful body. He cleared his throat. "It's not that I don't want you. It's just that uh-"

"That you'd rather have Imooni?" Bhriana asked.

"Imani?"

"Whatever her name is. You would rather do it with her."

"For the one hundredth time, Imani and I are just friends. Don't you have guy friends that you just hang out with? Take Steven for instance. I just found out that you two are friends but I trust both of you. I know that he would never take advantage of you and vice versa. It's the same thing with Imani and me. We're just friends and I would never have sex with her."

While Tyler made his speech, Bhriana's mind flashed back to Steven's bedroom. She had to admit that Steven did take care of her that night. She was surprised at how good he was in bed. Then again, she could have imagined it because she was drunk. Bhriana placed Tyler and Imani in the same scenario and it upset her. Tears streamed down her face.

"What's wrong?" He asked and embraced her.

130

Bhriana sobbed on Tyler's white tee shirt. The touch of Tyler's hands as they stroked her almost bare back felt so good. She wanted him to hold onto her forever. When he loosened up his hold, she leaned back against the white countertop.

"I don't have a lot of friends. My parents are divorced and my father doesn't have time for me," she sniffled and rubbed her eyes. Tyler handed her a pink napkin.

"I find a great guy...someone I truly care about and he pushes me away too. Just like my father." She turned her back to Tyler and bowed her head.

"Bhriana, listen to me. You're not the problem. I am. Can I tell you something that even Steven doesn't know?"

Bhriana turned around. "Sure, you can tell me anything, Tyler. Anything except that you're gay."

"Gay? Nooo that's not it," he responded and they both chuckled.

"Are you a virgin?" Bhriana asked in jest.

Tyler looked away.

Bhriana guided his face back to hers. "Hey, that's nothing to be ashamed of. I don't think any less of you just because you're a virgin. I think it's cute."

"Cute?"

"Not cute as in cute but cute as in that's okay. I'm honored to be with a popular athlete who doesn't fit into that 'I've conquered every girl I met' crap. And I'll be honest with you. I'm not a virgin but it will be my first time with you." Bhriana paused and pointed to her bosom. "Do you think any less of me?"

Tyler gawked at where Bhriana pointed and answered, "No."

Bhriana's full breasts heaved up and down as she was relieved to hear that. She embraced Tyler and nibbled on his ear lobe. His deep moan turned Bhriana on more. "Please, don't push me away again," she whispered.

FATIMA

"You can do this, Girl," Fatima told herself. She placed the torpedo shaped pill on the back of her tongue then loaded her mouth with tepid water. Fatima tilted her head back and swallowed. She gulped more water. But, her throat was tight. So tight with anger that it left little space for the medication to pass through. Every pill was a painful reminder of that day at the clinic.

"Chlamydia," the doctor told her.

"But how? I thought that was a nasty girl's disease. You know the girls who have sex with a lotta guys. That was my first time," Fatima said as a pool of tears filled her eyes.

"You can contract sexually transmitted diseases or get pregnant your first time or anytime for that matter. You're at greater risk if you have unprotected sex. And, the improper use of condoms or any method of

Jackie Hardrick

birth control qualifies as unprotected sex. *However, the only method that's 100% effective is abstinence."*

Fatima lowered her head.

"Don't be so hard on yourself. Many older women are just as naïve about the transmission of venereal diseases. Ignorance and the refusal to use condoms are the main reasons why AIDS, Gonorrhea, Syphilis, and Genital Warts are so wide-spread."

Fatima looked at the doctor who appeared young enough to be an older brother. Yet, he sounded old and wise enough to be somebody's grandfather.

"Chlamydia is one of the most common sexually transmitted diseases around and half of the women who have it don't know they have it until they're tested. That's why it's so important for sexually active women of all ages to visit a gynecologist at least once a year for an exam and a Pap smear."

"What about the guy?" Fatima asked.

"He must be treated as well. Otherwise, he will continue to pass the disease back to you. I hate to say this but if he's fooling around on you and having unprotected sex with other girls, they'll be infected, too."

Fatima replayed that same scene every time she took her medication. She laid across her bed and listened to Friday night club music and hoped that the upbeat tempo would raise her spirits. It didn't. The music only reminded her of the night she went to Club Paradise with Money and how they tore up the dance floor. But, that was two months ago.

For two months, she paged him 911 and no response. For two months, she listened as his mother or whoever answered the telephone said, "Sorry, he's not home." For two months, Fatima pondered what she did

134

wrong. After all, didn't he call her "his woman"? Wasn't it "all about her"? Then, where was he? She wanted to tell him that he had Chlamydia and needed medication then she would pop him in the mouth because he gave her the disease.

Two long, long, long months she was scared to death as she waited for her period and prayed to God that she wasn't pregnant. She was never late before. Fatima considered her regular monthly visitor a painful curse. But when her period finally arrived, she went to church with Grandma Rose and thanked God personally.

She got her answer from God and she wanted an answer from Money, too. If he didn't want to see her anymore, she could deal with that. What she couldn't deal with was the not knowing *why*. Her chocolate brown eyes glazed over but she refused to let one teardrop fall. She cried herself to sleep for too many nights and was determined to put an end to it.

Someone knocked on Fatima's door. She rubbed her eyes and told the person to come in. She was surprised to see tall and lean Imani in her doorway.

"Hey Girl! Ain't it past your bedtime?" Fatima asked.

"Forget you, Fatima. It's only six-thirty."

"Like I said. Ain't it past your bedtime?"

"I came over to cheer up your pitiful behind and this is how you say thank-you? Well like I said, forget you."

"I know you need cheering up too after losing that last game," Fatima said.

"What pisses me off the most is that may have been my last chance to get that scholarship," Imani replied.

"Just 'cause Westmoore ain't make the finals?"

"Well yeah. Why should they reward me with another scholarship if I can't lead the team to a State Championship? Dang, at least City."

"Oh, like you the whole dang team? What about all them other girls on the team? All y'all lost that last game not just you."

"That's what Tyler told me after the game. But, he doesn't know how desperate I am for that scholarship. He thinks that my family is well-off like his."

"Still lyin' to him huh, Girl," Fatima said and motioned her best friend to sit next to her. "Don't sweat it. Your grades got to count for somethin' too."

"I hope so."

Fatima's alto pitch climbed up to soprano when she said, "I know what will cheer you up. Girrrl, I got my period."

"Praise God," Imani said.

"I did that already 'cause Girrrl, I was petrified."

"It's about time something scared you. Maybe now you'll chill out," Imani said and then hugged her friend. "So how you feelin'?"

"I feel no different now than I felt before I knew I had Chlamydia. And that's a trip to be walking around with a disease down there and not know it."

"Dang," Imani said and shook her head.

"He said I was lucky 'cause we caught it early. But if I was walkin' round here like everythang's cool, it could have gotten real bad."

"I think we learned about that one in health class. Is Chlamydia the one where it could lead to uh...Pelvic...uh...Pelvic Inflam-"

"Yeah, Pelvic Inflammatory Disease or PID for short," Fatima said. That's some serious crap. You get pains in your stomach, throw-up, fever, and your tubes can get all messed up and make you sterile."

"Dang, the things us women go through," Imani said.

Fatima slapped Imani on her arm and said, "Uh-huh and let me tell you again Girl, forget what I said about giving it up to get Tyler. It ain't worth it."

"You don't have to tell me again. Anyway, Tyler's so wrapped up with Bhriana, I wouldn't even waste my time."

Fatima got closer into Imani's face.

"What's wrong with you?"

"That's what I was gonna ask you, Girlfriend. You know it ain't easy for us to blush but I swear you startin' to change color here. Whassup with that?" Fatima asked.

"W-e-l-l-l, things are going good with Jazz and me and oh, the boys team made it to the finals of the State Championship. Come to the game with me."

"So, are we rooting for Tyler or Jazz?" Fatima asked.

"They're both on the same team, Fatima."

"Yeah, but you're blushing again, Imani."

"I hope they both bring their best game with them. But, back to Jazz. I didn't want to talk about us because I didn't want to make you feel bad being all bummed out about Money and all."

"Pssst. Girrrl, don't worry about me. As soon as I track down that no good son of a-"

"Watch it," Imani cut in.

"What? I was gonna say son-of-a-gun. As soon as I catch up with his behind and get some answers, I'll be alright." Fatima continued to speak as she hugged her best friend. "I'm happy for you girl 'cause I know I don't have to worry about you doing anything stupid. So have fun."

"I'm happy that you're happy for me but back up a minute. I'm all for you trying to break out of the funk but why track him down? Get on with your life."

Fatima stood up and walked over to her dresser. Her bedroom was only large enough to fit the dresser and the twin-sized bed. The bed was the same one that her mother slept in when she was a child. Her boombox, a gift from an ex-boyfriend, sat on top of the dresser. Black hair care products were on one side of the box. Tubes of lipsticks, eyeliners and shadows, bottles of nail polish and nail files cluttered the other side.

Fatima studied her reflection in the mirror on top of the dresser. She slicked back her already smooth hair and shook her head. "It ain't like me to be buggin' like this and that's why I gotta find him. See what I'm sayin'?"

"I hear ya but you should just say fff-"

"Watch it," Fatima interjected.

"I was gonna say forget him and keep getting up. It's not like you're gonna have a hard time meeting another brotha."

"True dat. But, I don't appreciate being dissed without knowing what the deal is. Respect me damn it!"

"Well alrighty then Black woman. But how are you gonna find Money?"

Fatima swung around and smiled. "So does that mean you're down?"

"Down with what?" Imani asked in a higher pitched voice.

Fatima sat next to Imani and grabbed her hand. She knew what she was about to ask Imani to do was out of the question but she was desperate. She figured that if she begged and pleaded hard enough, Imani might cave in. "I need your help, Girl, so please don't say no. You know I would do anything to help you and we go waaay back so please help me out just this once. Okay I lie. This may not be the last time but I have learned my lesson and I promise that I won't make the same mistake again so please help me out and..."

"Will you plueeeze just tell me what you want?" Imani asked.

Fatima squeezed her best friend's hand tighter. "Plueeeze come with me to Club Paradise tonight because I know that's where Money is and I can get this nightmare over with and stop buggin'," Fatima rattled off then inhaled. "Being my girl and all, I know you wanna help me do that. And, I know you have a curfew but I promise it won't take me long to do what I have to do and I will cover for you and tell your parents whatever you want and..."

"Fatima! Shut up and breathe. You're driving me nuts."

"Sorry. It's just that-"

"Enough already, I heard you. Just be quiet and let me think."

She remained quiet as Imani asked her to. At least Imani had not said, "No."

"Is this club over on Central Avenue?" Imani asked.

"Yeah."

"Ummm...then this must be the same club Jazz said he likes. He claims he hasn't been there since we got together because he knows that I can't go. Buuut ... I am curious."

"Yeah sooo?"

"Sooo, I may be bold enough to sneak out tonight but I'm not bold enough to lie to my parents," Imani answered. Before Fatima could respond, Imani held up one finger and continued. "So what are you going to tell them?"

"Me?" Fatima asked as she pointed to herself.

"Didn't you say you would cover for me and-"

"Word up. Yeah oookay ummm, let me think," Fatima replied. Within seconds, Fatima snapped her fingers and ran down her plan to Imani. She told Imani to get into her bed and pretend that she was asleep and then Fatima would call Grandma Rose into the room to witness it. Then, Fatima would phone Imani's parents and tell them that Imani was so tired that she passed out and that it would be best if she spent the night there. She would put Grandma Rose on the telephone if Imani's parents didn't believe her.

"I don't know, Fatima. I hate bringing Grandma Rose into this lie."

"She wouldn't really be lying 'cause she'd only be telling what's she's seeing. It's not like she'd be making it up."

"True. True in a sick kinda way," Imani replied.

"Hey look. I really do want to wrap things up with Money tonight. But, you're my girl and if you're gonna be lookin' over your shoulders all night waiting for God to strike you down or something for lyin', I can go by myself. So if it's not cool with you, don't do it."

"It's not that I don't want to and okay say your plan works, look at me. I'm tall but I don't look 21 and neither do you."

"I'll work the make-up."

"I can't wear what I got on."

Fatima pointed to her closet.

"My hair's a mess."

"I'll hook that up, too."

"You got an answer for everything don't you?"

"Yup," Fatima said.

Imani exhaled and said, "Oh alright, Girl. Call in Grandma Rose."

Fatima hugged Imani, leaped off the bed, and threw her hands up in the air and shouted, "Yeees."

"Shhh… I'm asleep remember?"

Fatima whispered, "My bad," and motioned Imani to get underneath the covers. She left the room and moments later came back with Grandma Rose.

"…See what I mean, Grandma. I told Imani she works too hard. Look how early it is and she's knocked out."

Grandma Rose walked over to the bed and pulled the covers up under Imani's chin. Imani didn't move. Grandma Rose put her hands on her ample hips and said, "Um, um, ummm…I thought that chile looked a bit tired when she came here. I ain't gonna wake her so go on and call her mama. You can sleep with me tonight."

"I'll sleep on the couch, Grandma."

Jackie Hardrick

"Suit yourself but that girl's got a good idea. I'm turnin' in too."

Fatima gave her grandmother a good night kiss on the cheek. "If Mrs. Jackson wants to speak to you-"

"Just come git me, Baby." Grandma Rose took another glimpse of Imani. "Ump, I hope my snorin' don't wake her up."

Fatima closed the door behind Grandma Rose. She was thrilled with how smoothly that went but the toughest part was still ahead. She shook Imani and slowly she opened her eyes.

"I could fall asleep for real," Imani said in a groggy tone.

"Don't punk out on me now, Girl, we're almost there," Fatima said as she dialed Imani's number.

Imani covered her ears and told Fatima, "I don't wanna hear this."

Imani's mother answered the telephone and Fatima proceeded with her story. Mrs. Jackson bought it and said it was fine that Imani spent the night. Fatima quickly hung up the telephone just in case Mrs. Jackson changed her mind. The two girls buried their heads in the pillows and squealed. Fatima came up for air first. "Let's get beautiful, Girl."

* * * *

The exterior of Club Paradise blended in with the other run down buildings in the area. The only thing that looked out of place was the palm trees drawn on the "Club Paradise" banner draped across the top of the doorway. Spotlights lit up the florescent green painted sign. There was another sign posted on the outside of the black metal door. The sign read:

No Jeans

No Sneakers

No One Under 21

People arrived in old cars, new cars, taxis, and even limos. Some of the male motorists cruised by and gawked at the women who stood in line.

"Hey Baby, wanna ride?" was a common call out from them. The ladies blushed or rolled their eyes. The line stretched from the doorway, down the steps, and several feet from the building to the end of the corner.

"If that dang bus hadn't been late, we could have been way up there," Fatima said as she pointed towards the doorway.

"Why aren't they letting people in?" Imani asked.

"'Cause we're early. The Club doesn't open 'til ten so since we got a couple of minutes, stand out of line a little bit and let me give you the 411."

"Don't be startin' no mess out here. I can't be runnin' in these heels."

"I was wonderin' why you walkin' all funny like you bow legged," Fatima said and they both laughed. Soon after, Fatima told Imani, "Come on now, let's get serious. See that girl up there with the raggedy weave hangin' all down her back? She's tryin' to hide her face under that bushy bang 'cause she's only 14. The sistah behind her just had a baby last week and hangin' out here like she ain't got nothing better to do. She's only 14, too."

"Get outta here!" Imani exclaimed and then she covered her mouth.

"And oooh...that guy over there with those pleather black pants and floral fake silk shirt, like he's in Hawaii somewhere, he's a married man with five or six kids. But that ain't his wife he's smoochin' on."

"Oooh, I hate to cut you off, Fatima, but that guy over there in the bright red skin-tight tee shirt keeps staring at you."

"Girrl, I know you ain't talkin' about Mr. Puffed Up over there. He just got outta jail."

"Get outta here!"

"Ummm humm... and no she didn't!" Fatima exclaimed.

Both Fatima and Imani watched in disbelief as a forty-something full-figured woman with red painted on lips and red hair passed by them. Her large stomach rolled over the top of her black leather mini skirt. A black bra peeped through the white lace scoop neck top. Her thick brown legs were stuffed in her black fishnet stockings like pork in a sausage casing.

Fatima hollered and laughed so hard that tears streamed down her face. She ignored Imani's hushing sounds and continued to laugh.

"Keep on laughing, Fatima, but that could be you in 25 years."

"'Scuse me? Girrrl I ain't never gonna be that desperate."

"We'll see."

"No you won't see me profilin' like that," Fatima answered and wiped her eyes. She pulled out a paisley lipstick case that also contained a mirror on the inside flap and checked on her make-up. It was so dark out that it was hard for Fatima to see her reflection.

"How do I look?" she asked Imani.

"Fine, if you stop gnawing on that gum like a goat."

"I can't help it. I'm all hyped."

Imani nudged Fatima and motioned with her head to check out the guy to their left. Their eyes followed a handsome young man, about Fatima's height, decked out in a black suit and white shirt with no tie.

"Who died?" Fatima whispered to Imani.

"How y'all lovely ladies doing this fine evening?" the stranger asked as he approached them.

"Fine." Imani answered and nudged Fatima.

"Cool and you?"

"Can't complain," he said and introduced himself as Hanif and extended a handshake to Imani then Fatima. He held onto Fatima's hand a little longer.

Fatima removed her hand, returned his smile, and then turned away. When the line inched forward, she looked back at him and said, "W-e-l-l-l, maybe we'll see you inside."

"I hope you'll save at least one dance for me," he told Fatima.

Fatima shuffled along and didn't answer Hanif. When he walked to the back of the line, Fatima turned to Imani and said, "God he sounds country and what kinda name is that for a country boy?"

"Country or not he seems nice to me."

"Too nice. Something's up with him," Fatima said. She glanced over her shoulder at Hanif and added, "Too short, too."

"Too short for me but not for you," Imani said.

"I ain't that short."

"Yes you are."

"No I'm not."

Fatima and Imani continued the height debate all the way up to the club's entrance. The beat of the music pulsated through the door and underneath their feet. Fatima watched Imani as she chewed on her newly polished fingernails. "Chill, Girl, we'll get in," Fatima said as her jaws went into overdrive on her flavorless gum. The door swung open and the volume intensified.

"IDs ladies," an extremely tall and bulky man requested. He held his massive hand out to Imani. A buck-eyed Imani looked back at Fatima and a wide-eyed Fatima looked at Money's friend, Darnel.

"Yo Darnel. Remember me?" Fatima yelled.

He stepped up to her and checked her out from the feet up. "Do I know you?" he asked close to her ear.

"I'm Money's friend," she said loudly.

Darnel raised his brow then he glanced at his burly partner and nodded. "Go 'head in, Sistah."

"How much?" Fatima asked.

"It's on the house. Just go in and have a good time, gorgeous," he told Fatima then winked at Imani.

"Everything alright?" Imani yelled in her friend's ear.

"Yeah." Fatima shouted back.

Clouds of smoke and a foul odor greeted the girls inside of the club. The offensive smell seemed to be a mixture of cigarettes, liquor, sweet cologne or perfume, and underarm funk. Fatima forewarned Imani that the stench would attach to her hair and clothes and suggested that Imani wash her hair before she went back home.

The dim lighting made it difficult to see anyone's face from a distance so Fatima squinted as she entered the lounge area. The lounge was where the older crowd hung out. There was a bar on the left side near the entrance with a sign above it that read "Club Paradise" in neon green letters. Below the letters was a picture of a palm tree that was also lit up in green.

A small square shaped stage was on the right side and a tall deejay booth was opposite it on the left side of the room. Small round black tables ran down the center aisle and booths lined the walls. Groups of older women occupied those candle lit tables and booths. They chatted, laughed, smoked, and drank amongst themselves.

Fatima didn't expect to see Money in there because he disliked the mature clientele and the old R&B music that the deejay played. The volume of R&B competed with the thump, thump, thumping bass of the dance music that seeped through the ceiling above the lounge.

"Let's get outta this morgue and go upstairs," Fatima said.

"I'm not ready, yet. Let's hang here a little while longer," Imani suggested.

Fatima and Imani lucked out and found an empty booth. As soon as they sat down, a waitress approached them.

"I'm gonna assume since you're sitting here, you're old enough to drink. Am I right?"

"Sure you're right." Fatima answered. She felt a kick under the table from Imani but ignored it and maintained eye contact with the woman. "But uh we're tryin' to cut back on the liquor ya know so we'll uh order a-"

"A club soda with a twist of lime," Imani cut in.

The waitress gave the girls a suspicious look, repeated the order, and then walked away. Fatima turned to Imani and asked, "Club soda? Since when?"

"W-e-l-l-l, that's what those sophisticated ladies on TV and in the movies ask for."

"What did I tell you about buying into hype?" Fatima asked.

"Yeah, but you were talkin' about sex not club soda."

"May I join y'all lovely ladies?"

"Sure." Imani said.

Fatima kicked her under the table and Imani kicked her back. Both girls slid their hands under the table, rubbed their shins and smiled at Hanif. The waitress returned with their club sodas and asked for four dollars. Without hesitation, Hanif paid the woman.

"And what would the fine gentleman here like?" the waitress asked seductively.

"Pepsi ma'am. No ice."

The waitress leaned over towards Hanif and told him, "Do me a favor handsome and kill the ma'am. I ain't that old."

"Habit. Sorry, ma'...Miss."

Both girls chuckled then sipped their drinks. Their smiles disappeared at the taste of the club soda but they drank them anyway.

"You didn't have to pay for our drinks," Imani said.

"Naw, I didn't, but I wanted to."

"I love your accent, Hanif. Where you from?" Imani asked.

"I've been tryin' to ditch it ever since I came up here from North Carolina. Y'all really like it?"

"I do. Don't you, Fatima?"

Fatima gave her friend a "Girrrl plueeeze" look.

"Oooh, what a purdy name for a beautiful lady."

"Her name's even prudier?" Fatima said in his dialect. "It's Imani."

"Well I'll be...sho is," he said and continued to look at Fatima.

The threesome carried on a conversation about the meaning of their names. Imani explained that her name was Kiswahili and meant "faith." Hanif said that his name was Swahili and meant "believer." Fatima spoke last.

"Fatima's Muslim and it means 'weaned'." She cleared her throat and continued. "I guess my parents chose the right name since they were taken away from me when I was just a baby."

"I'm sorry," Hanif said.

Fatima stared into the remains of her club soda.

"If this is bothering you, we can change the subject," Hanif offered.

Fatima shrugged her shoulders.

So they talked about why Hanif left the south and college life as a Freshman. Hanif bought the girls a couple of rounds of sodas and Fatima warmed up to him as the conversation continued. She focused on what he said instead of how he said it.

"Some fellas on campus said I could meet a lotta honeys at dis here club. I keep tellin' 'em that all I need is one good woman. I don't need a whole mess of 'em."

Fatima and Imani agreed with Hanif. Fatima examined his face and decided that he wasn't ugly just too clean-cut for her taste. He had no moustache, no sideburns, no facial hair at all, except for eyebrows and lashes. Even so, he looked older than 19. His hair was low-cut which accentuated his big ears. It was too dark to tell the color of his eyes but it wasn't too dark to see the outline of his well defined lips.

"I must say that you two ladies are well put together."

"'Scuse me?" Imani asked as if insulted by that comment.

Hanif laughed and said, "Oh naw, I don't mean it like that. What I meant was your hair and make-up look great, classy." He looked about the room and pointed out all of the "overdone" women in the room.

"I see what you're saying and thanks for the compliment," Imani said and tapped her friend on the shoulder. "Fatima here deserves all the credit. She's the make-up artist and hair stylist."

"It's no big deal," Fatima said and waved her hand.

"Yes it is, Hanif. I keep trying to tell her that she could make big money if she wanted to with her skillz," Imani said.

"You'd better use what God gave you 'fore He takes it away," Hanif said.

"Amen Brother," Imani chimed in.

"I'm gonna go upstairs while you two have church," Fatima announced.

"Purdy, talented, and a sense of humor. You're too much, Fatima."

"I wasn't kiddin'. I am going upstairs." Fatima hit Imani's arm and said, "That's my song," and snapped her fingers in time with the beat.

"Fatima, come on and show me a thing or two on the dance floor." He took one last sip of his soda and added, "Let's boogie-woogie ladies."

"God, I hope nobody heard him say that," Fatima mumbled. Yet, she thought it would be useless to try to ditch the guy so she let Hanif tag along. She also liked the idea of dancing with another guy just in case Money was there. No doubt, he would be with someone else.

Fatima led Imani and Hanif up the winding staircase. The black iron staircase was congested with patrons in both directions. People checked each other out as they passed one another. Fatima did a double take on a girl she thought she recognized but couldn't recall where she had seen her before. The closer she got to the top of the landing the more her heart raced. She didn't know if it was the electrifying atmosphere or the possibility of confronting Money that excited her.

"Dang, it's hot up here," Imani said.

The threesome squeezed their way through the pack of people who blocked the aisle to the dance floor. Strobe lights flashed on the sweat-glistened faces and bodies in motion. Hands and arms flung about in the air in time with the beat. Hair, hips, and derrieres swayed in time, too. Mostly, the guys and girls danced together. Some showed off their skills, solo. Because the women outnumbered the men, groups of them partied together.

"All right ladies, let's do this," Hanif hollered out.

"Do what?" Imani yelled back.

Hanif took a hold of Fatima and Imani's hand and led them to a tiny vacant spot on the floor. Fatima watched Imani and Hanif and giggled as they settled into a simple two-step that even Grandma Rose could have done. Fatima kicked it into high gear and then motioned to Imani and Hanif to follow her moves. She laughed hysterically when Imani's long legs kicked Hanif by mistake.

"Oh just forget it you two," Fatima told them, "go back to whatever you were doing before."

"Don't give up on us," Hanif shouted.

The house lights came on and the deejay said something incomprehensible, yet, the crowd roared and more people rushed onto the floor. Although their tiny dance space limited their range of motion, the threesome continued to work up a sweat. Other dancers bumped into the trio but that didn't stop them. So when a guy and girl knocked into Fatima then brushed passed her, it didn't phase her. But when she focused in on their faces, she froze.

"Isn't that Money?" Imani asked.

"Where's money?" Hanif asked as he looked down at the floor.

"Not that kind of money," Imani yelled to him. "Fatima's boyfriend, I mean ex-boyfriend who pissed her off. He just walked by and his name is Money."

"Where?" Hanif asked.

Fatima snapped out of her trance and pointed in Money's direction. "The guy over there with his gray shirt wide open flashing all that gold." Fatima stared hard at the girl he was with, the same one she did a double take on earlier. When the girl smiled, Fatima remembered that she was the same sistah who pushed up on Money when they were at the mall. The same weave wearing sistah who Money said, "Ain't nobody."

Fatima kept the couple in view even when the deejay turned the house lights back off. She yelled to Imani and Hanif, "Imma go handle my business."

She felt Imani grab onto her arm. "Whatcha gonna do?" Imani screamed.

"You gonna be alright?" Hanif hollered.

"There ain't gonna be no mess unless that witch jumps bad with me. Now let me go Imani," she yelled and pulled away.

Fatima made her way to Money with a sense of purpose. She didn't know exactly what she wanted to do but she had plenty to say. They were face to face and she stared him down until she turned to the girl and yelled, "'Scuse you."

Money spoke in the girl's ear. She rolled her eyes at Fatima and then sauntered away. "Follow me," Fatima ordered. She led him to the lounge where it was quieter and sat in an empty booth.

"You stalkin' me?" Money asked.

"You playin' me?" Fatima retorted. She spit her lifeless gum out into a tin ashtray and then leaned across the table and into Money's face. "What was that night in Darnel's house all about?"

Money looked confused. Seconds later he said, "Oh that?" He waved his hand and added, "Pssst...an even exchange."

"What?"

"You knew the deal, Fatima. I bought you something and you gave me something in return." He hunched his shoulders, "So what's the big deal?"

"What about when you told me, 'it's all about me'?"

"It was right then and there."

"You no good son-of-a-"

"Hold up!" Money yelled. He was so close to her that she smelled the liquor on his breath. "It was good when we were kickin' it together. But, I ain't gonna be tied down to one woman and I ain't down with this emotional crap. It's over so deal with it."

"Just like that?"

"That's what I said."

Darnel came over and interrupted their stalemate glares. He said something to Money on the sly. Annoyance turned into rage across his face. He bolted from the booth and headed up the stairs with Darnel right behind him. Fatima figured it was a problem with the other woman and didn't bother to follow. She was still numb from what just went down. She dabbed the corners of her eyes with a napkin as she signaled for the waitress.

Fatima was oblivious to her surroundings until a loud commotion caught her attention. She looked towards the doorway and saw a mob of people hustle down the staircase. Immediately, she thought about Imani and Money.

"Call the cops!" someone yelled.

"Call an ambulance!" another voice screamed.

Fatima jumped up, ran to the door, and opened it. She heard the words "gunshots, killed, blood, and bathroom." Again, thoughts of Imani, Money, and even Hanif raced through her mind. She tried to force her way up the packed stairway but it was impossible.

"Imani!" Fatima screamed. She saw the overweight hoochie mama that she'd made fun of in line. "What happened?" Fatima yelled to her.

"Somebody got shot!"

"Imani!" Fatima hollered out as her floodgates opened.

"Fatima!" a voice shouted back.

She saw Imani caught up in the middle of the mob. Hanif was in front of Imani like a blocker for a running back. Fatima jumped up and down and waved her hands feverishly. The two friends tearfully embraced and Hanif led them out of the club.

A large crowd hung around outside to see what happened. Several policemen and paramedics stormed the club. "Ohmagod," Fatima said at the sight of Darnel in a blood soaked white shirt. She thought he was the wounded one but police officers escorted him to the squad car instead of the ambulance.

"Come on ladies, I'll drive y'all home," Hanif said.

"Yeah Fatima, let's get out of here before the police run us all in for questioning," Imani added.

Fatima ignored them. She fixed her eyes on the doorway and watched the back of a paramedic come through it. Once through, a stretcher was in full view. A black body bag rested on top of it.

"Ohmagod," spread throughout the crowd.

Fatima didn't blink. She didn't breathe.

"Monnneeey!" the pierced-tongued girl cried out. Police officers tried to restrain her. Somehow, she broke free and grabbed onto the body bag. "Monnneeey!" she screamed again.

* * * *

Fatima woke up the next morning to the ghastly smell of cigarette smoke from the clothes she wore the

155

night before. She looked about the room and saw Imani on the floor with the morning paper.

"What happened?"

"Hey Girl," Imani said. "You blacked out and poor Hanif had to carry you to his car. He said he would call today to see how you're doing."

"I gave him my number?"

"I gave it to him."

"That's cool," Fatima said and sat up slowly. She caught a glimpse of a picture of Money on the front page of the newspaper. Fatima closed her eyes tight and then opened them again. His photo was still there. "So I wasn't dreamin'?"

"Oooh nooo, Girrrl. Are you ready to deal with this?"

"Nooo, but tell me anyway."

"Well apparently, Money was pushin' drugs and it's thought that he owed somebody some money or something and when he didn't pay up they took him out. Whoever they are, which the cops don't know yet and…"

Fatima's mind drifted. The mall, the firecracker, the nail file, the baldheaded guy's warning, "this time". The club, the gold, the rage, the blood, the girl, the body bag all haunted her.

Fatima was in tears when she came back to the sound of Imani's voice. She lowered her head and her eyes fell on the gold bracelet Money bought her. "Drug money," she mumbled.

"What?"

"Drug money," Fatima repeated as she removed her bracelet and gold chain. She said it a third time as she took the gold stud earrings out of her lobes and the diamond stud earring out of her nose. Fatima tossed the jewelry on the floor then shuffled over to her closet. She mumbled, "Drug money," as she pulled out all of the clothes that Money had bought her.

Fatima dropped to her knees and leaned over the mound of material things. Black mascara mixed with the mocha foundation streaked down under her chin and onto the pile. She felt Imani's hand as it stroked her back. "You'll get through this."

"Maybe," Fatima said then looked up at Imani through blurred vision as she pointed to the pile. "But, is this crap worth dyin' for?"

Imani shook her head.

TYLER

The Westmoore Jaguars versus the Central Red Devils was the most hyped event of the year. Imani, Fatima, Hanif, Steven, and Mr. Powers were among the three hundred or so who came out for the State Championship Finals. Those in attendance came to see not only a Championship game but also an intense rivalry. Westmoore lost to the Red Devils by one point last year on Central's home court. But that was last year without their star, Tyler Powers.

Since the Jaguars had the better record, they hosted the Championship game. Cool-sky blue and white packed the Westmoore stands. On the opposite side of the court, most of the Central High fans wore their school colors, fiery red and black. Several security guards dressed in navy blue uniforms stood in the four corners of the gym. Increased security was a safety measure used in case some rowdy fans didn't like the outcome of the game and resorted to violence.

There was a war of the fans in terms of who cheered for their team the loudest. Westmoore's mascot, a boy dressed in a Jaguar costume pumped up his crowd. While the Central mascot, outfitted in a Red Devil costume led his side. There was also the half-time battle of the cheerleaders. Central's squad performed more of a rap and hip-hop type routine. In contrast, Bhriana led her squad in the more traditional high kicks, flips, and chants. She demonstrated her athletic ability and flaunted her beauty. It wasn't hard for her to spur on the males in the crowd. Even the Central guys shot out "dog calls" at her.

That was halftime. Once the game resumed in the second half, the Red Devil fans supported their own. Tension mounted even more in the fourth quarter. Westmoore called a time out with thirty seconds remaining and behind by one point. Tyler looked up into the stands and spotted his father. Mr. DuPree put his fist up in the air and Tyler returned the gesture. A few rows up, his eyes met Imani's. Although he was nervous, she was able to put a smile on his face.

"...You got that, Tyler!" his coach yelled above the roar of the spectators.

"I heard you, Coach!" Tyler screamed back.

"Good, now get out there and do it!"

The play that the coach ordered, the team had executed many times that season and with much success. Tyler was to drive to the basket to force a double team then kick the ball out to the open man, usually Jazz, for a jump shot. The buzzer signaled both teams back onto the floor.

Tyler caught the inbound pass from Jazz. He dribbled the basketball and gazed up at the time clock.

Twenty-five seconds remained then down to twenty ... fifteen ... ten. Tyler charged towards the basket. His defender stuck to him like velcro. Another Red Devil player attempted to steal the ball but he hit Tyler's hand. The referee's whistle was barely audible over the roar of the crowd. Westmoore fans screamed for the foul call. The Central fans yelled, "No foul." The referee signaled a foul and sent Tyler to the free throw line for two shots.

"You can do this," Tyler mumbled to himself as he stood at the line.

He tried to block out the "miss, miss, miss" chanted by the Red Devil tormentors. The Jaguar side was silent. Sweat rolled into Tyler's eyes and stung. The basket looked blurry. He rubbed his eyes with his forearm until his vision cleared and then he bounced the ball a few times.

"You've done this a million times," he said before he arched the ball high up in the air. The ball swooped down and bounced off the front of the rim.

"Aw..." exhaled the Jaguar fans while the Central crowd cheered wildly. Tyler stepped back from the free throw line.

"Walk it off, Man, we only need one to tie," one of his teammates said and patted Tyler on the butt.

Tyler nodded and walked up to the line. The referee fired the ball to him. The ball felt like dead weight in Tyler's hands. He pounded the ball on the court three or four times then paused. Again, one side of the gym was quiet while the other screamed "choke, choke, choke..."

Tyler stared at the rim. "Just one, just one..." he repeated as he bounced the ball again. He stopped, took a deep breath, then released the ball. When it landed, the ball circled the red rim. Slowly, it slipped off the left side and a Red Devil player grabbed the rebound. The buzzer sounded.

The celebration of the Central team and their supporters echoed into Westmoore's locker room. Some of the players were in the showers while most sat in front of their lockers with heads bowed. Speechless. The pep talk from their coach about what a great season they had didn't relieve the pain, especially Tyler's. He sat alone.

"I was open, Man," someone yelled from across the room.

Tyler recognized the voice and focused in on Jazz but he didn't reply.

"Did you hear me?"

Tyler remained silent.

"I was open, Man!"

"What the hell can I do about that now!" Tyler yelled back.

"You should have made one of those freebies but you choked, Maaan."

Tyler couldn't defend himself. He felt he choked, too. He replayed those missed shots in his mind as he made his way to the shower.

"Maybe Imani can give you a little something tonight to make you feel better," another teammate told Jazz and Tyler overheard it.

"And if she don't, I'll call up another female. But sooner or later, Imani's got to give it up," Jazz said.

"You playin' Imani?" Tyler asked.

"What's it to you?" Jazz replied and stepped up in Tyler's face. "You want her too?"

"I don't want her to get played. Understand?"

A few of their teammates surrounded them. Some stood with white towels wrapped around their waist. Others were dressed in street clothes and on their way out the door until the tone in Tyler's and Jazz's voices caught their attention. Their eyes darted back and forth from Tyler to Jazz.

"You're a trip, Man. First, you take my starting position and then you take the last shot of the game when I was wide open. Then you have the ballz to get up in my face talkin' 'bout how I should handle my girl. You must be crazy."

All eyes shot back to Tyler.

"If you think I'm gonna let you hurt Imani, then you're the one who's crazy."

"Mind your business, Man."

"Imani is my business, Man."

"You don't own me Rich Boy so back off!" Jazz said and shoved Tyler.

Tyler threw a hard right cross that landed on the corner of Jazz's lip. Blood trickled down from the opened wound as the brawl ensued. The two slammed into the metal lockers and stumbled over wooden benches. It was apparent that they would fight to the death, so the bystanders stepped in and separated them.

"Killing each other won't change the score," their burly center said.

"And if Imani wants to be with a playa, well then that's her business Tyler, not yours," a Jazz supporter offered.

Tyler pulled away from the guy who held him back and stepped back up to Jazz. "Imani has no idea who she's dealing with and if you hurt-"

Another teammate wrapped his arms around Tyler from behind and joked, "Doesn't it hurt you two to know that you played your last game together?" Everyone laughed except Tyler and Jazz.

Minutes later, the warriors met Imani and crew outside. Other than the solemn expression on the boys' faces, no one could have imagined what took place in the locker room. Imani approached Tyler first. She hugged him and whispered, "If you wanna talk, call me."

Bhriana and Jazz appeared agitated by Tyler and Imani's tender moment. "What about me?" Jazz asked Imani and held his arms out. Imani walked over and embraced him. Jazz sneered at Tyler as he continued to embrace her. Bhriana followed suit and wrapped her arms around Tyler. Steven took a break from his cell phone conversation and told Tyler, "Sorry T-Man. I've got to run and pick up Porsche. Maybe we can get together tomorrow."

Mr. Powers approached Bhriana and Tyler and patted his son on the back.

"You gave it your best shot. Didn't you son?"

"What kind of question is that, Dad? You think I missed on purpose?"

"Of course he gave it his best shot," Imani jumped in. "With all due respect Sir," Imani added then backed away.

"I wasn't criticizing you, Son. I guess I'm just as shocked as everyone else." He tapped Tyler on the back of his head. "I'll give you a ride home."

"If you don't mind Mr. Powers, I'll give him a lift," Bhriana said. She turned to Tyler and kissed him on the cheek. "I think your son needs a little cheering up first."

Mr. Powers looked at Bhriana as if he tried to read between the lines. A smile crossed his face and his large hand landed heavily on Tyler's shoulder. "Don't keep my son out too late," he told Bhriana while he kept an eye on Tyler.

"Before you go Tyler, I'd like you to meet my best friend Fatima and a new friend of ours, Hanif," Imani said. Tyler in turn introduced Bhriana to Fatima and Hanif. Bhriana and Fatima checked each other out then rolled their eyes.

"We're gonna pull up outta here, Girrrl. You ready?" Fatima asked Imani.

"Obviously, you are not a Westmoore student, Farina." Bhriana said.

"It's Fa-ti-ma," Imani and Fatima said in unison. "And no, I don't go to this uppity school but obviously you do and actually I was talkin' to my girl not you," Fatima said and rolled her eyes at Bhriana again. "This whole town gives me the creeps. Comin', Girrrl?" she asked Imani.

"Since Imooni lives in this uppity town, I can take her home and you can head back to wherever you came from," Bhriana insisted.

"Imani doesn't-"

"Imani doesn't wanna go home. She's staying with me tonight," Fatima said as she cut Hanif off.

"Actually, you think Imooni would want to be with Jazz tonight to comfort him in his time of need," Bhriana said and zeroed in on Jazz.

"You got a speech problem or something? My girl's name is E-mon-nee," Fatima enunciated slowly.

Jazz followed Bhriana's lead and told Imani, "I was hoping you would hang with me tonight." Imani took hold of Jazz's hand and pulled him aside. Tyler watched the expressions on their faces as they engaged in a private discussion.

"Even though y'all lost tonight, I like your game," Hanif told Tyler. "It's hard as heck making 'em free throws under pressure. So don't go beatin' yourself up."

"Thanks, Man," Tyler replied and the two shook hands. "Maybe we can get together and play sometime."

"Sounds like a plan."

"Yeah, I could tell you got skillz. You'll take it next year," Fatima said.

A car cruised by with a Red Devil sign posted on the side of it. Central fans packed the vehicle. They saw Tyler and a chorus of "Choke ...choke ... choke..." rang out from the window.

"Don't even listen to those stupid retards, Tyler," Fatima said.

"Yeah, don't sweat it, Man," Hanif chimed in.

Tyler ran his hand across his wavy wet hair then shook his head. "It's gonna be a long summer."

"Pssst. You'll be surprised how quickly you'll git over it. I've been there."

"Thanks, Hanif, but right now I just wanna get out of here."

"It's about time. I've been ready. Nice meeting you, Hanif," Bhriana said and surveyed Fatima from the cement up. "Bye Fa ...Fa ...oh forget it. You know your name."

"And that ain't all I know. I've got your number you little-"

"Uh, Fatima," Imani jumped in, "I'm gonna take off with Jazz."

Tyler wanted to warn Imani about Jazz but he wasn't sure how to go about it. He did know that the girl who held his hand embarrassed him.

"I never realized until tonight just how rude you could be, Bhriana."

She stopped and planted her hands on her hips. "What?"

"You totally disrespected Imani and her friend, Fatima. What makes you think you're any better than they are?"

Bhriana turned to the right, then to the left, and then spun her entire body around. "You talking to me?" she inquired and pointed to her chest.

Tyler didn't respond.

"I know you're upset about blowing the game but don't take it out on me. Everybody has problems. Did I tell you the latest episode that my parents had?"

"Only a thousand times, Bhriana. Actually, all we do is talk about your problems, your life, your parents, your shopping sprees, your car, your-"

"Hey Tyler," someone from a jeep yelled, "you wanna see the instant replay?" Loud sounds of laughter traveled from the vehicle and echoed in Tyler's head. Bhriana and Tyler picked up their pace. Once inside Bhriana's car, Tyler closed his eyes and laid his head back against the headrest.

"You know, Bhriana, it's one thing to take crap from them and even my own team, but to hear you say I blew the game...that's messed up."

"I didn't mean it like that, Tyler. Why are you turning on me tonight? Don't you think I'm upset too? It makes me nauseous. I'm the cheerleading captain and I have to deal with the gloating from the Central cheerleaders. I-"

"I really don't want to be rude but just take me home," Tyler interrupted.

"I thought we were going to spend time together. I want to make love to you again. Do you realize we've only done it once? I want-"

"Shhh..." Tyler said with his finger to his lips. He sat up straight in his seat. "*I* don't want to hear another 'I' from you. Tonight is not about what *you* want so for the last time, take me home. Thank you."

* * * *

"Did I wake you?" Tyler asked. "I would have called last night but I thought you were out with Jazz."

"I've been up cramming for finals and no I wasn't out with Jazz last night. He wanted to hang but it was past my curfew."

"Curfew? I thought your friend said you were going to her house. So how would you parents know?"

"Uh ... I changed my mind and decided to go home because ummm...I wanted to get up early today and study. But anyway, how are you doing?"

Tyler exhaled and then laid back against his headboard and rubbed his beet-red eyes. His tensed body tossed and turned all night. Every time he closed his eyes, the missed shots, the taunting of the Central fans and the disagreement with Bhriana was an endless video in his head.

"I don't look forward to facing everybody at school Monday but I won't blame them if they're pissed off at me."

"And if they are, they were never down with you from jump. Plus, any true athlete knows that this can happen to the best of us, even me," Imani said then laughed. Tyler laughed too and it felt good.

"I needed that. Thanks, Imani."

"What's so funny? I am the greatest!" She said and Tyler laughed on.

"I owe you one, Imani."

"No you don't. It's a corny cliché but that's what friends are for."

"Well at least let me treat you to dinner or a movie or something."

"I don't think Bhriana would appreciate that."

"She knows that we're friends. But, what about Jazz?"

"We don't keep secrets from one another. He knows that we're buddies."

Tyler wanted to ask Imani if she was sure that Jazz was on the up and up with her but he decided not to. "So, may I take my buddy out?"

"How about ice cream?" Imani asked.

"Sounds good but where?"

"W-e-l-l-l, how about the North Pole Fountain?"

"That's the best ice cream parlor in town."

"What if I meet you there at about noon?" Imani asked.

"I could borrow Steven's jeep and pick you up."

"No. I mean thanks but no thanks. I'll meet you there."

"Are you sure?"

"Did you know that a black man was the first to reach the North Pole?" Imani asked rather than answer Tyler's question.

"Matthew Henson, I knew that," Tyler answered with pride. "I'm glad we don't have to go that far for a banana split sundae. And thanks to you, I've got my appetite back..."

That telephone conversation with Imani seemed like only minutes ago instead of hours. Yet, it was noon and Tyler sat in a booth at the back of the North Pole Fountain. Tyler looked about the parlor to see if he recognized any of the patrons as Westmoore students. He was relieved to see a bunch of whiny little kids with their mothers and some teens that he didn't know. Tyler glanced down at his sports watch then back up to the door.

A tiny silver bell above the doorway rang whenever the door opened. Each time it did so, Tyler's eyes darted back in that direction. In between bell rings, he salivated at the larger than life poster of waffle filled cones topped with rainbow sprinkles. Next to that was one of pastel hued sherbets accompanied by its matching fruits of oranges, lemon, and coconut.

Refrigerators on the right side of the parlor stocked take home items. A long counter with red leather covered high stools was on the left side. Behind the counter, Fountain personnel dressed in red and white uniforms prepared eat-in orders. One of the waitresses approached Tyler. "May I take your order?"

"I'm waiting for someone," Tyler replied. The silver bell above the door sounded. Tyler peeked around the waitress and his tired eyelids raised up. A broad smile crossed his handsome face.

"There she is," he told the waitress. Tyler stood up and waved to catch Imani's attention. Their eyes connected and they both smiled.

169

"I'll give you two a minute," the waitress said and attended another table.

Imani plopped down in the seat opposite Tyler. She seemed out of breath and beads of perspiration dotted her forehead. She wore a pair of jeans and a white Jaguar tee shirt tucked inside. No nail polish, no jewelry, and no make-up. Her long braids hung about her shoulders. No hair ornaments. Yet, Tyler could not wipe the smile off his face. Her deep bronze eyes captivated him.

"I brought you a present," Imani said and pointed to the wrapped box on the table. Tyler followed her long finger down to the gift. He couldn't believe that he hadn't noticed the navy with gold stars wrapped package. A gold bow and a little gift card decorated the top of the box.

"It's too early for Christmas and my birthday's not until September. So what's up?"

"It's a cheer you up type thing that's all," Imani answered.

"You did that over the phone."

"Just open it."

Tyler stroked the top of the box then the gold bow. He removed the gift card and opened it. It was a handwritten message inside. He read it to himself and smiled. Then he read it again out loud.

"I'm not a poet
never claimed to be but you
have a friend in me."

Tyler shook his head in disbelief.

"It rhymes but it's not real poetry like what you write," Imani insisted.

"Yes it is, Imani."

"Well, I did follow that 5-7-5 syllable formula. Did you catch that?"

"I caught that," Tyler said as his eyes remained fixed on the white card.

"I'm glad you picked up on it but come on now and open up your gift," Imani told him and tapped on the box.

Tyler lifted the box and shook it. He couldn't hear anything to give him a clue of what was inside. He peeled back the paper and exposed a brown square box. He opened the lid and a sweet cinnamon aroma seeped out and engulfed him.

"Did you bake this?"

Imani nodded up and down.

"I can't believe you did this for me," he said then signaled the waitress. "We're ready to order." He asked Imani, "What flavor ice cream you want with this?"

"You don't have to eat it now. You may not even like it."

Tyler asked Imani again what flavor ice cream she wanted. Both agreed on plain vanilla with whipped cream topping. As soon as the waitress returned with their order and a knife, they dug into the sweet potato pie. The first taste on Tyler's tongue brought back a memory of his mother. He was in grammar school and had just met Bhriana for the first time.

"There's this girl at school and she's the prettiest girl ever."

"What's her name?" his mother asked.

"Bhri-a-na," young Tyler managed to say with a mouthful of pie.

Mrs. Powers smiled as she picked up a yellow paper napkin and gently wiped away the crumbs from the corners of his mouth. "That's a pretty name."

"Uh huh."

"Did you introduce yourself?"

He shook his head from side to side.

"Why not?"

Tyler stopped eating and lowered his head.

"What's the matter?" she asked Tyler and lifted his head until their eyes met.

"She won't like me. None of the girls like me 'cause I look goofy."

"Oh no you don't," his mother said and hugged him. "You look...uh...unique."

"Huh?"

"You know...not ordinary or common. You have your own look...that's what unique means," she said. "And let me tell you," she continued, "the most unique looking boys turn out to be the most gorgeous men."

"You're just saying that."

"Baby, your father wasn't always so handsome."

"Dad?"

"He looked like Bugs Bunny with those two front teeth all poked out."

"Dad?" Tyler asked her again with his face all scrunched up.

"And, if a gust of wind caught up under his Dumbo ears, his scrawny little body would have taken flight."

"My dad?" Tyler asked and then giggled.

"Yes, your dad," his mom replied and giggled along with him. She leaned over to kiss Tyler but he backed away.

"Dad said I'm too old for you to be kissing on me."

"As long as I'm alive, you'll *never* be too old," his mother said and planted a big kiss on his chubby cheek.

"What's the matter?" Imani asked.

"Huh? Oh...nothing. Why?" Tyler asked.

"Your hand was like this," Imani began and then showed him, "on the side of your face and you seemed so... far away. Were you trying to think of a way to tell me that my pie sucks?"

"No...this tastes so good that it took me back to when I was a kid gettin' down on my mom's pie." Tyler shoveled in a couple of spoonfuls and several "umms" echoed from his mouth.

Imani smiled.

"You don't know how happy I am right now. It's not just the pie it's everything," Tyler said and put his spoon down. "I just don't get it. I always thought that if I had a girl like Bhriana that I would be on top of the world." Tyler stopped there and tried to search for the right words.

"I see it all the time," Imani said. "The light-skinned girl with the long straight hair and great body with a rich daddy gets all the guys."

"You're a beautiful rich girl too but you're different," Tyler insisted. "You care about people like your friend Fatima and everything she went through with that guy who was killed and how you tried to help her through it."

"You remember that story?"

"How could I forget? And by the way, I want to apologize for the way Bhriana treated her and you last night. Fatima and Hanif are pretty cool. Maybe we can all hang out sometime."

"Maybe...but you shouldn't have to apologize for Bhriana's behavior. She's old enough to know better."

"Yeah I know and that's part of my point. You're down to earth and would never diss anybody like that," Tyler responded.

"Help me out, Tyler, because I'm new to this dating game. What is it about Bhriana other than her looks, clothes, and money, that attracts you to her?"

"It's not about money," Tyler said then paused and rubbed his chin.

"Is it that little boy crush that you had on her in grammar school?"

"I never thought about it like that but I dunno...I guess Bhriana's like a trophy. You work hard to get what everybody else wants and then when you win it, you put it up on the mantle and when the boyz come around, you show it off. But..."

"But what?"

Tyler shrugged his shoulders and shook his head. "Something's missing. I don't know what it is but this is not what I thought it was gonna be." Tyler leaned forward and lowered his voice. "I'm not the type of guy to kiss and tell but can I make a confession?"

"You can trust me," Imani said and crossed her heart.

"Steven doesn't even know and I feel kinda funny telling a girl about it-"

"Tyler just spit it out," Imani interrupted.

"Okay. Bhriana and I...um...you know...did you know what a couple of weeks ago and I only mention it because even after that, there's still something wrong." He looked at Imani's solemn face and regretted that he told her.

"Do you uh, do you love her?"

"I don't think so. Maybe, that's a part of the problem. I do care about her," Tyler said then paused again and fixed his eyes on Imani's. "Do you love Jazz?"

Imani cleared her throat. "I dunno. I'm sorta embarrassed to say that I'm just glad to have a boyfriend. I hear girls talking about their boyfriends and now I finally have someone to talk about and, I'll have a date for the Junior Prom."

"Pretty lame reasons to stick with a brotha like Jazz."

"Your reasons for seeing a girl like Bhriana are pretty lame, too. And, I'm quite sure that you'll be at the Prom with her."

"Touché."

A few moments of silence went by before Tyler asked his next question. "You two got a serious thing goin' on?"

"We haven't 'done it' if that's what you're asking. He's tried a couple of times but he respects the fact that I'm not ready. I guess that's why I like him because he's willing to wait and to play by my father's rules."

Tyler sighed and sat back in his seat. That explained why Jazz hadn't bragged about having sex with Imani. What Tyler couldn't figure out was why Jazz was being so patient with her. "Does Jazz ever ask you for money?"

"Jazz knows I don't have – I mean no, he's never asked."

"Just be careful and don't let him use you and make sure he's not playin' you."

"I know Jazz likes me and he swears that he's not seeing anybody else."

175

"Guys talk Imani and I'm just telling you what I've heard Jazz tell other guys. He claims that he has this long list of females and I don't want you to be just another number."

Tyler hated that he unloaded the real deal on her, but, he had to warn her. He touched Imani's hands then held on to them. "I'm sorry but I'm not making this stuff up."

"Like you said, guys talk. I know how y'all brag and try to outdo one another. So that's all Jazz is doing. He hasn't given me any reason not to believe him and until he does, I'll trust him. And quite frankly, I'm more concerned about finals than I am Jazz."

"Why are you so hard on yourself?"

Imani sighed then looked away. Tyler shook her hands to get her attention. She turned back to him. "You don't understand, Tyler. I got into Westmoore on a basketball scholarship. We didn't get into the City Finals so now I'm counting on my grades to get another scholarship for next year."

"What's the worst thing that could happen if you don't get it?" Your father's a doctor so can't he afford to pay your tuition?"

"So how was that pie ala mode?" their waitress asked.

"Fan-tas-tic!" Tyler exclaimed and then turned to Imani. "Do you want anything else?"

"Nooo, I'm stuffed plus I really gotta go now."

"I guess you can bring the check," Tyler told the waitress. When the waitress walked away, Tyler turned back to a sad looking Imani. "Is your family having money problems?"

"My mother doesn't work so everything falls on my dad. Sooo, if I get the scholarship, that would be one less burden on him," Imani said and her eyes filled with water. She turned away but Tyler already noticed.

"Talk to me, Imani."

"Tyler you don't understand. I guess it's my fault because when I told you that my father worked in a hospital and you assumed he was a doctor, I went along with it."

"So your father's not a doctor?"

"No...and that's not all-"

"Here you go," the waitress said and turned the check face down in front of Tyler. "You two make such a really cute couple," she added.

Tyler and Imani blushed. Tyler's hands felt warm. He looked down and saw that they were still locked in Imani's hands. Another smile came over him and she smiled back. "What were you saying, Imani?"

"Oh, nothing. Everything's gonna be alright."

STEVEN

"Jazz is dropping by in a few and then I'll swing by your place after he leaves," Steven told Porsche. He placed the receiver between his ear and shoulder and continued with the conversation. "You know I can't wait to see you. I can see your gorgeous face right now."

The vision Steven referred to was the sketch of Porsche's face that he completed. It didn't take him long to convince Porsche to go all the way. He signed and dated the sketch on the front of the portrait. He turned the picture over and put Porsche's initials, "PT" on it. Steven kissed the portrait then congratulated himself with a gulp of beer.

"See you later," he said then hung up the telephone and knocked off his third can of beer. His eyes scanned the sketches of past conquests strewn about his bed. Steven felt proud to have swayed so many pretty girls. His most favorite piece of work was the portrait of Bhriana. For once, he'd gotten something that Tyler didn't have.

The doorbell rang and Steven tried to stand. His equilibrium was off kilter so he sat back down. The doorbell sounded three or four more times in rapid succession. Steven succeeded in his second attempt to stand and he reached the balcony. He leaned over and yelled, "The door's open!"

Jazz came through the doorway. He surveyed the vacant foyer then spotted Steven as he hung over the railing. "What took you so long?"

"Relax, Man," Steven said."

"And if you're gonna jump, can you pay me first?"

"Pay you for what?" Steven asked and laughed hysterically until he felt the blood rush to his head. He straightened up and motioned Jazz to follow him.

"Three hundred dollars was the deal for me to date Imani and so far all you've paid me is a hundred. I got the girl now give me the other two hundred."

"You don't have the girl, Jazz, and you won't get another penny until you do."

"I do have her, rich boy," Jazz said as he looked about the room and threw his hands up in the air. "This place is laid out and you're gonna try and hold out on me?"

"I'm not holding out but I'm not putting out until Imani does. Get my drift?"

"Having sex with Imani wasn't a part of the deal. I was supposed to date her to keep her away from Tyler until Bhriana wrapped him up."

"My point exactly. If you don't nail Imani, she'll never leave T-Man alone. They're still hanging out together so what's your problem? I thought you street guys had all the moves," Steven said then laughed.

"I ain't got no problem, Man!"

Steven laughed again and reached for a couple of beers. "Chill, Maaan, and have a brew."

"Stop tryin' to sound black," Jazz shot at him. "Am I supposed to be a smooth talkin' drunk from the 'hood, too?" he asked. "Keep your beer."

"See, if you were to get with Imani, you wouldn't be so uptight."

"I get more action in a week than you probably do in a month 'cause athletes got it that way, Tubby, and don't you forget it."

"Not with Imani you don't."

"Imani's different."

"How, Jazz? And who you callin', Tubby?" Steven added after he realized that Jazz had cracked on him.

Jazz ran down all of the rules that her parents enforced. He explained how difficult it was to get time alone with her and how it interfered with his program. He blamed that and the fact that Imani has her own activity packed agenda. "She lives right by me but I can't get with her everyday and..."

"Hold up," Steven said with a raised can of beer in his hand.

"Didn't I tell you to stop tryin' to sound black, Mr. Softie."

"I'm not soft," Steven said and sucked in his gut.

"You could have fooled me."

"Forget you, Man, just get back to Imani. Where did you say she lives?"

"Up the hill from me."

Steven laughed so hard that beer almost shot out of his nose. He dialed a number into his telephone and shook his head while he waited for a voice on the other end. "May I speak to Bhriana?"

"What are you doing?" Jazz asked.

"Shhh...oh hey, Bhriana, it's Steven. Jazz gave me some interesting information that I know will make your day. Guess where Imani lives?" Steven asked then put Bhriana on speakerphone.

"Where?"

"In the ghetto with Jazz. They're slum-mates."

"Why you gotta say it like that?" Jazz jumped in.

"Who's that in the background?" Bhriana asked.

"Your good-news boy, Jazz."

"I'm nobody's boy!"

"You two can argue later but right now I want all the dirt," Bhriana insisted.

"Anymore dirt?" Steven asked as he rocked back and forth.

"Yeah, I got more dirt. Your boy Steven is an alcoholic."

"What? I offer you a can of beer and that makes me an alky?"

"Are you drunk, Steven?" she asked.

"No."

"Then can we get back to business?" Bhriana asked and let out a deep breath. "I knew she was hiding something. Does Tyler know about this?"

In unison, both boys answered, "I doubt it."

"I don't want either of you to tell him. Leave that to me. Do you hear me?"

"Why should you have all the fun?" Steven asked.

"He's my boyfriend that's why. So keep your big mouths shut."

"She must be talking to you, Steven, 'cause I know she ain't hollering at me like I'm some little kid or something."

"Oh that's right you're a man, Jazz. A man who's supposed to keep that wench away from Tyler but don't seem to be man enough to do it."

"Like you're woman enough to keep your man in check?" Jazz retorted.

On that note, beer shot out of Steven's mouth then he doubled over in laughter. He slid off his bed and onto the floor and hollered out, "You two are killing me."

"You must be high, Steven. What's so funny? I thought you were on my side. And, take me off of that stupid speaker!"

"I'm sorry, Bhriana," Steven said. He tried to restrain himself as he listened to Bhriana rant and rave about Tyler and Imani's lunch date. He endured complaints of displeasure with Jazz and his inability to get the job done. "Oh yes, I do remember that night Bhriana...no that's not too much to ask in return...I'll take care of it," he said then hung up the telephone.

"She's the only female that I've ever met that I can't stand and I should have known that this was her idea. That witch should be payin' me," Jazz said as he browsed through the drawings on the bed.

"Not bad huh?" Steven asked and ignored Jazzs' statement. Steven proceeded to explain to Jazz what the portraits represented.

"Cool system but I'll stick with my good ole little black book. Actually, I've got a couple of black books now.   But daaag Man, you've got a whole portfolio here. You could open up an art gallery."

"Ummm, yeah I could huh?" Steven responded and they both laughed.

Jazzs' laughter came to a halt as he picked up a picture and examined it more closely.   There were no initials but it had Steven's signature and a date.   "Is this who I think it is?"

"Yup."

"Same date as your party?"

"Yup."

"You nailed your boy's girl after the party?   Sooo, that's what you got out of the deal with the devil," Jazz said and shook his head.   "Don't ever consider me one of your boyz."

"Oh come on Jazz, you make it sound like I did it on purpose.   We were both drunk and it kinda like, you know, happened.   I haven't touched that girl since."

"You rich people are a trip, Man.   How can y'all judge people like me when y'all do some low down dirty crap, too?"

"Hey, you're cool people and to prove it to you, I'm gonna sweeten our deal."

"Don't front, Steven.   You're gonna sweeten the deal 'cause you don't want me to blow the whistle on you and Bhriana."

"Plueeeze, T-Man wouldn't believe you.   The both of you hate each other's guts and I heard how he kicked your butt in the locker room after the game."

"Now I know you're drunk 'cause ain't nobody kick my behind," Jazz shot back and slammed his fist into the palm of his other hand.

"Yeah yeah, whatever whatever, but anyway, Bhriana won't admit to it so it doesn't matter what you say. But like I said, I'm gonna sweetin' this up."

"And like I said, Tyler didn't jack me up."

"Oh Man, just calm down," Steven told Jazz then wrote out a check for two hundred dollars and handed it to him. "I'll pay you another three hundred in cash if you get Imani in check on or before prom night. And if that means sexing her, then a man's gotta do what a man's gotta do."

Jazz seemed to have cooled off after he received the check. He slid it into his back pocket and asked, "How long am I supposed to play this game?"

"When are you leaving for college?"

"August."

"There you go," Steven replied.

"I ain't wasting my last summer here with her, Man. I got too many females to say good-bye to and you know what I mean."

"So hang with Imani by day and creep with your other females by night like you're doing now. What's the big deal?"

Jazz nodded his head in agreement then told Steven, "Just for the record, I have nothing against Imani. She's an alright sistah."

"This ain't personal, Jazz, it's business. So can you handle it?"

"No doubt."

"No doubt what?"

"You're hopeless, Man," Jazz said then laughed.

* * * *

Steven's speedometer hit 55 mph. The speed limit on the usually busy Route 1 was 45 mph. Entry onto the two-lane road occurred from the left and right of it. Steven steered his black jeep recklessly in and out of lanes while Jazz searched through the glove compartment full of CDs.

"There's gotta be something in here I can jam to," Jazz said.

"I'm doing you a favor by dropping you off at a check cashing place and you turn around and dish my music."

"It's diss not 'dish'."

"You know what I mean," Steven said and then he pressed down on the accelerator. The speedometer climbed to 60 mph.

"Man, why don't you just slow down? What's the rush?" Jazz asked as he fastened his seatbelt.

"Porsche's waiting for me."

"How long you plan on keeping her around?" Jazz asked.

"Why? You want her next?"

"Naw, Man, I ain't feelin' her. She's too skinny and pale for me. I like em' thick and chocolate like ummm, like uh, Imani's friend, Fatima. Shoot, I would get with her but it's too tricky 'cause they're tight."

"She's not worth messing up our game plan and don't be dishing-"

"Dissing," Jazz corrected.

"Forget that. Don't disrespect my girl, Porsche."

"Hey, if that's the way you like your coffee, then drink it up," Jazz said then made a slurping sound.

"Drink it all up then lick the bottom of the cup," Steven blurted out.

"That's what I'm talkin' 'bout. And not the same old flavor day in and day out."

"Keep a variety on hand and rotate."

"Yeah, you gotta mix it up," Jazz agreed then slurped again and Steven joined in. "You're having too much fun, Man, concentrate on these big old trucks that are whizzing around you."

"Who's afraid of the big bad wolf? I mean, who's afraid of the big bad trucks, the big bad trucks," Steven sang as he watched Jazz. "This baby floats at 100. You wanna see?"

"I wanna see my 19th birthday so stop staring at me and keep your eyes on the road, fool," Jazz replied and pointed straight ahead.

"You are sooo uptight," Steven said while he continued to look at Jazz.

"I could chill out if you had some slammin' jams up in here and pull your drunk behind over and let me drive," Jazz said as Steven drifted back into the right lane.

"For the last time, I'm not drunk and I don't need a co-pilot."

A bullhorn blared and tires squealed. Steven checked his rearview and side mirrors. He gasped.

"Get out of his way, Man!" Jazz yelled.

"I can't!"

"Well let go!" Jazz screamed and tried to pry Steven's hands off the wheel.

Steven froze. His hands were glued to the wheel and his bucked eyes fixated on the smoke that rose from under the truck's tires. He felt Jazzs' hands on his but there was no where to go. They were sandwiched in between a car on their left and the oncoming truck on their right.

"Faster Man!" Jazz screamed. Just then, the truck crashed into the jeep.

"We're gonna die!" Jazz cried out.

* * * *

A steady stream of doctors and nurses filed in and out of the hospital room. The police officers that sat in the room hoped that Steven regained consciousness so they could get his side of the story. The truck driver had already given the officers his version of the accident.

"I saw him coming into my lane and I swear to God I tried my best to stop," the teary-eyed truck driver said. He paused and then added, "I have three teenaged boys at home so I know how foolish they can be but you never want to see anything tragic happen to them."

"We could tell by the skid marks that you tried to stop your truck. If you hadn't been alert and hit those boys at full speed, they would have died instantly," the police officer said.

"Talking about alert, thank God the driver in that left lane had his wits about him and was able to get out of the way," the truck driver replied. He looked into the steel gray eyes of the officer. "I want to speak to the boys' parents and tell them how sorry I am."

"Unfortunately, we haven't been able to locate the driver's parents. The passenger's mother is on her way here," the officer said.

"I'll wait for her and in the meantime, I'll be praying for those kids."

In addition to what the truck driver told them, the officers also knew from the blood test results, that Steven was under the influence. Police officers called it DUI for short. They checked his license and discovered that wasn't his first DUI offense. Even if the truck driver didn't sue, Steven faced serious charges.

"How's the other boy doing?" an officer asked one of the nurses.

"He's still unconscious, too. He suffered similar injuries, a severe concussion, fractured ribs, cuts and contusions to the hands and face. We're running tests to make sure there's no internal bleeding or brain damage. From what I overheard that driver telling you, these boys are blessed to be alive."

"If they didn't have their seat belts on, they would have been two dead kids," the officer said.

"Shhh…" the nurse said and turned to Steven as if she heard him speak.

"I caaan't," Steven moaned.

Within seconds, a team of doctors and nurses surrounded Steven's bed. They called out his name as they checked his vital signs. Steven's eyelids quivered then slowly opened. He tried to focus in on his surroundings but his vision was blurred. His head throbbed and the voices of those around him were muffled. It looked as if they lip-synced.

Steven tried to speak again but the words caught in his parched throat. He decided that it was too difficult and tried to go back to sleep but the blurred images around him wouldn't leave him alone. He opened his eyes again to try to see who kept calling his name. He recognized the uniforms and it finally occurred to him that he was in a hospital.

"Wha, what hap...pened," Steven managed to say between cracked lips.

"You were in a serious car accident, Steven. Do you remember being in the accident?" a doctor asked.

"N... no."

"Do you know what day it is Steven?"

"N... no."

"Where are you parents?"

"T-Man."

"Who's T-Man?"

"T-Ty-ler Po-Pow-ers," Steven whispered. It took all the energy he had to say Tyler's name. Steven drifted back off.

The next time that Steven woke up, Tyler was at his bedside and held his hand. His chapped lips curved up to a semi-smile.

"Hey goof off, it's about time you woke up," Tyler said. Steven followed Tyler's finger as he pointed to his left leg, "Oh yeah, I hope you don't mind but I signed your cast. I wrote on there 'what a lousy way to try and ditch final exams, friends to the end, T-Man'."

"Nooo po-em?" Steven asked and tried to laugh but his headache intensified. He touched his bandaged wrapped head and closed his eyes.

"There's plenty of room on that big thing to write one if you really want it."

Steven nodded, "no."

"I hear that you don't remember what happened. I'm glad that you remembered me."

Steven opened his eyes and gave Tyler's hand a light squeeze.

"It's scary how the cops can track you down. They called me and I called Imani and told her about

Jazz. Then I jumped into my father's old car and shot over here. I was gonna pick Imani up but she said she'll meet me here."

"Ja-Jazz?"

"Jazz was in the jeep with you. He's next door in pretty bad shape too." Tyler paused and then asked, "So you really don't remember anything that happened do you?"

Steven tried to follow as his friend repeated the details of the accident that the police officer told Tyler. Steven searched his mind to find that information but he couldn't locate it. However, it was clear to him that he was in big trouble. And if Jazz died, it would be his fault. Steven moaned and sobbed.

"Are you in pain? I'll get the nurse," Tyler said then bolted out of the room.

A couple of nurses rushed in with Tyler. Steven held his head and nodded "yes" when one of the nurses asked if he was in pain.

"I'm sorry young man but we're going to have to cut your visit short. Steven must rest now," the nurse told a teary-eyed Tyler.

"I finally ran that police officer out of here. I told him that this kid is in no condition to answer questions today," the other nurse told her co-worker.

"K-keys?" Steven asked in a low tone.

"What keys, Steven?" the nurse nearest to him asked.

"House," Steven said and looked to Tyler to fill in the blanks.

"You want the nurse to give me your house keys, Steven?"

Steven nodded "yes." He inhaled deeply and got up enough wind to form a complete sentence. "Find my folks."

* * * *

Tyler felt like a burglar when he entered Steven's dark and quiet home. He ran his hand across the walls and located a light switch. The sunken living room lit up. Tyler was in search of the phone number where Steven's parents could be reached. Steven couldn't recall where he'd placed the paper with the number on it. He couldn't even remember what state or city they were in.

Tyler searched all of the obvious places. He checked by each telephone and even the refrigerator door and found nothing. Tyler stood still and surveyed the lower level of the house. It was immaculate. That's when it hit Tyler that the Clark's had a maid and she would know how to contact them.

Tyler entered Mr. Clark's den, on the upper level, in search of the maid's number. Framed degrees, family photos, and photos of Mr. Clark with prestigious people lined the back wall. In front of it was a massive cherry wood desk and burgundy leather chair. Tyler found a Rolodex on top of the desk.

"Wow, this man's got connections," Tyler said aloud. He continued to scan through the index cards of who's who in education, politics, and sports. He got to the "M" section and found the maid service card. Their maid's name, Rachel, and her home telephone number was printed on it. Tyler picked up the receiver and then put it back down.

"What am I gonna say? Don't tell her Steven's in the hospital, she might freak out. Just tell her you need the Clark's number and you'll explain later," Tyler debated with himself.

His plan worked. He stared at the Clark's phone number and then the telephone then back to the phone number and decided to let his father handle it. Tyler didn't know how Steven's mother would react and he knew that his father would know all of the right things to say.

Tyler noticed that a light was on in Steven's bedroom so he went in to turn it off. He knew that his friend was a slob but never had he seen his room in such a disastrous condition. What shocked him the most was the number of beer cans on the floor beside the unmade bed.

He remembered what the police officer told him. "I think your friend has a drinking problem. This isn't his first DUI."

Tyler placed his hands on top of his head. How did he not know that Steven had a problem? Yeah, he had seen Steven down a couple of beers before but he didn't think it was a big deal. "I'll come back tomorrow and clean this mess up," he said aloud as he picked up Steven's checkbook off the floor.

Tyler leafed through the blue checkbook that contained carbon copies of checks that Steven had written. "Let's see who's been selling him alcohol." Tyler was about to close it when he didn't find any checks written to liquor stores, but then he caught a glimpse of the name, Jazz. He saw that a check was written out that day to Jazz Timmons for two hundred dollars.

"What's up with this?" Tyler asked aloud. He made a mental note to ask Steven about it. Tyler placed the checkbook onto the nightstand and reached to turn off the lamp. From the corner of his eye, he noticed the drawings spread out across the bed. He figured they were nothing new until he looked closer.

"So he scored with Porsche, huh?" Tyler shook his head and smiled. "Let's see who else he's got under here," he said and slid Porsche's portrait off to the side. His smile disappeared as familiar light eyes stared up at him. *This can't be,* he thought and pulled the drawing closer to him. Tyler scanned every inch of the portrait and looked for some facial feature that did not resemble Bhriana. He couldn't find one.

Tyler spotted Steven's signature and a date on the front. Although the girl's initials were absent on the back, he knew that it was Bhriana. "There's got to be a good explanation for this," he said to the picture. "Steven probably planned on giving me this for my birthday but he drew this back in March and my birthday's not until September. Then again, Bhriana will be away at college in September so maybe that's why he did it early."

Tyler paused and searched deeply into the eyes of Bhriana. "Or, maybe it's a 'something-to-remember-me-by present' from Bhriana to me. Yeah, that's it," he said and kissed the lips in the portrait.

IMANI

The month of June arrived and excitement and anticipation filled the halls of Westmoore High School. Yearbook signings, graduation day, college acceptance letters, and off-campus parties preoccupied the minds of upper classmen, like Bhriana.

Juniors like Imani and Tyler prepared for final exams and the Junior Prom. Foremost in Imani's mind was final exams and Jazz. She sacrificed much of her study time to help Jazz as he recovered from the accident. Imani picked up Jazz's homework from his teachers and delivered it to him each day. Then she took his completed assignments back to school the next day.

Imani walked by the bulletin board in the cafeteria and a fluorescent orange flyer jumped out at her. She stopped and blinked in disbelief. *Who did this?* Imani asked herself and scanned about the cafeteria. She couldn't imagine who added her name to the ballot for prom queen. Imani read the names of the other entrants and shook her head. She figured that she didn't have a chance against any of them.

"You can thank me now," a voice rang out from behind her.

Imani spun around and Bhriana stood there with a smirk on her face. As Imani checked her out, there was something different about Bhriana but Imani couldn't figure it out.

"Thank you for what?"

Bhriana pointed to the flyer. "I want to publicly prove a point to you."

"What?"

"Well, we all know that Tyler will be king at the prom. And, all those girls vying for queen know that they will only be the queen of the prom, not Tyler's queen." Bhriana paused and then added, "But that's not my point. My point is that you're not in Tyler's league and since you don't believe me, maybe you'll believe the 100 or so juniors when they elect someone else."

Imani felt a lump in her throat and her body tensed up. She wanted so badly to snatch Bhriana up by her long neck and shake the evil out of her. She decided that wouldn't be a good idea because there were too many witnesses in the cafeteria. *She ain't worth serving time in jail*, Imani thought.

"Speaking of being out of Tyler's league, does he know where you live?"

Imani was unaware of her clenched fists until she attempted to point at Bhriana. "You don't know," Imani managed to release from her tight throat.

Bhriana moved in so close to Imani that the scent of her perfume made Imani nauseous. "Yes I do, poor girl."

"You're bluffin'." Imani spat out.

Bhriana nodded her head. "Stay away from him and it'll be our secret."

A war raged inside of Imani. If she popped Bhriana, she'd be suspended. If she cried, victory would be Bhriana's. If she said nothing and just walked away, she would look like a punk.

"Hey ladies," a male voice called out and broke their harsh gaze.

"Hey baby," Bhriana said in a soft tone. Imani watched as Bhriana publicly displayed her affection for Tyler.

"Where you been, Imani?" Tyler asked.

Imani cleared her throat and tried to calm down. Yet, the sight of such a nice guy involved with such a trifling being only intensified Imani's rage. She felt the perspiration ooze through the pores of her forehead and hoped Tyler didn't notice. Imani forced a smile and said, "You know I'm always busy."

"Yeah, I know. So...how's Jazz?"

"Not bad. He still gets headaches but the cuts on his hands and face have almost healed."

"Will he be escorting you to the prom?" Bhriana asked and then slid her arm around Tyler's waist.

"Of course."

Bhriana turned to Tyler and said, "We should share our limo with Imani and Jazz. We could swing by and pick them up from their homes."

"No!" shot out of Imani's mouth so quickly and loudly, she startled them and herself. In a calmer tone she added, "Thanks, but we have our own ride." Imani felt an urgent need to change the subject. "So Tyler, how's Steven?"

A somber expression crossed Tyler's face. "I feel for him. He's dealing with the broken leg and cuts and bruises. But, there are some things that he still can't remember and some other stuff. Stuff I can't go into."

"How many times must I hear this?" Bhriana huffed.

Tyler ignored her and continued. "His license was suspended for a year and before he can get it back, he's got to take refresher driving courses."

"Really?" Imani asked.

"Yeah, and his parents had to pay all sorts of fines and stuff."

"What about school?"

"His parents got him a tutor so he might get his diploma by the end of the summer. But, he probably won't start college until January." Tyler shook his head. "He really messed up his senior year and it didn't have to go down that way. I had no idea..." Tyler didn't complete the sentence.

Imani felt that her friend really needed her. She sensed that if Bhriana wasn't glued to him, he would have confided in her.

"Oh for Christ sakes, enough of these sad stories, I'm hungry, Tyler. Let's go eat."

Tyler pulled away from Bhriana and just stared at her as if he was at a loss for words. Imani's eyes darted back and forth from Tyler to Bhriana.

"What?" Bhriana asked and held on to Tyler's glare.

Tyler released a deep sigh and turned to Imani. "I'll catch you later."

"Wait. I'll come with you but let's eat first, Tyler. I told you I'm hungry," Bhriana said.

"You stay here and eat," Tyler said and took off.

"What's wrong with him?" Bhriana asked Imani.

"I dunno," Imani said, "he's your man." As Imani turned away and walked out of the cafeteria, she felt the heat of Bhriana's caustic amber eyes as they seared through the back of her head.

Imani thought about that scene between Bhriana and Tyler as she sprinted up the 13 flights to Jazz's apartment. She was energized as she maneuvered around cans, bottles, broken toys, and other debris that laid on the stairs. Once outside of Jazz's door, Imani tried to catch her breath. She covered her nose and mouth with her hands and breathed deeply into them.

Perspiration slid down her temples and onto her hands. *I must look a mess*, Imani thought as she knocked on the door. Imani heard the sound of locks and chains. To Imani's surprise, Jazz opened the door instead of his mother who usually greeted her.

"Hey, how ya doing?" Imani asked and kissed Jazz on the lips.

"Better than yesterday. Come on in."

The scent of pine somewhat masked the putrid urine smell that seeped in from the hallway and into the tiny living room. The room was large enough for a couch, television, and a black halogen lamp. Instead of an antenna, Jazz's trophies adorned the top of the twenty something inch television.

"You're killin' me with all that homework you keep bringing up here."

"Sorry."

Jazz smirked. "Relax, I'll get with you in a sec'." He motioned Imani to take a seat and then limped to the beige telephone that rested on top of a square metal table in the kitchen. "I can't talk right now," he told the caller, "check you later."

Imani remembered that Tyler had warned her about Jazz. It came to mind the days she'd visited Jazz at the hospital and there was a different girl in the room each time. And at his home, the telephone rang non-stop. Most of the time, Jazz's mother answered and took messages. Occasionally, Jazz answered and told the person he'd call back.

Imani watched how gingerly Jazz sat down next to her on the nubby plaid cloth-covered couch. "Sorry to see you like this."

"Don't feel sorry," he said and looked down at his bandaged left hand and then back up to Imani. "You're too good for me."

Imani tried to read between the lines. She searched his sad face and only found the physical scars. A long dark scab ran down the left side his high cheekbone to the top of his swollen lip. Whitish marks dotted his brown forehead where scabs formed and shed. She inhaled the sweet smell of Cocoa Butter that he used on them.

"You look like you need cheering up," Imani said and bumped her shoulder into his. "You wanna hear something funny? Well, it's not really funny and I was pissed off when I found out who did it but it is funny to think that it could really happen to me..."

"Slow down, Imani, you're making me dizzy."

"Sorry," Imani said then took a deep breath. "My least favorite person in the universe nominated me for Prom Queen to teach me a lesson. Do you believe that?"

"If you're talkin' about crazy-behind Bhriana, I'll believe anything."

Imani noticed that Jazz still wore a serious expression on his face. "Sooo, why aren't you laughing?"

"'Cause ain't nothing funny. I can't stand that scheming witch either, but you have just as much a chance of winning as any of those other females...I mean girls. You've got my vote."

"You don't really mean that," Imani said and bumped him again.

"I wouldn't lie...about that," Jazz said as he played with her long braids. "You're tall, tan, and totally all dat."

"Yeah right, if you say so. Well anyway, I'll feel better knowing that I'll have you there to lean on when I lose," Imani said and reached over and hugged him."

Jazz backed away. "So...what else happened at school today?"

Imani was deep in thought. *Is it my imagination or did he just push me away? Why is he changing the subject?*

"Imani."

"Oh yeah, ummm let me see. Okay, yeah, I ummm ran into Tyler today and he told me that Steven's having a tough time recovering. I don't really know him that well but maybe I'll send him a get well card."

"Don't waste your stamp," Jazz said.

"What?"

"What I mean is I'm sure Steven's getting enough sympathy from his nurses and maids and what have you."

"Well have you spoken to him since the accident and why were you in his jeep to begin with? I didn't know you two were runnin' buddies."

"You're breaking the speed limit again. Slow it down, Imani."

"Sorry."

The phone rang and they both stared at it as if their glares would make it stop. "I was on my way to the kitchen anyway. You want something to drink?"

"Water."

"Well I hope you like tap 'cause we're out of the bottled stuff. My momz went out food shopping."

"I was wondering where she was," Imani said as she followed Jazz's tall frame all the way with her eyes. He looked like he'd lost weight but he didn't shed his muscular upper body. His sleeveless white tee shirt was wet with sweat. It clung to him and his brown skin showed through the thin cotton. Imani fanned herself with her hands and wondered if it was the weather or her hormones that made her temperature rise.

"Hello," Jazz said after he finally reached the receiver. He hunched his shoulders. "Whoever it was couldn't wait."

"I knew you were popular but daaang," Imani said in an irritated tone.

"Just friends calling up wishing me well," Jazz said then placed his hand to his head. "Now what were we talkin' about. Oh yeah, I haven't talked to Steven since the day I checked out of the hospital." He handed Imani a plastic cup filled with ice and water then eased down next to her and shook his head. "I never should have let him drive. He was drunk as hell."

"Drunk?"

"Stupid drunk."

Ring…ring…ring…

Imani rolled her eyes at another interruption. Jazz excused himself and pulled the telephone wire out of the jack.

"Thank you," Imani mumbled. In a louder tone she said, "Tyler mentioned that Steven had other problems. Is drinking one of them?"

"The boy's a straight up alcoholic. He drinks beer like it's spring water. But I ain't mad at him about the accident 'cause it was both our faults," Jazz said and nodded. "Like I said, I never should have let him drive. I just wanted to get to the check-cashing place before it closed. I still ain't made it there yet."

"I can try and cash it for you."

"Naaaw, you've done too much for me already."

"You sure?"

Jazz looked away from her.

Imani gently stroked the right side of his face. "What's buggin' you?"

He turned back to her but Imani didn't give him a chance to answer. She placed her lips onto his. His puffy lips didn't move. Imani traced the edges of them with her tongue. She glided along the crease and he parted them slightly. Imani probed until their tongues met. Jazz jerked back and opened his eyes.

"Did I hurt you?"

"I can't do this anymore," Jazz said and shook his head.

"You can't kiss with sore lips?"

"That's not it."

"You can't kiss with a sore hand or ribs or head?" Imani joked and laughed. She noticed that Jazz's serious expression had not changed. "Come on and lighten up. That's what everybody tells me. Lighten up."

Jazz released a deep breath and eyed the scuffed wood floor. "I've gotta be straight up with you. Being on lockdown since the accident, I've had time to think and one of the things I've been thinking about is how you've stuck by me."

Imani rubbed his back and felt his wet skin through the tee shirt. "I really like you Jazz and maybe it's love that made me want to see you through this."

"That's what I can't do anymore," Jazz said and looked into Imani's eyes. "I can't use you."

"What are you talking about? You're not using me. I want to be with you."

Jazz took hold of Imani's hands. She felt the rough bandage in one and sweaty palms in the other. It was so quiet in the apartment that she heard her own heartbeat. Or, was it his?

"I don't deserve you Imani..."

Imani opened her mouth. Jazz put a finger to her lips and said, "Shhh...let me finish. I'm not feelin' you the way you're feelin' me. You're too good a sistah to just string along. I can't play you like that, anymore."

"What are you sayin', Jazz?"

"I'm saying that you deserve to be somebody's number one. Not just another player coming off the bench. See what I'm sayin'?"

Imani nodded her head in the affirmative. "Yeah, I see." Imani withdrew her hands from Jazz's and continued, "I wasn't the only girl you were seeing and I was a fool to think that any guy would want only me." Imani fought back the tears that threatened to spill from her brown eyes.

"If anybody's a fool, it's me, Imani, not you. I'm crazy enough to let a good thing get away. And yeah, you are a good thing but just not the one for me."

"That makes me feel a whole lot better," Imani responded sarcastically.

"This probably won't make you feel better either but I am sorry, Imani. I shouldn't have let it go this far."

Through blurry eyes, she opened her vinyl backpack and took out Jazz's homework. She handed the papers to him and his eyes met the floor again.

"My momz can do this from now on."

Imani didn't reply. She blew her nose, dabbed at her eyes, and headed for the door. Before she turned the knob, Imani felt Jazz's hand grip her arm. "Wait, Imani."

She refused to turn and face him.

"The least I can do is to take you to the prom."

"Don't do me any favors."

"It'll be my way of paying you back for everything you've done for me."

Imani snatched her arm from his grasp and swung around towards him. "Pay me back? Is this some type of business deal?"

"Nooo, Imani. That's not it. I'm just trying to do the right thing."

"The right thing? You should have told me from jump how you felt instead of playin' me. It's goodbye now, Jazz, not prom night."

* * * *

Imani walked through the door and her mother pointed the receiver at her. "Come on over here and talk to Roberta."

Imani shook her head, "no."

Mrs. Jackson placed her free hand on her ample hip. "Girl, you better git over here and talk to your sister."

Imani's head ached from the tears she held back all the way from Jazz's to her apartment. All she wanted to do was run to her room and release the pressure. But, she knew that to disobey her mother's orders would only add to her misery. Imani shuffled over and held the receiver to her ear.

"Well say something, Chile. I'm payin' for this long distance call," Mrs. Jackson said and tapped Imani on her back.

"Hello," was all she could muster.

Imani listened to all of the latest happenings in her sister's life. The 3.90 average, the boyfriend, the track record, the athletic awards, the Dean's list...

When Roberta turned the table and asked her little sister a series of questions, Imani gave curt replies.

"Fine."

"No."

"Yeah."

"I dunno."

The prom question opened the floodgate. The pressure lessened as tears cascaded down her cheeks and onto the phone. "Maybe" was her last word before she handed the wet receiver back to her mother. Imani raced to her room and shut the door. Clothes that hung from a nail on the back of the door fell to the floor from the force. Imani ignored them and dove face first into her pillow.

Imani wallowed so deep in sorrow that she didn't know that her mother was in the room. She recognized the touch of her mother's hand on her back and she bawled even more.

"What's wrong with you?"

Imani continued to soil her faded pink cotton pillowcase.

"Okaaay, you don't have to talk but hear me out. Whatever happened to you today was not Roberta's fault. I know you two are not that close and it's probably 'cause of your age differences, but she loves you and she didn't deserve the treatment you just gave her."

"You don't understand," Imani managed to say in between sobs.

"Tell me then."

Imani peeled her face from the soggy pillowcase and accepted a white hankie from her mother. Mrs. Jackson pulled back her daughter's braids away from her tear stained face.

"I can't compete with her or anybody else," Imani cried out then buried her face in her mother's ample bosom.

"What on earth are you competing for?"

Imani tried to gather her thoughts. She knew what she felt in her heart but struggled with how to express it.

"People say I'm smart but I have to fight for every 'A'." They say I've got skillz but I couldn't take my team to the City Finals. Fatima says I'm pretty but there's no way I'll ever be prom queen. Some guy says I'm a good thing and yet, and yet…" It was too painful for Imani to go on. She tried to bury her head back in her mother's bosom but Mrs. Jackson held her back.

"Do you know who your main competitor is?"

"Who?"

"You," Mrs. Jackson said and pointed her index finger at Imani.

"Me?"

"That's what I said, Baby Girl. You compete with yourself everyday to be the best *Imani* that you can be. Not the best Roberta or anyone else, get it?"

"Not really."

"Every time you take a test or play in a game you're in competition with yourself to do better than you did, not than Roberta did, the last time. Every time you practice or workout and exercise, you're in competition with yourself to make Imani better and stronger than before. Get it?"

"But it's harder for me because I'm constantly reminded about how great Roberta is. I feel like I'm walking in her shadow," Imani said then buried her face in her hands.

"You better step out from that shadow you talkin' about and concentrate on what Imani wants to do, not what Roberta has done. Everybody's got their own special gifts. Everybody's got their own history to create."

Mrs. Jackson was quick to add, "Roberta's gone through the same trials and tribulations that you have, black woman. That's why her accomplishments are so sweet and we go on and on about them. We're not doing that to make you feel bad because her victories are your victories and ours too. You should be proud not jealous of her because she's family."

Mrs. Jackson took a breather then pointed at Imani's window. "It's a mean world out there. Some people take joy in bringing other people down. I'm telling you not to tear down your own but to be proud and toot her horn and your own. I'm always tooting both my girls horns."

"What do you mean, toot my own horn?" Imani asked and wiped her face.

"I mean if you don't believe in yourself and act like you do, you're leaving yourself wide open for a butt kicking, excuse my expression."

Imani eyes widened.

"If you believe that you're smart, beautiful, and as you young folks say, 'got skillz', then it won't matter what anybody says about you. They can't tear you down 'cause you're strong. Don't look for somebody else to praise you, praise yourself. See what I'm sayin'?"

"I guess."

"Do you guess or do you know? If you're not sure, I'll run it down again."

"No mama, I got it."

"Then tell me how you feel about yourself. I don't want to hear again what other people say about you."

"Oh, Ma."

"Don't oh Ma me. Talk to me, Sistah."

Imani was embarrassed. No one had ever asked her to do that before. "W-e-l-l-l, I am smart. I mean it's harder to pull A's and B's at Westmoore but I'm doing it."

"Okaaay," her mother said and nodded her head.

"I did get a basketball scholarship so I must have some skillz."

"But did they just give you that scholarship out of the kindness of their hearts or did you earn it."

"I worked my tail off for it."

"Alrighty then. And, how you lookin' baby?"

Imani paused before she answered. She stared into her mother's face and saw an older reflection of herself. "I'm lookin' good 'cause I look just like you and daddy. I'm family."

"Oh yes you are and mama loves you," Mrs. Jackson said and kissed her daughter's damp forehead and then embraced her.

* * * *

Fatima huffed as she unbraided Imani's hair. "You make up your mind at the last second to go to the prom then you expect me to work a miracle. Ain't no telling what's up in here."

Imani found it hard to sit still as Fatima toiled for hours on her hair. Yet, she sat and listened as Fatima complained. All the while Imani knew that her friend was in her glory.

"I can't believe how my hair grew!" Imani exclaimed. Her thick and course dark brown crinkled tresses landed at her chin.

"I gotta cut these raggedy ends though."

"Cut? I dunno, Fatima."

"Chill girl, it's just this much," Fatima replied and pinched about one half inch of hair between her fingers. "Once I straighten this stuff out with a perm, you won't even miss it."

Imani smiled then caught Fatima as she stared at her in the mirror. "What?"

"How do you do it?" Fatima asked.

"Do what?"

"How do you get over being dumped by a brotha so fast?"

"He was never all mine to begin with but it's his loss not mines."

"Since he was never all yours, you can't lose what you never had, right?"

"Right," they said in unison and high-fived.

"I wished that playa wannabe could see you tonight. When I hook up your hair and make-up, you're gonna be Da Bomb of the Prom. And, I hope that Bhriana's plan backfires and they name you Queen."

Imani sucked her teeth. "Every clique will be voting for their own and I don't even care anymore. I don't need anybody telling me that I look good, I know I do."

"Well excuse you Miss Thang," Fatima said and snapped her fingers two times. "Boooy, your mama's sermon put a whoopin' on you, huh?"

"Yeah," Imani replied and shared more of her mother's wisdom with her best friend. It appeared that Fatima soaked it up like a sponge.

"So hold up," Fatima said at one point. "You mean to tell me that when I step out of the house lookin' all fly and stuff, I ain't competing with Big Butt Barbara or Weavin' Wanda?"

"Nope."

"So I compete with myself everyday to look better than the day before?"

"Yup."

"Daaang. The competition's fierce!" Fatima said and the girls laughed.

After the laughter subsided, Fatima said, "That Bhriana must think that you're competing with her. I wish I could be there too 'cause if she gave you any lip tonight, I would physically whoop her a-"

"Fatima."

"W-e-l-l-l, she deserves it," Fatima said as she cracked her knuckles. "If she works your nerves, just threaten to scratch her evil eyes out with your cheap press on nails. I could have givin' you a real manicure if you'd givin' me more notice. They make better weapons, too."

"You know I'm not a violent person."

"I know. That's why I wish I could be there," Fatima replied and made a snapping sound with her scissors. "And another thing," she continued, "how did she find out where you live?"

"I dunno but the only student at Westmoore who knew was Jazz. But he promised... he said... oh dang, he probably did it."

"Wouldn't surprise me none," Fatima offered.

"But why tell her?"

Fatima shook her head. "Who knows. You can't trust those trifling brothas out here."

Imani thought about that comment. The last of her braids unraveled and she told Fatima, "We know a couple of cool brothas."

"Like who?"

"Tyler and Hanif seem to be on the up-and-up."

"True dat. But, how do you think Tyler's gonna react when Bhriana tells him? Will he still claim to be your friend?"

Imani had lost touch with Tyler since Jazz's accident. But, he had not called her either. Even so, she shivered at the thought of him knowing the truth.

"Be still," Fatima said as she yanked on a braid.

"I'll go with my head lookin' just like this if you do that one more time," Imani warned. She turned around to see if Fatima got the point and it looked as if she did. "If the situation was reversed, I would still be his friend."

"That's not what I asked you."

Imani hunched her shoulders and said, "I hope he does. But if not, then I guess he was never my friend from jump."

"Hey, my offer still stands. If you want Hanif to take you, that's cool with me 'cause Bhriana ain't loanin' out Tyler."

The image of Tyler's face, the last time she saw him with Bhriana, flashed in Imani's mind. It wasn't the same happy face that he wore when they spent time together. She remembered his smile and the way his eyes squinted when he laughed. She recalled his calmness when he recited impromptu poems.

"I really don't think he's happy with her."

"Happy or not, he's still with the troll. Which brings me back to what I asked you before, do you want Hanif to go with you tonight?"

Imani nodded her head from side to side.

"Come on Girrrl, you know that you gotta show up with someone as phat as Tyler."

Imani nodded her head again.

"You remember my cousin Shonda, right?"

"Yeah."

"You know the one who works part-time over at that doctor's office."

"Yes Fatima, I said I remember her."

"Well we tight and talk about some of everything and everybody. Anyway, she could hook you up tonight. Shonda knows a lot of fly brothas."

"Girrrl, you scared me there for a moment. I thought you were trying to hook me up with her," Imani said and they both laughed.

"Naaaw, you ain't her type."

"S'cuse me? She ain't my type either."

"You know I'm just jokin'. Both y'all straight."

"You got that right. But naw Girl, I'd rather go by myself. That way, there's no pressure to do what I don't want to do or doing it and worrying about what I've done later on." Imani paused then asked, "Did that make sense?"

"Yeah...but at least let us drive you. It's kinda tacky rollin' up in a taxi."

"Hey, I didn't think of that. Now that's an offer I won't refuse."

And, she didn't refuse. A few hours later, Imani stepped out of Hanif's sports car and onto the curb of the Hillside Cliff Manor. Limousines and antique cars decorated the circular driveway. Glamorously attired young couples emerged from them with smiles brighter than the stars that twinkled in the crystal blue sky. From patent leather shoes and satin lapels, to the glitter-embellished dresses, and the diamond jewelry, everything sparkled.

All eyes seemed to shine upon the entranceway in unison. There stood a statuesque beauty draped in a simple red spaghetti strapped form-fitting gown. Maybe, the color red caught their attention. Maybe, the plain yet elegant satin gown was a change of pace from all the glitter and lacy frills. Maybe, it was the way she wore the gown with her head held high as she stood there. Unescorted.

Whatever the reason, Imani got their attention. She felt their eyes upon her so she smiled and hoped that *everything was tucked in.* The gown accentuated all the positives that she kept hidden under baggy clothes and sweats. Her mother made the dress and thought it was too tight in the rear but she didn't have time to adjust it. Mother and daughter were both surprised to see that an "onion" had blossomed back there.

Okaaay. Head up, shoulders back, one foot in front of the other, and whatever you do, don't trip... The crowd on the dance floor parted like the Red Sea as Imani tipped through in high heels.

"Lookin' good Girrl."

"You go, Girrl."

"Imani? I can't believe it's you."

"You're wearin' that dress."

"Wow, your hair looks great!"

Imani heard those call outs from male and female classmates. Even guys who never acknowledged her presence all year long gave her compliments. She graciously accepted them with "thank you," smiles and nods until she reached her destination.

Once inside the posh ladies room, Imani leaned her back against the white door. She looked up towards the ceiling and released a deep sigh of relief. *Oooh, I made it without falling on my face*, she said then looked down at her sling backs. "But dang, my feet hurt!"

She glanced around the vanity section of the bathroom and was glad to see that no one was there. "Daaang, this room is bigger than my living room." Imani crossed the plush canary carpet and sat in one of several vanilla-colored chairs that faced a mirror. "You're here and looking good but now what?" she asked her reflection.

Imani flinched and covered her mouth when she heard someone vomit from the other side of the room. A sour smell filled the air and Imani pinched her nose. *Well, you can't hide in here all night*, she told herself and turned back to the mirror for a final inspection.

"Imani? Is that you?"

Imani recognized that voice but the face wasn't the same. Dark brown mascara streaked the otherwise colorless puffy face. The whites of her eyes were red and the hazel center was dull.

"Bhriana? Is that you?"

"Don't get cute with me," Bhriana warned.

Imani stood up and towered over Bhriana. "And, don't jump bad with me."

"What is that, some type of ghetto talk?"

Imani backed away when she smelled Bhriana's funky breath. "I don't think you're in any condition to mess with me tonight. Your breath stinks, your attitude stinks, your whole disposition, stinks, stinks, stinks…"

"Excuse me?" Bhriana asked in a soprano voice.

"You're excused so get outta of my face," Imani demanded and turned up her nose. "And, go clean yourself up 'cause you're lookin' kinda scary," she said and shooed Bhriana away.

Just as Imani stepped out of the ladies room, a guy from her English class, John Marc, took hold of her hand. "You wanna dance?" he asked.

Got some nerve. Ain't said boo to me all year now he wants to dance?

"Sure," Imani told him.

John Marc was about an inch taller than Imani. His hair was cut so low that he almost looked bald which made his thick black eye brows and jet black eyes stand out even more.

"Girrrl, you're killin' that dress," he yelled above the loud music.

Imani smiled.

"You here by yourself?"

Imani nodded. "Are you?" she asked.

"Yeah, I like going solo."

"It's not so bad." Imani admitted and the couple smiled in agreement.

They danced and danced until the music stopped. The spotlight lit up the stage and the MC addressed the audience and asked for everyone's attention.

"What's going on?" Imani asked John Marc.

"They're probably gonna announce the queen and king," he said and his eyes roamed her body from bottom to top. "I wish I had voted for you now."

"Who did you vote for?"

"My old girlfriend, Tiffany."

"Go figure. A member of Bhriana's clique," Imani mumbled.

"Let's do something different tonight. How about crowning the king first?" the MC asked." The crowd roared in agreement.

Oh great. Just delay the agony, Imani thought. She stuck a long painted fingernail between her teeth and bit down. *Dang acrylic!*

"And the king is..." the MC began but then he hesitated. While he paused, the audience shouted out the names of their favorites.

Tyler, Tyler, Tyler ... Imani chanted to herself.

"Tyler Powers," the MC said and the ladies in the crowd went wild.

"He ain't all dat," John Marc said in Imani's ear.

"Yes he is."

"How do you know?"

"Because he's a friend of mine."

"Well lucky for your friend that he didn't have to compete against me," John Marc said and tugged on his lapels.

Plueeeze, Imani said to herself and strained to get a glimpse of Tyler. Once she focused in on him, Imani smiled brighter than the flash bulbs that lit up the room as Tyler was crowned king. She took a mental photograph of him and carried on her own conversation. *Maybe it's the tux but he looks finer and taller and the hair is shinier and that smile, wooow...*

She imagined sharing the stage with him as queen. They would hug each other and then turn to the crowd, wave, and blow kisses. When Imani blew a kiss in Bhriana's pale face, it would erase like chalk from a blackboard. Just the thought of it thrilled Imani.

"... and now the moment you've all been waiting for," the MC said and interrupted Imani's dream.

She felt her heart bang against the wall of her chest.

"The junior queen of Westmoore High..."

Imani inhaled and held it.

"And, here she is..."

Imani didn't blink.

"Tiffany Ellis."

Imani exhaled.

"It should have been you," John Marc said.

"No big deal," Imani replied and clapped along with the other girls while the guys barked their approval. *Look at Bhriana up there right in the middle of them like she won something. She's probably making sure Tiffany doesn't get too comfortable up there with Tyler. Dang, she don't even trust her girl? Look at her. I can't believe she's profiling and posing for pictures. The girl's whacked.*

"After this, I'll never be able to get next to her again," John Marc said.

Imani forgot that he was there. "Why? You want her back?"

"Naaay, I'm lookin' for something new."

Imani frowned. "Some thing or someone?"

"Somebody new, like you," he said. He grabbed hold of Imani's hand. "Let's go somewhere we can talk."

"How about over there at the fountain, I'm thirsty," Imani said and she tagged behind John Marc.

"It's quieter over here," John Marc said.

"Isn't it beautiful?" Imani asked about the five-tier silver fountain. Red punched flowed down from the top on all sides. Crystal punch cups surrounded the base of the fountain.

"You're beautiful," John Marc said and handed her a cup and a napkin.

"Imani tried not to stare into John Marc's jet black eyes. She looked away and noticed that Tyler headed in her direction. Along the way, he received quick hugs and high fives. Imani took her sky blue cocktail napkin and dabbed it across her face to kill the shine that she sensed was there.

When their eyes united, Imani felt like she had hit the pause button on a VCR. Time froze. The cup quivered in her hand. "Hold this," she told John Marc. Imani glided over towards Tyler and the closer she got, the harder her heart pounded.

"Hey, Queen," Tyler whispered in her ear as they embraced.

"Hey, King," she whispered back. The sweet smell of his cologne went straight to her head as if she had drunk alcohol. She held on tight. *Get a grip girl. Let go of him before Bhriana gets ugly. Now come on legs, hold me up.*

"I better let you go before Jazz rolls up on me," Tyler said.

"He's not here."

"What?" Tyler asked as the twosome parted.

"We broke up. W-e-l-l-l actually, he broke it off."

"I'm gonna break off a piece of his a-"

"Nooo, that's not necessary," Imani said and then laughed."

"What's so funny?"

"I'm okaaay," she replied but from the look on his face, Imani didn't think Tyler believed her. She took his hands in hers. "Really, I'm fine."

"You look better than fine. You look ... wooow ... incredible. I mean you look beautiful every time I see you but Queen, you've taken it to another level."

Imani was speechless. Her face felt flushed. If Imani were a few shades lighter, it would have been as red as her dress.

"Who's here with you then?" Tyler asked as he scanned the room.

"Me."

"Get outta here."

"Nope." Just then Imani remembered John Marc and added, "I came here solo but John Marc has been tagging along all night. I left him over there by the fountain." Imani watched as Tyler looked over in that direction but she didn't want to see the expression on John Marc's face. "Is he staring at us?"

"Yeah. But he's frontin' like he's not."

They both chuckled about that. Imani realized just how much she'd missed talking to him. "How come you stopped calling me?"

"Way to go, Tyler," someone said and slapped him on his back.

"Thanks, Man," Tyler replied then turned back to Imani. "You have no idea how much I-"

"There you are," Bhriana said.

"Imani, you want this punch?" John Marc asked as he walked up on her.

Well dang, why don't everybody just come on over, Imani said to herself.

"You're here with her, John Marc? So where the heck is Jazz?" Bhriana inquired.

"Obviously not here," Imani said in a sarcastic tone.

"You two are still together. Aren't you?" Bhriana asked then looped her arm around Tyler's.

"Evidently not."

"Steven didn't tell me that happened," Bhriana blurted out.

"Why would Steven tell you?" Tyler asked.

"Steven? I didn't say Steven. What I said was I can't even imagine what happened."

"Nooo, that's not what you said the first time," Tyler insisted.

"Baby this music's so loud, I can hardly hear myself!" Bhriana yelled.

"What are you screaming for, Bhriana? The music isn't that loud," Imani said in a normal tone.

Imani watched a pinkish red creep under Bhriana's translucent skin. She knew that she had hit a nerve but didn't know why.

"I bet you heard who's Prom Queen," Bhriana told Imani and laughed. "By the way, Tiffany and a group of us have rented out suites for the night over at the Princess Hotel. Of course you're gonna join us, John Marc," Bhriana said.

Imani's eyes left Bhriana's and focused on John Marc.

"Sure, sounds like fun. Count us in."

"Us?" Imani asked.

"You wanna go, right?"

"No."

"Oh come on, Imani. It'll give us a chance to get to know one another better."

"I have friends picking me up in an hour, sorry."

"Call 'em and tell 'em you got a ride. I'll take you home in the morning."

"Thanks, but no thanks."

"But-"

"But the lady said no, John Marc. So back off," Tyler said in an unusually deep voice. All eyes turned to him as if in total surprise.

"Hey," John Marc began and put his hands up, "can't blame a brotha for tryin'." He turned to Imani and said, "Maybe we can hook up some other time."

"Sounds good," Imani said. She accepted the red punch from John Marc and he gave Tyler one last gaze before he turned and walked away.

"You're on a roll, girl," Bhriana said. "Oh well, come on Tyler, let's go."

"Are you sure you're gonna be alright here by yourself? I could give you a ride home now if you want," Tyler offered.

"Imooni came here by herself, so why are you making a big deal about this?" Bhriana asked Tyler then placed her hands on her hips.

"You know my name, Bhriana."

Tyler put his index finger to his lips and shook his head from side to side. Imani took that as a signal for her not to say another word. Tyler then slid his hand into the inside pocket of his black blazer. He pulled out a piece of paper and handed it to Bhriana. In a calm tone he said, "Do me a favor. Tell the valet to have our chauffeur bring the car around and I'll meet you outside."

"Why? You wanna spend some time alone with her?"

"Hey look Tyler, just go. Really, I'll be fine so just go on," Imani said to avoid a scene.

"Since when does my man need permission from you to do anything?" Bhriana asked and stepped up to Imani.

Imani looked around and noticed that a few people overheard and they gawked at them. She always hated to see two girls fighting over a guy in public. As much as she despised Bhriana and adored Tyler, she didn't want to go there. Yet, she refused to back down from Bhriana. It was about respect, not Tyler.

"I'm tired of your yapping and your 'I'm better than everybody' else attitude. I'm sick of your threats and your naming calling. So for the last time, get out of my face little girl and grow up!"

Imani didn't realize just how loud she was until she heard voices around her. She turned about and noticed that a small crowd with surprised looks on their faces gathered around them. Bhriana must have noticed it too because her face was a deep rich red.

"I'll meet you at the car," Bhriana told Tyler then stalked away.

"I'm sorry, Tyler, but she just pushes and pushes and-"

"I know," he said and led Imani over to a more secluded spot.

Don't cry. Girrrl, you better not cry. Fatima will kill you if you mess up this make-up... Imani tried to think of anything humorous to keep from shedding a tear. She was embarrassed yet she felt so safe with him.

"Everything you told Bhriana about herself was true so don't feel bad about it. I've got to go and talk to her because we're not working out."

Imani sucked in her cheeks as she attempted to keep a straight face.

"I'll call you soon, if that's okay with you?" he asked.

Imani nodded, "yes."

Imani felt the light touch of his hand on her face. She wished it could stay there forever. But just as quick as it was there, it was gone. Tyler headed for the door. Her brows arched when he made an about face and sauntered over to her.

"I wanna give you something."

"What?" Imani asked then held her breath.

Imani followed Tyler's hands as he removed the white rose from his lapel and pinned it onto her dress. "Just a little something for my Queen."

BHRIANA

Bhriana's tanned legs and feet hung over the edge of the in-ground swimming pool. The cool blue water did little to offset the 90-degree temperature and thick humidity. Yet, she sat there in an oversized white tee shirt and khaki shorts and sipped seltzer with lemon. The ice had long melted under July's bright yellow sun.

The ripples that she made with her feet hypnotized Bhriana. Her mind took her away from the physical heat to the emotional fire of prom night. Although that was weeks ago, the smoke lingered and the charred ego remained. She saw Tyler's face as they argued in the car that night. She heard the hurt in her voice as she replayed the heated conversation for the thousandth time.

"I can't believe you let that girl talk to me like that in front of all of those people. How could you do that to me, Tyler?"

"Do what? Stand by and watch my girl get read like a book? I hate to tell you but it's not fiction. Everything Imani said about you is true."

Bhriana gasped and covered her mouth.

"Look Bhriana, I don't wanna hurt you."

"Then take back what you said!"

Tyler sat in silence.

"I thought this was going to be a perfect night," Bhriana huffed. "I always dreamed that I'd wear this incredible gown, be escorted by a gorgeous guy, and spend the entire night with him." Tears leaked from the corners of her eyes. She grabbed Tyler's hands and squeezed them tight. "I love you, Tyler. Please don't ruin my dream. Let's go to the Hotel and make up."

The sound of footsteps behind her broke her trance. She shaded her eyes from the sun as she looked up and Tyler towered over her. She wiped away a combination of sweat and tears from her golden honey face then turned away from him and stared back into the water.

"Who let you in?"

"I let myself in. The door was unlocked."

The birds chirped at one another in the trees and that was the only noise that came between Bhriana and Tyler's silence. Bhriana placed one hand on her stomach and sipped seltzer with the other.

"We've got to talk, Bhriana."

"Oooh yes we do," Bhriana said as she nodded her head. She rose, toweled off her legs and feet, and brushed past Tyler. The quick change in temperature from the outside to the air-conditioned living room gave Bhriana an instant headache. She sat down on the couch and placed her head in her hands.

"You alright?"

"What do you think?" Bhriana countered as she looked up at him. "Never mind, don't answer that," she said before Tyler responded. "But maybe you can tell me why I've only heard from you a couple of times since the prom. And where, or should I say who, you've been with because it hasn't been with me…"

"If you give me a chance I can tell you."

"And…why didn't you meet my parents and me at the restaurant for dinner after my graduation? We waited for you and you didn't even have the decency to call and say that you weren't coming."

Tyler's eyes met the plush carpet.

"Do you realize how hurt I am? Even my parents called it a truce and didn't start a war over dinner. The only thing that could have made that night perfect was you."

Tyler's head remained bowed.

"Well you wanted to talk so speak up!" Bhriana snapped.

"I messed up. I messed up by not telling you prom night. I should have told you then that it's over," he said then sat down in a loveseat opposite Bhriana.

Bhriana just looked at him or rather, through Tyler.

"I have always been sprung on you. But, I don't love you, Bhriana. And to be honest, now that I know the real you, I don't even…how do I say this… l don't even like you anymore." He paused as if he waited for a violent reaction from Bhriana. He didn't get one so he continued.

"I haven't been playin' you. Just avoiding you and concentrating on finals."

"I bet you spend time with that poor lying ghetto girl."

"Who are you talking about?"

"I guess Imooni didn't tell you that she and Jazz are neighbors, huh?"

"For the last time, that's not her name."

Bhriana waved her hand. "It's not important. She's not important. It doesn't even matter whether or not you love me. I still love you and if you think you're gonna ride off into the sunset with that low-life Ipooni, Irooni-"

"Imani!"

"Whatever! You're sadly mistaken."

"It's not like we're married."

"Not yet."

"Not ever."

"Tell that to our baby!" Bhriana yelled and lifted her shirt.

Tyler looked stunned. His mouth was wide open but no words came out.

"This is all that matters now, get it," she said and pulled her top back down over her swollen belly.

"How do you know it's mine? You told me that you weren't a virgin and we only did it once. One time, Bhriana," he said and held up one finger.

"It only takes one time, Tyler, and it's yours."

Bhriana watched Tyler pace back and forth. He stopped for a second then paced again. "Will you cut it out, you're making me nauseous," Bhriana told him.

"I can't believe this." He paced some more then stopped dead in his tracks. "Wait a minute. It could be Justin's baby. You were with him before me."

"Don't even try it, Tyler. This baby is yours not his. Justin was history a long time ago."

"It wasn't that long ago and what did the doctor say?"

Bhriana looked away from Tyler. Her period was way overdue and her size 6 clothes were tight in the waist. So out of curiosity, she took a home pregnancy test and it turned up positive.

"I was hoping that I felt sick to the stomach from something I ate or this gut was just a weight gain but I don't eat that much anymore and it won't go away. Look at me," she said. She pulled her shirt up again then burst into tears. "I'm scared, Tyler. I know I have to go to the doctor to be sure but then again, I don't wanna know," Bhriana admitted as she rocked back and forth.

When Tyler sat down next to her, she stopped and looked into his eyes. She finally had his full attention and felt closer to him than ever before. His expression seemed to soften and she knew that was the time to get as much sympathy from him as she could take.

"What am I gonna do?" she asked then buried her head into his chest. Tyler's strong arms engulfed her and Bhriana's entire body went limp.

"You've got to go to a doctor, that's for sure," he said.

Bhriana thought about Tyler's advice long after he left. She sat in the middle of her bed and combed through the yellow pages of the telephone book. The names of gynecologists seemed endless. "The ones in my town are definitely out of the question," Bhriana said aloud. She took a pencil and crossed those doctors off. "And, I don't want some strange man examining me either," she said then crossed off all of the male doctors.

"Eenie, meenie, mynie, mooo ..." was the way Bhriana selected one of the gynecologists. Her finger landed on Dr. Janice Murphy and she fixed her eyes on the doctor's telephone number. The sound of her mother's footsteps startled her. She slammed the thick book shut and tossed it to the floor.

"Bhriana, baby, I went shopping today and picked you up a couple of cute shorts and tops," Ms. Austin said then pulled them out of the shopping bag. "I took one look at these and just knew you'd love them."

Bhriana sized up the petite outfits and figured there was no way she could fit into them.

"Sooo, was I right? Are these you or what? Come on and try them on," her mother said then put the shorts up to her waist. "Once upon a time I could strut around in these," Ms. Austin added and shook her head.

"Me too," Bhriana let slip.

"What?" her mother asked.

"I said I know they'll fit me. I don't have to try them on and of course I like them. You always had great taste in clothes."

"Speaking of which, when does my Princeton freshman want to go shopping for school clothes? All you will need is a few pair of jeans to go with the shirts and sweaters that you already have. And, would you believe the stores are stocked with fall fashions already? Here it is darn near 100 degrees in July, and they're trying to sell wool jackets, sweaters, turtlenecks, and you name it."

"Actually Mother, I have enough clothes to start the first semester. I would rather use that money to go, ummm, to go away. Yeah, to go away with Tiffany and a couple of other girlfriends to an island somewhere. You know, just to get away and have fun before school starts."

"What does your father think about that?"

"I haven't asked him yet but I'm quite sure he'll say yes if you say yes."

"You do deserve a nice vacation and I'm so proud of my college girl," her mother replied and walked over and hugged Bhriana. "Give me a day or two to think about it and discuss it with your father," Ms. Austin said then headed towards the door. She stopped by Bhriana's dresser. "Will you look at me, I'm still holding these clothes," she said and pulled open the top drawer.

Bhriana heard her mother shuffle through the unopened boxes of tampons. *You idiot. You should have thrown them away*, Bhriana told herself.

"Bhriana?"

"I knew it," Bhriana mumbled under her breath. "Yes, mother?"

"What's going on here? When was the last time you used these?"

"I don't remember," Bhriana whispered.

"Excuse me. What did you say?" Ms. Austin asked and made an about face to her daughter.

Bhriana couldn't maintain the intense eye contact. She picked at the threads of her bedspread and repeated herself. "I don't remember."

"How many times have I suggested that you keep track of your period by using a calendar. Every month I put a circle around the day that my period began. Bhriana, look at me when I'm speaking to you."

Bhriana raised her head and their eyes met.

"Did you get your period this month?"

"No."

"What about last month?"

"No."

"And the month before that?" she asked but that time her voice trembled."

"I don't remember," Bhriana said as water filled her eyes.

"Lift up that baggy shirt, Bhriana," Ms. Austin demanded.

Just go ahead and show her. I'm sick of trying to keep this a secret. She's gonna kill me. Maybe not physically, but her ranting and raving will. I can't win. God, I'm in big trouble...

"Bhriana Sharise DuPree."

The sound of her full name interrupted Bhriana's private conversation.

"Either you lift up that shirt or I'll do it for you."

She's serious. I know she'll do it. You just had to cry, didn't you? You messed up. Now what? God, she's gonna freak but she wants to see so show her. Bhriana sucked in her belly and lifted up her shirt. She looked down at it instead of her mother. Even when she sucked it in, her stomach still appeared larger than normal.

"Put your shoes on and let's go," her mother said in a forceful tone. Yet, her face was expressionless.

"Where?"

"You have five minutes to meet me downstairs," Ms. Austin said and walked out of the room and slammed the door behind her. Bhriana got up and put her ear to the door to hear if she had walked away but she heard no footsteps. All she heard was a faint cry.

* * * *

As soon as Bhriana stepped inside, the odor reminded her of why she hated doctor offices. The smell of alcohol and the stuffiness in the small waiting room made her queasy. Her legs shook as she followed behind her mother up to the receptionist's window.

"I'm Ms. Vanessa Austin and I have a four o'clock appointment with Dr. Parker," she told the young woman behind the desk.

The receptionist scanned down the list of names in her appointment book. "Sorry ma'am, but I don't have you scheduled here," she said but didn't bother to look up at Ms. Austin.

"I spoke with David on my way here and he said he could squeeze me in at four."

The young woman raised her head and eyed Ms. Austin. "Excuse me while I go and verify this," she said and sauntered off.

"We could come back another day, Mother."

Ms. Austin just looked at her daughter as if to say, "don't even try it."

Bhriana saw the irritation in her mother's face and decided not to press the issue. Instead, her eyes roamed the bright white room. Framed pictures of smiling babies put a smile of Bhriana's face and held her attention the longest. The horrific prints of the outward signs of sexually transmitted diseases like blisters, warts, and scabs, made her stomach churn.

Bhriana left that gross scene and scanned other parts of the room. Magazines seemed to be everywhere: on the rack by the plants in the corner, on the center table, and strewn about empty chairs. She didn't want to make direct eye contact with anyone there for fear someone would recognize her. But in a quick glance, she saw that the room was filled with women of various ages and only one or two of them had a man by their side.

"Doctor Parker has confirmed your appointment ma'am. I'll need your daughter to fill out these forms and bring them back to me."

"Thank-you, ummm, Shonda," Ms. Austin said as she noted the receptionists name tag.

Shonda smiled at Ms. Austin and then Bhriana. "You can sit right over there and fill these out," she said to Bhriana.

Mother and daughter took a seat and worked on the papers together. "Do I have to use my real name?" Bhriana asked.

Ms. Austin calmly asked, "What name did you use when you got yourself into this condition?"

Bhriana knew her mother well enough to know that she really didn't want an answer to that question because it wasn't a question. It was a statement. *Score another one for Mother*, Bhriana said in her mind and then worked quickly to complete the forms. Once finished, she handed them to Shonda.

"Bhriana S. DuPree," the receptionist said as she examined the paperwork. "Your name sounds familiar. Have we ever met?"

Bhriana stared at the young woman and thought she resembled someone she had met once before but couldn't remember who. "I don't think so."

"Well if we have, it'll come to me," Shonda said and then told Bhriana, "have a seat and relax. The nurse will call you soon."

I know it's just a matter of time before she explodes, Bhriana said to herself as her eyes darted from her mother to the door. *I could slip out of here without her seeing me, but, where would I go? This can't be happening to me. This must be a bad dream. Yeah, that's all it is, a bad dream. Wake up right now and everything will be all right...*

"Bhriana DuPree, the doctor will see you now."

Bhriana was still in her own world and didn't comprehend what the woman said. Her mother tugged on her arm and she followed her.

"Please be seated and the doctor will be right with you," the short nurse said.

Bhriana's legs went limp and she plopped down into the green leather chair. The back of her moist legs stuck to the seat. She crossed and uncrossed them but couldn't get comfortable. She wished she could take the perspiration that dripped down her back and her temples and wet her arid mouth. Bhriana glanced over at her mother and saw a very calm and very dry woman.

"Good afternoon, ladies."

"Well hello, David," Ms. Austin said and stood and embraced him.

"Boy oh boy, you look younger and younger every year."

"Oooh, David," Ms. Austin said and her cheeks became flushed.

"Aren't you overdue for your annual check-up, young lady?"

"I've been so busy lately, David, that it has totally slipped my mine. But, I'll make an appointment on my way out."

"You do just that, the doctor said then pointed at Bhriana. "Is this the same baby I delivered?" And, how many years ago?"

"Seventeen."

"My, my, you two could be twins."

Bhriana squirmed around in the chair and tried not to linger too long in his eyes. *Maybe he can tell just by looking at me that I'm pregnant*, she thought.

"What seems to be the problem, young lady."

Bhriana tried to swallow but there was no saliva. "Well, ummm, sir I guess I'm here because it's been a while since, ummm, since I've had my ummm, my ummm, period."

"Well, it's not uncommon for young girls to experience irregular cycles and skip a month here or there. So tell me, how many months have you missed and is this the first time it's ever happened?"

"David, this has never-"

"Vanessa, let the girl speak."

"I dunno. T-two, or th-three...I dunno."

"Just relax," he said and smiled. Then he jotted something down on her chart. "In general," he added, "how have you been feeling these past few months?"

"Stressed out with finals and college entrance exams and stuff."

"She's been accepted into Princeton," Ms. Austin jumped in.

"Princeton, well, you're intelligent and beautiful. Great combination."

Bhriana blushed.

"That type of pressure could throw your cycle off as well. Are you experiencing any sleeping or eating disorders?"

"No, not really. But, I do have a problem keeping my food down. Stuff I used to love to eat is upsetting my stomach so I don't eat that much."

"I see," Dr. Parker replied and took more notes.

"I hadn't noticed any weight gain in her until today," Ms. Austin said.

"I know this is a tough question to answer, especially, in front of your mother but I need to know."

"Oh God," Bhriana mumbled and squeezed the armrests on the chair.

"Are you sexually active?"

Perspiration released from every pore of her body. Her heart seemed to bang against the wall of her chest and all air expelled from her lungs. She wanted to high tail it out of that claustrophobic office but her feet felt like they were nailed down to the wood floor.

"Answer him, Bhriana," her mother said in a raised tone.

"Well..."

"Well what, Bhriana?"

"Vanessa, please, let the child speak," Dr. Parker insisted.

"Well...once in a while, I am."

Ms. Austin's gasp was so loud that it surprised Bhriana. "Every time I asked you that same question you told me 'no'. Every time."

"Calm down, Vanessa. I understand you're upset and yes it's unfortunate that the parent is usually the last to know but please calm down." Dr. Parker's big eyes landed on Bhriana again. "So you're active occasionally but I hope you know that you could get pregnant anytime. Especially, if you have unprotected sex. Did you use any type of contraceptive each time you engaged in sexual intercourse?"

Bhriana shook her head "no."

"Have you ever used any kind of protection?"

"Condoms, sometimes."

Ms. Austin shot up out of her seat. "How many times have we had this discussion?" She asked but didn't wait for her daughter to answer. "Several times Bhriana, several. I blame myself for not seeing the warning signs sooner. The vomiting and the tummy-bulge, but, I'll be damn if I blame myself for not educating you about safe sex because I have. I guess you're like hundreds of thousands of girls who think that this won't happen to them."

"Vanessa," Dr. Parker said as he stood up. "You have every right to be upset. However, let me examine Bhriana and test her urine and blood to see if she is indeed pregnant."

He turned his attention to Bhriana, "Even if you're not pregnant, you could have contracted a sexually transmitted disease and I'll test you for those as well."

He leaned over his desk and got into Bhriana's face. "I hope that the pain on your mother's face and the fear that's probably raging within you will deter you from ever having unprotected sex again."

Tears ran down her face. She hoped he would feel sorry for her and end his speech. She was wrong.

"Better yet, no sex until you're ready to deal with the emotional, physical, and financial consequences of your actions."

* * * *

Bhriana and Tyler's parents agreed to meet at Vanessa Austin's house for a group discussion. Both families wanted to decide on a course of action. Bhriana answered the door and embraced her father. "I'm sorry, Daddy," she said and sobbed like a baby. When she felt his bear hug tighten, she knew that he was not angry with her.

"Shhh...come on now, stop crying. Are Andrew and Tyler here yet?"

"No."

"Hello, Brandon," Ms. Austin said.

"Vanessa. And, how are you doing?"

"Not so good. And you?"

"Hangin' in there," he replied.

"May I get you something to drink?"

"Not right now, but thank you."

The doorbell rang and Bhriana wiped her face and smoothed back her ponytail while her father answered the door. The adults exchanged hugs and pleasantries while Bhriana and Tyler traded nervous glances.

"What can I get you all to drink?" Ms. Austin asked.

"Anything with ice in it will be fine with me," Mr. Powers said. "How about you, Son?"

"Nothing, ma'am."

"Me either, Mother."

Bhriana's parents went into the kitchen and returned with beverages and platters of fruits and vegetables. Bhriana gagged at the sight of it and covered her mouth. She was relieved that no one noticed.

"Please, help yourselves," Ms. Austin said as she motioned to the food. The grown-ups did just that as Bhriana and Tyler watched.

"The AC feels good, Vanessa. It's hot as heck outside," Mr. Powers said.

"I can't wait for this heat wave to end," she replied and everyone nodded.

The crunchy sounds of carrots, celery, broccoli, and cauliflower replaced the small talk. Bhriana checked out her nails and Tyler stared down at the carpet. Not that she was anxious to hear what the adults had to say, however, Bhriana wished that somebody would break the silence.

"Can we get on with why we're here?" Tyler suggested.

"Sounds good to me," Ms. Austin chimed in. "Why don't we go around the room and one by one articulate our feelings about this situation and what should be done about it. Starting with you, Andrew."

All eyes and ears turned to Mr. Powers. He leaned forward and clasped his hands in front of him. "Initially I was mad as hell when I heard about this. Although I've calmed down some, I'm still very disappointed in my son. I apologize to you, Vanessa, and to you too, Brandon, for my son's irresponsible behavior. Even though it takes two to tangle, I promise you that Tyler will do right by your daughter."

"What does that mean? Do right by her?" Tyler asked.

"It means owning up to your responsibilities," his father said.

"Let's move on to Brandon, if you're finished, Andrew," Ms. Austin said. Mr. Powers nodded.

Mr. DuPree turned to his daughter. "Well first, let me just say that I love my baby girl. And, I never want to see her hurt the way she's hurting right now. Yes, she's brought it all on herself, with Tyler's help, but that doesn't make me feel any better. All I want is for her to be happy. So, whatever she decides, I'll support."

"We're her parents, Brandon. This cannot be that child's decision alone."

"Can we at least let her speak?" he asked.

Bhriana pointed to herself and asked, "Me? Now?" She looked about the room and the adults nodded "yes." She zoomed in on Tyler and smiled at him. "I want to begin by saying that I love Tyler and I want to be with him. I know this is not the ideal way to start a family but I want to keep this baby and marry Tyler after he graduates from Westmoore."

"What!" Tyler and Ms. Austin shouted out at Bhriana in tandem.

"Hey wait a minute," Mr. DuPree began, "I thought we agreed to listen to everyone. You will have your turn," he said and pointed to Ms. Austin and Tyler.

When Bhriana saw the red creep under her mother's skin and in her eyes, she knew that her mother was about to erupt. "That's all I wanted to say, for now," Bhriana ended.

"If Bhriana wants to have that baby, then I will support it. But, ain't no way I'm gonna marry her. Bhriana knows that I don't love her and with all due respect, Mr. & Mrs. DuPree, I don't even like her."

"You liked her enough to knock her up, didn't you?" Mr. DuPree asked.

"Let him speak," Ms. Austin countered.

"That was before I really got to know her, sir. And like I said, I'll work as much as I can while I'm in school to help support the baby, but I will not get stuck with someone I don't want to be with."

"Shooot, you should have thought of that before you stuck my daughter with this baby," Mr. DuPree said.

"We heard you the first time, Brandon, it's my turn now," his ex-wife said.

Bhriana braced herself for the wrath. She took hold of her father's hand and held on tight.

"Being the only adult female in this room, I want to address all of you from first hand experience. What I have to say is nothing new to Brandon or Bhriana but it's worth repeating.

"To marry so young and to someone who doesn't love you, and worse yet, doesn't even like you, is wrong. You are not going to be able to change Tyler's mind and he will resent you even more.

"It's not fair to that baby to have a child raise it. And, for you Bhriana, to put your life on hold in an attempt to do so, is not being fair to yourself, either-"

"But-"

"But let me finish, Bhriana," Ms. Austin said then took a breath before she continued. "There are thousands of infertile married couples out there who are emotionally and financially ready to adopt."

"So are you sayin' that you wished that you had given me up for adoption?"

"No, that's not what I'm saying. What I am suggesting is that if you are determined to carry that baby to term-"

"And I am."

"Then, I suggest that you give the baby up for adoption so that it can be raised in a household with two loving parents who are able to give that child all the love and support it deserves. And, so you can give yourself all of the opportunities that you deserve."

"Just because things didn't work out with you and daddy, doesn't mean that's how Tyler and I will end up," Bhriana said.

"You're not listening, Bhriana. He just told you how he felt about you."

"Yeah, I wished he had discovered that before he slept with my daughter," Mr. DuPree said in a bitter tone.

"Well it's too late for that now. But, that doesn't mean Bhriana has to ruin her entire life. Think about it, girl. While Tyler's away at college, and trust me, his father is going to make sure Tyler goes to college."

"You damn right," Mr. Powers said.

"Where will you be?" Ms. Austin asked.

Bhriana shrugged her shoulders.

"I'll tell you where you'll be. You'll be stuck at home changing nasty diapers, wiping spit up, rocking a crying baby not knowing what's wrong with it, feeding it at all hours in the night and talking baby talk. How often do you think Tyler's going to come home from college to help you care for that baby?"

Ms. Austin caught her breath and then pointed at Tyler. "And where will he be when that baby's sick in the middle of the night? Tyler will be pledging for a fraternity, playing in a basketball game, cashing in on his popularity with all the girls, partying till the wee hours of the morning, and earning his degree."

"Why can't I have it all, Daddy?"

"What do you want, Sweetheart?"

"I could take a year off to have the baby and then Tyler could join me at Princeton next year and we'll get married and live off-campus. We could schedule our classes so that one of us is with the baby at all times."

"That might work," Mr. DuPree said.

Ms. Austin shook her head and threw her hands up in the air. "There is no reasoning with you or your father. I assume that since you have your father's full support, you will be living with him for the next year. My diaper changing days ended a long time ago."

"Surely, you're not going to put our daughter out of our house!" her ex-husband exclaimed.

"Surely, I've made all of the sacrifices that I'm going to make so don't ask me to put my dreams on the back burner again. I have raised my child. I am not about to raise hers!"

"And a deaf child at that-"

"Hey, boy! You better watch what you say about my daughter," Mr. DuPree warned.

"And for the last time, I'm not gonna marry her," Tyler shot back.

"You're in no position to be disrespectful, Tyler, so watch your mouth," his father told him. Mr. Powers reprimanded him further with his eyes before he turned to Bhriana. "I didn't think that was such a bad idea. Back in the day, a boy got a girl pregnant and there was no question what happened next. I'm sure my business partner will agree that we will finance your tuition, living expenses, and childcare services. That way, neither one of you will have to worry about working and can concentrate on school and the baby."

"How dare y'all plan my life for me! I'm not going to Princeton and I'm not hooking up with her."

"You 'hooked up' with my daughter the day you slept with her and got her pregnant."

"It's not all his fault," Ms. Austin said in Tyler's defense.

"It doesn't matter whose fault it is, the bottom line is that Tyler was man enough to have sex with her, then he's got to be man enough to deal with the consequences," Mr. Powers said.

"How long I gotta pay for one mistake?" Tyler asked.

"I'd say anywhere from 18 to 22 years or more depending on when your kid's ready to leave home," Mr. DuPree said then shot a look at Ms. Austin.

"Tyler, I know that you'll feel differently about me when you take one look at our baby."

"Dream on, Bhriana," he replied.

"Mr. Powers, Tyler and I were doing just fine until this poor ghetto girl, Imooni, started chasing after him."

"E-who?" Mr. Powers asked with a frown on his face.

"So you think you're gonna to do a hit and run on my daughter? You've got to be out of your mind."

"I'll work on him, Brandon, don't you worry," Mr. Powers said.

"And you can come and live with me, Sweetie," Bhriana's father told her.

Bhriana beamed with confidence. She hadn't felt that good in months.

FATIMA

"Girrrl, I almost broke a nail dialin' your number so fast."

"This must be some really hot stuff. So what's going on?" Imani asked.

Fatima frowned at the new shorter length acrylic tips. "I don't know about this summer j.o.b. at the Chicken Shack, Girrrl. It's messin' with my nails and it's all hot up in there. I can't keep a decent perm no more and..."

"I know this ain't the 4-1-1 you were in such a hurry to lay on me," Imani said. "And, kill the gum, will you?"

"Fatima! You better come on out here and finish this schoolwork. I ain't playin' with you," Grandma Rose's voice sounded.

"I'm comin' Grandma," Fatima said and smacked on her chewing gum.

Imani laughed.

"You think that's funny? She's riding me like a jockey," Fatima said then sucked her teeth. "Shooot,

246

don't get me started on summer school. It's really jackin' up my program. I tell you what. You'll never catch me in summer school again. I'm comin' correct my senior year."

"Well alrighty then. Now hurry up, little filly, and tell me what's going on before Grandma Rose whips you."

"Ha. Ha. Enough of the horse jokes already. But speaking of animals, guess who's gonna be lookin' like a fat oink, oink?"

"You're late, Tyler already told me. He ran down all the gory details of the so-called family conference that they had at Bhriana's house. They're tryin' to force him into marrying that spoiled witch."

"What! Tyler's the baby's daddy!"

"Yup. It's a mess."

"Daaang," Fatima said then shook her head in disbelief.

"Tyler's hurtin'. Big time. But wait a minute, how did you find out?"

"I got connections ya know. My cousin, Shonda, works down at Dr. Parker's office and she asked me if Bhriana's name sounded familiar 'cause you know we talk about everybody-"

"I know."

"I only say good things about you cuz you're my girl. Anyway, she said that the nurse said that Bhriana was there to take a pregnancy test but that's all she knows. Actually, I know Shonda knows more than that but she ain't gonna tell me 'cause she ain't about to lose her job by givin' out confidential stuff."

Only the rapid gum popping came across the telephone lines as both girls were silent. Fatima heard

Grandma Rose shuffle around in the living room and knew it was just a matter of time before she came her way. In a hushed tone Fatima said, "She did tell me that the test results are in and if I wanted to know all the details, we would have to get it ourselves."

"We?"

"Yeah, we. Don't you wanna know the real deal? Maybe Bhriana's lyin'. Maybe she's really not pregnant. Maybe she is pregnant but maybe Tyler's not the baby's daddy and who knows what else we could find out," Fatima said.

"And how on earth do you propose that *we* get this information?"

"I got that covered."

"Oh, God," Imani let out.

"Check this out. See, my cousin Shonda could conveniently leave the doctor's office unlocked for us to sneak in-"

"What!" Imani exclaimed.

"To sneak in after hours," Fatima continued. We could read Bhriana's file, put it back where we got it from, and then lock the door on the way out. Simple."

"Simple minded is more like it," Imani snapped. This is not some mystery on TV. This is real life, Fatima, and if we get caught-"

"We ain't gonna get caught."

"The last time I let you talk me into something crazy, Money got shot. Remember, Snoop Fatima?"

"Ain't nobody gonna get shot up in the doctor's office, Girrrl. Here's your chance to play detective. Are you down or what?"

After a few seconds of silence, Imani said, "I don't know, Fatima."

"What you got to lose, Girrl? The worst thing that could happen is that you find out that Bhriana's really pregnant and Tyler's really the baby's daddy. But on the flip side, it ain't got to be that way and then the two people who should be together can finally hook up. I'm just tryin' to help my girl out 'cause I know you're feelin' Tyler. See what I'm sayin'?"

"I wouldn't be doing this just to try and get with Tyler. He's a good guy and a friend and I would hate to see him get railroaded. He doesn't deserve that," Imani said. "Plus, I owe him one for tryin' to warn me about Jazz but I was too stupid to listen."

"Yeah yeah, whatever whatever. Are we gonna do this tonight or what?"

"Tonight!"

"If you hurry up and get off the phone, I can catch Shonda at the office before she leaves and tell her not to lock the door," Fatima said as she looked at her watch. "Just meet me here at nine o'clock tonight."

"Why so late?" Imani asked.

"What? You wanna do this is broad daylight? I don't think so," Fatima said as she answered her own question.

"What? Like my parents are gonna let me walk outta here so late? I don't think so."

Fatima slapped her forehead. "Oh, doggone it. Ummm, well, ooookay, how about you tell them that you're spendin' the night? Yeah, you're stayin' here to help me cram for a test and ummm they know how slow I am and it could take all night."

"I hate lyin' to them," Imani said.

"Hey, if it'll make you feel better, come on over now and do my homework and that way it won't be a total lie."

"Oh, you would love that," Imani began, "I'll see you at nine."

A few hours later, Imani arrived at Fatima's apartment at exactly nine o'clock. She appeared surprised to see Hanif on the couch with Grandma Rose. Imani grabbed hold of Fatima's hand and yanked her into her bedroom.

"Ouch, I'll need this arm you know," Fatima said as she rubbed it.

"What is he doing here?" Imani asked through clenched teeth.

"He's driving the getaway car."

"For what?" Imani said loudly and then lowered her voice. "We're not knocking off a bank."

"And, we ain't gonna be able to get a bus cross town and we can't afford a cab over there so we need a driver."

"I don't wanna drag Hanif into this mess," Imani pleaded.

"Hanif volunteered 'cause he didn't like the way Bhriana dissed us after that game. Remember? Plus, he's got my back and I always got your back, so everythang's everythang. Except."

"Except what?"

"Except, you can't go dressed like that. You stand out like a traffic light. That bright yellow tee shirt has gotta go. Here," Fatima said and handed Imani a black tee shirt.

"I was wondering why you and Hanif were dressed down in all black and here it is 70-something degrees outside."

"Let me show you something else," Fatima said and directed Imani to the black plastic bag on her bed.

Fatima pulled out a couple of flashlights, black leather gloves, ski masks, sunglasses, paper, an ink pen, and a magnifying glass. Fatima looked at Imani and noticed that her mouth was wide open.

"What's wrong with you?"

"This is pretty scary. No, you're pretty scary 'cause if I didn't know any better, which I'm beginning to doubt, I would swear that you've done this before."

"If that's your way of saying that I've got everything covered, then thank you very much," Fatima replied and patted herself on the back.

Fatima's confidence held up as she led Imani to the back door of the doctor's office. Imani reached around her to turn the doorknob and Fatima whacked her hand. "Where are your gloves?" she asked in a low whisper.

"I must have left them in the car. I'll go back and get them."

Fatima grabbed hold of Imani's shirt. "Forget it. Here, take one of mine."

Fatima gave up her left glove then turned the knob with her right hand. She was relieved that the knob turned all the way. As the door opened, it's hinges squeaked. Both ski-masked girls looked behind them to see if the noise caught anyone's attention. But luckily, no bystanders were around. The only other person in the parking lot was Hanif. He was inside the car with the engine running.

"God, it's dark in here. Is this a light switch?" Imani asked and reached for it.

Fatima slapped her hand again. "What's wrong with you? Use the flashlight I gave you."

"It's in the car with the gloves," Imani said.

Fatima let out an exasperated sigh.

"I can't help it. I'm nervous," Imani said.

Fatima flicked on her flashlight and took hold of Imani's hand. "Follow me and don't touch a thing." The girls stepped through the waiting room. Each time the floor crackled beneath the carpet, they stopped and held their breath.

"Shonda said the file cabinets are right behind that window," Fatima said as she flashed the light to her left. The glare bounced off the gray-metal file drawers. "Bingo," the girls said in unison.

"One of us has to hold the light while the other search through the files," Imani suggested.

"I'll hold. You look." Fatima said.

"Give me that other glove then."

"Now you're getting with the program," Fatima said and handed her the other glove.

Imani fingered through the files.

"Shhh..." Fatima said and both girls froze.

There was a faint popping sound and they strained to locate where it came from. Fatima felt a smack upside her head.

"Spit that dang gum out," Imani told her.

"Oh, my bad," Fatima said then swallowed it.

"Now, can we get back to this?" Imani asked and then proceeded to call out the last names of patients as she ran across them. "Davis...Day...Dent...Douglass... DuMont.... DuPree, Bhriana DuPree!"

"Shhh...hurry up and read what it says," Fatima said.

Imani opened it then slammed it shut. "I can't do it. Here, you read it."

"Give me the gloves first you big chicken."

Fatima read the report and then looked up at her friend. There was no easy way to break the bad news to her. "It says that the slut's pregnant. She's four and a half months pregnant."

Imani mumbled four and a half months over and over again and then she yelled out, "Hold it!"

Stunned, Fatima dropped the folder and threw her hands up as if the cops busted her. "Girrrl, don't ever scare me like that again."

"My bad but check it again, Fatima."

Fatima bent down, picked the loose papers off the floor and read the results again. "Look Ms. Brain, it says 18 weeks. Four and a half months equal 18 weeks and even I don't need a calculator to figure that out."

"Tyler told me that they slept together only once and that was back in early May. And if that's the case, Bhriana would only be about three months pregnant, not four and a half."

"Oh snap!" Fatima exclaimed.

The two girls embraced and jumped up and down as they sang, "It's not Tyler's baby...it's not Tyler's baby..."

* * * *

The West Side Diner was a popular after party hangout. It was open 24-7. Not the most fancy or cleanest diner but no one went there for the ambience.

The food was cheap, the portions were huge, and the service was fast.

Fatima, Imani, and Hanif occupied a booth near the back of the diner. The two girls faced the doorway and Hanif sat opposite them.

"Lordy, Lordy. I'm so glad to be sittin' here with Snoop and Sherlock instead of in some jail cell. I was gonna give y'all two mo' minutes," Hanif said as he held up two fingers. "Then," he continued, "I was gonna go in there and snatch y'all up. What took y'all so long anyway?"

"Good reading," Imani answered and pulled out a piece of paper. "We got Bhriana's address and phone number. I may have to pay her a visit."

"Can I come with you? Please, please..." Fatima begged.

"Nooo, I've got to use a more smooth approach. I have to trick her into telling me who the baby's daddy is, not beat it out of her."

"Hanif, don't listen to her. I'm not the violent type."

"Not my Boo," he said then took hold of her hand and smiled.

Their waitress placed a basket of golden fries in the center of the table. "Your sandwiches will be out in a minute."

"Three more soda pops, ma'am," Hanif told the frail looking woman. The words "ma'am" or "soda pops" must have gotten her attention. She stared at Hanif like he was an alien.

"You ain't from around here, are you?"

"No ma'am."

"That's what I thought," the waitress said before she went on her way.

"I gotta git rid of dis Southern thang," Hanif told the girls.

"Don't sweat it, Handsome, I like you just as you are," Fatima said in a southern accent.

"There's nothing wrong with being different," Imani added as she tucked the piece of paper away.

Their sandwiches arrived and the threesome devoured them. "So Snoop, what's the latest with summer school?" Hanif asked.

"You know how English lit' is, a lot of reading," she said and looked up towards the door.

"If you ever need help, you can sho nuf call me," Hanif said.

"I hope you're not reading any mysteries because I can't take too many more of your adventures," Imani said.

"That's him." Fatima mumbled as her black eyes remained fixed on a tall, bald-headed brother in the doorway.

"Who?" Hanif asked and was about to look until Fatima kicked him.

"The guy who rolled up on Money at the mall. Some of his boyz look familiar too. I bet he took Money out."

"Oooh, no Snoop, that's one case I'm not about to solve. Call the police and tell them what you know but ain't no way *we*'re gonna get involved with that one," Imani insisted.

"Do I look crazy?" Fatima asked.

"With or without the ski mask?" Hanif teased.

"That was a good one," Imani said and gave Hanif a high-five.

"Y'all got my back right?" Fatima asked.

"Sho nuf, why?"

"'Cause he's comin' this way."

"Uh-oh," Imani said.

Fatima's eyes jetted back and forth from that guy to the table. She wanted a weapon. But, there were no utensils on the table.

"You packin'?" Fatima asked Hanif between clenched teeth.

"A pack of gum."

"Oh great."

The tall boy stopped at Fatima's table and four guys were right behind him. He stared at her, then Imani and then Hanif. "Which one is yours?" he asked Hanif.

"Both of 'em."

"No disrespect, Man. I'm just curious 'cause the short one looks familiar."

A chorus of "straight up" echoed from the background.

"I don't know you," Fatima told the boy.

"No disrespect to you either, brother ummm…"

"Mad D."

"No disrespect to you either, brother Mad D., but my lady said that she doesn't know you. So, you and your posse can move on," Hanif said in a street tone without a hint of his southern accent.

"You gonna let him talk to you like that, Mad D.?" one of his boys asked.

"Everythang's cool. It ain't my style to be pushin' up on another man's female," he answered while he glared at Hanif. Then he turned to Fatima. "But, if I remember who you are and it's a bad memory, you will be seein' my face again."

"And if anything should ever happen to my woman, you will be seeing my face again," Hanif told him then eyed each one in the group.

"Lookin' forward to it," the leader said and then extended his hand.

Hanif stared at the large brown hand but he didn't shake it.

"So it's like that, huh?" the leader asked then withdrew his hand. "We will definitely meet again," he added then signaled his boys to move on.

Fatima made sure they were far enough away before she spoke. Even then, she whispered, "Why you hafta come at him like that? I ain't never heard you talk like that before. Now, we're both on his hit list."

"Girl, you know Hanif wasn't about to get over on him with that Southern charm thing. It was real smooth how Hanif got that thug's name."

"That's right. But, that's not all. I wasn't sitting here contemplating whether to shake his hand, I was checkin' out his tattoo."

"Go 'head, Smooth," Fatima began, "you wanna hook up with Snoop and Sherlock's detective agency?"

Imani and Hanif shot her a look. "You better call the police and tell them about Mad D.," Imani warned.

"Don't forget to mention that he has a red pit bull with a sword clenched between his teeth tattooed on his right hand. 'Mad D.' was printed underneath the paws of the dog," Hanif said.

"Where's that piece of paper, Imani? I won't remember all this."

IMANI

Gorgeous homes filled the window of the bus like framed paintings in a museum. They were the same houses that Imani passed everyday on her ride to school. Yet, they looked more impressive. Maybe, it was because the bus wasn't crowded and she had a clear full view. Or, maybe it was that Imani's mind wasn't pre-occupied with schoolwork or basketball.

She assumed that Bhriana's house must be just as awesome. But, Imani wasn't interested in a tour of her home because her visit wasn't a social call. Imani smiled as she recalled their telephone conversation that morning.

"Bhriana, it's Imani."

"How did you get my number?"

"I got it from the senior yearbook," Imani lied. "And, I'm calling to see if you're going to be home today because I want to drop by."

"You must be joking. We have nothing to talk about."

"Oh yes we do. I could discuss it with Tyler first and let him relay the message to you, or, we can handle this."

"Didn't I tell you to stay away from him? What's your problem?"

"You're the one with the problem and like I said, we can talk about it or I'm callin' Tyler."

"Can't we do this over the phone?"

"No."

"You are such a-"

"A what?" Imani jumped in.

"Look, since you got my number, you must know where I live. But, I hope you're not gonna have some hoodlums escorting you."

"I don't know any hoodlums."

"Well, I have things to do so if you're not here by noon, too bad," Bhriana said then hung up on Imani.

"Oak Tree Lane," the bus driver yelled. "Who wanted Oak Tree Lane?" he repeated as he looked in his rearview mirror.

Imani rose from her seat and headed out the door of the air-conditioned bus. "Daaang it's hot," she said as the heat and humidity slapped her. She put on the shades that Fatima gave her and she squinted to make out the numbers on the houses. Imani read the house numbers aloud as she passed each one. "Two-twenty-two, two-twenty-four, the next one should be, yup, two-twenty-six."

Imani spotted Bhriana's white convertible in the circular driveway and knew for sure that she had the right house. She pressed the white doorbell button then surveyed her surroundings while she waited for someone to answer. *Is this place laid out or what?* She asked herself as she soaked up the exquisite scenery. An abundance of green leaves decorated big old trees. The sprawling rich green lawn and hedges were manicured and free of any debris. The only things that occupied a portion of the lawn were matching water fountains on both sides of the driveway. *They probably light up at night,* Imani thought.

The sunrays penetrated through Imani's shirt and sweat rolled down her back. She pressed the button three or four more times. Seconds later, the large white door swung open and there stood Bhriana. She wore a sleeveless oversized peach colored tank top that was so long that it covered up whatever bottom she had on underneath. Her peach painted toenails peeked through the opening of her brown flat sandals.

"You know that's rude, right? I heard you the first time."

Imani opened her mouth then closed it. *Play it cool. That's the best way to get what you need from her,* she told herself.

Once inside the spacious living room, Imani screamed to herself. *Wow, check this out!* Yet, she kept a stoic demeanor as she discreetly eyed the furniture, paintings, African art, sculptures, and figurines. Even the squishy plush carpet beneath her feet, grabbed her attention. When she spotted the floral luggage at the bottom of the spiral staircase, Imani eyes widened.

"Going somewhere?"

Bhriana smiled and said, "I'm moving in with my father today." Her smile disappeared when she added, "That's why I'm in a hurry. So speak fast."

Imani didn't bother to ask her why because Tyler told her that issue came out in their family conference. She just stared at Bhriana's mid section.

"What?" Bhriana asked then looked down at the bulge.

"I just can't get over how great you look. You look so...so small. What are you just a month or two pregnant?"

"Who told you?"

"Tyler. But, you know how guys are. When I asked him how far along you were, he wasn't sure."

"Why did he tell you about this? This is none of your doggone business!" Bhriana shouted then sat down. Imani wanted to join her but she felt too sweaty and greasy. Instead, she sat down on the carpet and faced Bhriana.

"We have chairs in my home."

"I'm nice and comfy right here," Imani said as she patted the thick carpet. Imani paused and looked at Bhriana's stomach again. "There was a girl at church who was twice your size at two months. But then again, she didn't have your great body to begin with."

Bhriana stroked her belly. "I do look good at four and a half months."

"Wow, you're that far along? So you got pregnant back in March, huh?"

"I guess," Bhriana said.

"Sooo...if you're four and a half months pregnant, then, you had sex with somebody back in March."

"That somebody was Tyler and, in a year or so, he'll be my husband and that just burns you up, doesn't it?"

"Not anymore."

"Yeah right. I don't buy that crap. And another thing," Bhriana said then pointed a finger in Imani's face, "Stop calling my man."

Imani bit the inside of her lip.

"Is this what you wanted to see?" Bhriana asked then lifted up her shirt. "Now, get the hell out of my house."

Imani's long legs uncoiled and she rose from the squishy carpet.

"You're just so jealous of me. You've always been jealous. And now you wish that you were having Tyler's baby," Bhriana rattled off.

"By the way, Bhriana, who was the better lover? Tyler or what's his name? You know, the guy you dated before Tyler."

"Why? You wanted to sleep with Justin, too?" Bhriana asked. She stood up and crossed her arms under her bosom. "Or, are you one of those funny girl jocks and you wished you could have been in the bedroom with Justin and me?"

If she wasn't pregnant, I'd choke the life out of her! Imani screamed inside.

"You obviously can't get a man of your own, on your own," Bhriana said and her lips curled up.

"You don't know me," Imani said in as calm a tone as she could muster.

"I know that you didn't land Jazz on your own. The boy got paid to be with you."

"You're lyin', Bhriana. Just like you're lying about who the father of that baby is. And when that baby comes out lookin' like Justin, what lie are you gonna use to cover that up?"

Lines formed on Bhriana's forehead as she leaned forward. "Look poor girl, a good friend of mine's father knows most of the Westmoore school board members. And, I'm talking about the ones who issue the scholarships. So if you ever want to see the inside of Westmoore again, you'd better keep that silly butt notion to yourself."

"You threatening me again?"

"There you go talking what you don't know. I'm not threatening you. I am making a sincere promise to you. And if you think I'm lying, try me."

She's crazy. She'll do it, Imani thought as they stared one another down.

"You called me poor but let me tell you, Bhriana," Imani began as she pointed a long finger in Bhriana's face. "I would rather be me than you any day because even with all this," Imani said in reference to Bhriana's incredible home, "you are one miserable, trifling...evil ingrate. Correction, you are a low life. A low down and dirty no good low life."

"Get outta here!" Bhriana yelled and pointed to the door.

Imani walked passed Bhriana en route to the door. She spun around and added, "I feel sorry for that baby...and its daddy."

On the bus ride home, Imani carried the image of an outraged Bhriana with her. Imani's game plan worked but she didn't feel victorious or that she had a reason to celebrate. The scholarship threat rocked her and probably shelved part two of her plan, which was to tell Tyler that Bhriana admitted, inadvertently, that he was not the father.

Imani laid her head back and closed her eyes. The feud with Bhriana all year wore her down. *I should just back off and let Tyler figure this out on his own. I need that scholarship.*

In addition to the scholarship, she wondered about the comment Bhriana made about Jazz.

Did she say that about Jazz just to hurt me? Then again, why lie when she knows I could pick up the phone and call him. I should have known something was up the first time he called talkin' bout he called me because he was too shy to approach me in person. Yeah right, shy my behind. Dang, am I that naïve?

Imani opened her eyes and wiped the water away. She thought about that question and asked herself a couple more. *Who would pay him to do that? Why?*

She searched for the suspect in her mind. Mental images of everyone she knew at school flashed by one by one. *This doesn't make any sense. Why don't I ask Jazz? Oh yeah, like he's gonna rat out the person. You may never solve this one,* Imani told herself as she rested her head against the window.

* * * *

It was a clear and bright Sunday morning. The humidity lifted but the heat wave was still on. At seven-thirty, the temperature was near seventy degrees. The sole air-conditioner, located in the dining room window of Imani's apartment, whined under the strain of around the clock usage. It put out cool air instead of cold even when set at the highest level. Imani slept on the couch in the living room to be closer to the air conditioner because it wasn't powerful enough to project the cool air into her room. The heat in her tiny bedroom was unbearable.

"Get up sleepy head, it's time to get ready for church," her mother said as she tapped on Imani's back.

Imani was already awake. She decided to play sick today so that she could have the place all to herself for a few hours. Imani grunted as she turned over. "I am sooo...s...sick, Ma..." Imani moaned and rubbed her stomach.

"Was it something you ate?" Mrs. Jackson asked.

"I think it's that and the heat. I just can't go out there today."

"Well alright then but sit up a minute and let me give you something to settle that stomach."

Nothing's ever easy, is it? Imani asked herself.

In an instant, her mother was back with a big tablespoon and a bottle of pink medicine. The thick pink liquid oozed out of the bottle and dripped onto the tablespoon. "Open up," Mrs. Jackson said and shoved the spoon into Imani's mouth.

Imani frowned as the chalky taste engulfed her mouth.

"Swallow it, Imani."

Imani swallowed hard yet the medicine slid down at a snail's pace.

"Open up."

In went another overflowing dose. Imani gagged and hollered out, "Auuug!" then wiped her lips.

She laid back down and faked being asleep until her parents left. When she rose, the sweet smell of her mother's perfume mixed with the strong scent of her father's cologne topped with the thought of what she was about to do really made her stomach queasy.

Imani leaned back against the kitchen wall and dialed the telephone. She stroked her flat stomach to the beat of the ringing sound.

"May I speak to Tyler, please."

"Who's calling?"

"Imani."

"I'm his father. What do you want with Tyler?"

"Dad, I've got it," Tyler said and then his father hung up.

"Boooy, he wasn't too thrilled to hear from me, huh?"

"He thinks you're the reason why I don't want to marry Bhriana."

"What! Where did he get that idea?"

"Bhriana."

"Enough said," Imani replied as she twisted an already knotted beige telephone cord between her long fingers. "Can I see you today?"

"Sure, where do you wanna meet?" he asked.

"He...here."

Tyler didn't answer.

"Is that okay?" she asked.

"Well yeah. I'm just kinda surprised, that's all. But, gimme your address and I'll be right over."

"W-e-l-l-l, it's not that simple," Imani said and the phone cord became a coiled ball in her hand. "I don't live that close to you."

"Give me the directions. I'll borrow my father's car."

"You know Tyler, maybe it's not such a good idea after all," Imani began. "I don't think you'll ever find this place, plus…"

"Can I be straight up with you, Imani?"

"Sure."

"I already have some idea of where you live. Bhriana told me that you live near Jazz. I didn't want to be the first one to bring it up because I figured that one day you would tell me."

"She warned me a while ago that if I didn't stay away from you, she was gonna do that."

"She threatened you?"

"Yeah, but I don't care about that now. It's just that my address was a secret that I kept from everybody not just you. I don't even know how she found out."

"She told me that she heard it from Steven who heard it from Jazz."

"I had a feeling that Jazz opened up his big mouth although he promised that he wouldn't."

"I don't care how word got out. I don't care where you live. When I see you or talk to you, I don't think, 'I wonder what type of neighborhood she lives in'. I do wonder why it took me so long to realize that-"

"That what?" Imani interrupted.

"That I wanna be with you."

Imani grinned so hard that her lips hurt. "Hold that thought until you get here," she said and proceeded to give him detailed directions.

Imani placed the receiver back on the hook and leaped high into the air. After her feet landed back on the linoleum, Imani snatched the receiver up again and frantically pushed the buttons. "Come on Girl, pick up."

"You know who you called so speak," the person said in a groggy-toned voice.

Imani screamed so loud into the mouthpiece that she scared herself.

"Who the heck's screaming in my ear? Is this a freakin' crank call!" Fatima yelled.

"It's me, Fatima. Tyler's on his way over here so I can't talk right now 'cause I gotta hurry and clean up this place and then take a shower," Imani said then smacked her forehead. "Ohmagod, what am I gonna wear? My hair's a sweaty mess. Gotta go, bye." Imani caught her breath then hung up the receiver.

Seconds later the telephone rang. Imani placed the receiver to her ear.

"Hair up, white shorts, and your hot pink shirt." Click.

"That's my girl," Imani said then smiled.

Imani cleaned up the apartment in record time. It even smelled good. Imani used an air freshening disinfectant instead of roach spray to kill the bugs. The ones that survived the disinfectant got squashed. Imani knew that she couldn't control when they would make an unwanted appearance, so she decided to keep Tyler away from their most popular hang out, the kitchen.

Imani figured that she didn't have that much time left to primp, so she took Fatima's advice. After a quick shower and a generous amount of lotion, she pulled her braids up and secured them with a white ponytail holder. She was relieved that the cotton white shorts and hot pink top didn't need ironing and quickly threw them on.

Slow it down, Girl, you're startin' to sweat, Imani warned herself. She searched her room but couldn't find the match to the one pink sweat sock. "Forget the socks, where are your white sneakers?" She asked aloud.

She found one under the bed and the other in the corner. Imani didn't bother to untie them. She stuffed and wiggled her size 10 feet into them and then froze when she heard a knock on the door.

Just don't leave him standing out there, answer the door," she told herself. Imani smoothed down the front of her outfit and looked around the apartment one more time before she opened the door.

He was the most gorgeous thing that ever graced her doorway. The clothes didn't make the man because all he wore was a plain white tee shirt and long denim shorts.

"Any problems with my directions?" she asked as he walked in.

"Nooo, they were on the money but I had a tough time finding your building. Did you know that the numbers are-"

"Out of sequence," Imani completed for Tyler. "I forgot to mention that."

"Don't sweat it," Tyler replied as he looked about the small apartment.

Imani followed his eyes and said, "Now you see why I never invited you here before. It's home but it's not a place I like to show off. There's no big tour I can take you on. What you see here is all there is. Except for the bathroom and two bedrooms in the back..." Imani nervously rambled on.

"I didn't come for a tour of your place, I came here to see you," he said and pointed at her. "Let me ask you this. How would you feel about me if I told you that I lived right across the street from you instead of cross town?"

"That wouldn't faze me," Imani replied without hesitation.

"Why not?"

"Because."

"Because what?"

"Because it wouldn't change who you are. You're a real cool brotha and a good friend."

"Change the word brotha to sistah and that's exactly how I feel about you."

Dang, he always knows the right thing to say to make me blush, she told herself. "It's a little warm in here. You want something to drink?"

"A glass of iced water would be great right about now."

Imani searched the white metal and rust stained cabinet for two matching glasses. She found a pair that wasn't chipped or cracked. *I hope no bugs are in there entertaining him,* she thought, and rushed to get back to the room.

"Where are your parents?"

"Church. Just about every Sunday, we're all in church," Imani said and handed him a cold glass.

"We used to go a lot before my mother died. Come to think of it, we haven't been in a church since her funeral."

"Well, you can visit my church whenever you want."

"I may check it out sometime," he said.

"Speaking of church, I have another confession to make," Imani began. "See the guy in that picture over there with the navy overalls? That's my dad in his work uniform. He's a custodial worker at the hospital," she said then lowered her head.

Imani felt Tyler's hand under her chin. Gently, he guided her back to eye level. "Why are you telling me all of this now?"

"Because, I'm tired of hiding. Anyone I claim to be my friend knows all of this stuff. I don't want to leave you out anymore. I would have told you sooner but I thought if you knew the truth, you would be ashamed to be with me. But the more I got to know you, the more I realized that you're not a spoiled rich brat who turns his nose up at people like me."

"People like you? I wished I knew more people like you and what you have or don't have ain't got nothing to do with it. You're cool, down to earth people."

Imani smiled.

"That's better," he said and smiled back.

"Can I ask you something, now?"

"Sure, go ahead."

"Oookaaay. Forget about me for a minute and say you didn't know me and Bhriana and you were in the exact situation you're in now, would you marry her?

"No."

"Why not?"

"I don't love her. I don't like her. So even if I didn't know you, I wouldn't wanna be with Bhriana. Period."

"And, how exactly do you feel about...you know... me?" Imani asked then held her breath.

Tyler smiled as he stroked her chin. "From the first day we met in the gym, I knew there was something special about you. I tried to ignore it. Maybe, because what I felt for you, I mean, feel for you

271

is real. I was sprung on Bhriana but you already knew that. But, what you don't know is that I've fallen in love with you. And thanks to you, I know the difference."

"Wow," was all Imani could say. She wanted to call Fatima and scream into the telephone again. *Tell him how you feel,* she urged herself.

"Well, ummm...I've been in denial too. I never thought I had a chance to get with you. Sooo, I tried to convince myself that I didn't want you. Then when Jazz came along, I turned all of my attention to him but, you were, I mean are, always on my mind."

"Sooo, even after everything that's gone down with Bhriana, you want to be with me?"

Imani didn't answer, Tyler. Instead, she leaned forward and their full lips met. When they parted, the two sighed with relief.

"I can't even put into a poem how I feel right now," Tyler said.

"Well, I hate to ruin this moment but I have something serious to tell you."

"Please don't tell me you're dying or moving out of state or changing high schools or-"

"Well, after I tell you this, I may be looking for a new school."

"What?"

Imani stood up and paced the floor. It had been a few days since her meeting with Bhriana and she'd wrestled with whether or not to tell Tyler ever since. After Tyler's confession, she decided to go for it.

"I saw Bhriana the other day and discovered something that if I told you, she promised me that I won't get another scholarship."

"She threatened you, again?"

"Nooo, according to her, that was a promise. But hear me out," Imani said when she saw Tyler's mouth open again. "I'm willing to take that chance because I wouldn't be able to sleep at night knowing what I know and not tell you. I wouldn't be able to face you, either."

Imani sat back down next to him. "Follow me now. Bhriana admitted that she's four and a half months pregnant. That means that if what you told me was true, that you only had sex with her once back in May, then there's no way that you could be the father. She would only be two or three months pregnant."

"I swear that I told you the truth." His face lit up. "Then you're right, I can't be the father!" he exclaimed then wrapped his arms around Imani and held on tight. He let go and added, "You have no idea the pressure I've been under. Maaan, this is incredible!" He took a deep breath then added, "I can't wait to tell my father. His plans for Bhriana and me just blew up in his face!"

Tyler's happy expression became somber as he continued. "I can understand Mr. DuPree giving in to his daughter, but for my father to support her so hard and strong and so fast, that hurt. You don't know how badly I wanted my mother to be in that room. I..."

Tyler stopped talking and looked up towards the ceiling. Imani noticed the anguish in his face and the veins that protruded in his neck. Imani gathered him up in her long arms and he placed his head on her shoulder.

After a minute or two, he whispered, "Thanks for believing in me."

"You're welcome," she whispered back.

They held onto one another for a few more minutes before Tyler broke the silence. "I wonder who's the daddy?"

"I can't be sure but I think it's Justin," Imani said. She released her hold on Tyler and wiped the tears off her cheeks. Imani sniffled then continued, "She kinda admitted that the two of them had sex back in March." Imani left out the freaky-deaky accusation that Bhriana threw at her.

Tyler's red eyes held onto Imani's. "I was talking to Bhriana then but I swear nothing happened between us back in March. When I asked her about Justin, she said they were just friends. Supposedly, they broke up a while ago."

"Maybe they broke up then made up if you know what I mean," Imani said.

"I can't believe she played me like that. If she knows that Justin's the father, why doesn't she go after him?"

"Hummm…W-e-l-l-l, didn't Justin transfer out of Westmoore when his family moved out of town?" Imani asked.

"They moved because his father went bankrupt," Tyler explained.

"Bingo," Imani said and snapped her fingers. "Material girl wants a rich daddy for her baby. And in her sick twisted mind, she may really believe that she loves you."

Tyler shook his head as if in disbelief. "First, she threatens you-"

"And that's not all. There's something else that you don't know," Imani interrupted.

"Oh God," Tyler sighed.

"She told me that Jazz was paid to go out with me. I have absolutely no proof that she was involved, but, I wouldn't be surprised if she paid him to keep me away from you."

"What is this? A soap opera? Actually for us, it's a freakin' horror flick starring that devil." It appeared that every exposed muscle on his body tightened up. "Steven always said that Jazz was a serious hustler, but maaan, that was beyond foul," Tyler said and leaped off the couch.

Imani had never seen Tyler so angry. She had seen his fierce competitive game face on the court but this was different. Imani gasped from the loud sound his fist made when he pounded into his palm.

"I feel like punching somebody, anybody right now. It's one thing for her to try and wreck my life. But I be damned if I'm gonna sit back and let her bring you down too! And if this thing with Jazz is true, I swear-"

"I swear I don't want you to do anything crazy and end up in jail. Then they'll win anyway because we still won't be together."

That seemed to calm Tyler down a little.

"All I want is for you to be happy, Tyler."

Tyler walked over to the couch. He pulled Imani up and hugged her. Tyler kissed her on the cheek and whispered in her ear. "I have some business to take care of before that can happen."

Tyler pulled away and she tried to grab his hand but he was out of reach. "Where you going?" she asked as he opened the door.

"I love you, Imani," was all she heard before the door slammed shut.

TYLER

Tyler's initial reaction to Bhriana's broad smile was to not only loosen every tooth she displayed but also the ones waaay in the back of her mouth.

"Don't ever hit a girl," he heard his mother say. "Boys are physically stronger so you can use that strength to restrain her then walk away."

"What are you waiting for, Baby? Come on in here," Bhriana said as she motioned him into her father's condominium.

"Have a seat."

"I'll stand," Tyler answered dryly.

Bhriana hunched her shoulders. "Suit yourself," she replied then sat down on a black leather sofa. "But, I hope you're gonna stay a while."

Tyler scanned around the black, burgundy, and ivory decorated room and asked, "Where's your father?"

A strange look crossed her full face, "Didn't you see him at your house? He went there hours ago to talk business with your father."

"I left early and haven't been home since."

"Where you been?"

"None of your business," Tyler snapped.

Bhriana's eyes widen and she walked over to Tyler and draped her arms over his shoulders. "My my, aren't we uptight," Bhriana told him and stroked the back of his head. "My bedroom is right around that corner and I could relieve all this tension for you. And just think how fun it'll be because we don't have to worry about me getting pregnant," she said then broke out in laughter.

Tyler pushed her arms away. "No thank you. I made that mistake once back in May, Bhriana, and I'm not about to do it again."

Bhriana stepped back and placed a finger to her chin. "Hmmm...no...that wasn't May, Sweetie. It was March. I'll never forget that. Ever."

You know ain't nothing happen in March so chill and go in for the kill, Tyler encouraged himself.

Tyler walked away and sat on the sofa. He leaned back and his eyes roamed Bhriana's body. When their eyes met, Tyler licked his lips and said, "I'll never forget what you wore that day. You looked so hot in that light green bathing suit," he said then shook his head. "Shooot, you were packin' that outfit."

Bhriana blushed then added, "I did look good in that little two piece."

Tyler laughed aloud. "So you remember that too, huh?"

"Of course I remember. I'll never forget the way your mouth hit the floor when I untied my cover-up," Bhriana replied and sat down next to Tyler.

Tyler's smile faded as he maintained eye contact with her. "Why in the *hell* would you wear a skimpy behind bathing suit in March? Nobody around here, in their right mind, is gonna swim outdoors in March."

"But it was hot, remember?" Bhriana pleaded.

"You and whoever you had sex with may have been hot but the weather wasn't hot enough for me to hit the pool. So who's the baby's daddy, Bhriana?"

Smaaack.

Bhriana's open-handed slap surprised Tyler and the pain clung to the side of his face. He wanted to rub where it hurt but he didn't want to move his hands for fear of what else he might do with them.

"You're the father and how dare you accuse me of sleeping around," Bhriana said as she caressed the hand that landed the blow.

"I'm not accusing you, I am telling you that I'm not the father and unless this is some type of Virgin Mary thing, somebody nailed you in March."

Smaaack.

I'm sorry Mama but one more of those and I can't promise you that I'm gonna just walk away, Tyler thought as the pain traveled up the other side of his face. "Since you're so sure that I'm the baby's daddy, you won't have a problem with me taking a paternity test, right?"

"What?" Bhriana asked as she massaged her other hand.

"You heard me."

"You wouldn't, Tyler."

"Try me."

"That ghetto jock chick brainwashed you with this crap. Can't you see she's a liar? Can't you see what she's trying to do?" Bhriana asked as she shook her finger in Tyler's face.

Tyler stood up and towered over her. He gazed down at Bhriana and wondered how could anyone that pretty be so evil. "I know you hate Imani but I never understood why, until now. Just how far were you willing to go to keep Imani away from me?"

"What?"

"You paid Jazz to go out with Imani and now you're dangling a scholarship in her face."

"Pssst. Now I know that witch has turned you against me," Bhriana responded and began to cry. "Why do you always believe her?"

"So Jazz wasn't paid?"

"He was but I didn't do it. I swear I didn't," Bhriana pleaded. "You're always doubting me and then taking up for your so-called friends like her and Steven."

"Steven? What does he have to do this?"

"Since you're so smart, you tell me? Or, go and ask your ghetto psychic girlfriend since she knows every doggone thing."

Tyler exhaled loudly. "I'm tired of playing games and I'm tired of your lies. You have no chance of being with me so the truth won't hurt anymore."

Bhriana wiped away her tears. "The truth could hurt you, though."

"If you ever threaten Imani again, you will get hurt."

Tyler caught hold of Bhriana's right wrist as her hand reached within inches of his face. Within seconds, he grabbed her left wrist before it connected. He had no idea how strong Bhriana was until he tried to restrain her. He held on tight as she struggled to pull away. The sight of tears spilling from her hazel eyes didn't faze him. He continued to clench his hands around her flesh.

"You're hurting me!"

"I'm not letting you go until you tell me the real deal, Bhriana," Tyler said and squeezed even tighter.

"Ooouch, okaaay, okaaay, I'll tell you but don't hurt Steven's baby!"

Tyler felt the veins in his neck fill with blood. He imagined that his eyes were bloodshot. His sweaty palms slipped up Bhriana's wrist as she tried to pull away but he caught hold of her hands.

"Stop lyin' Bhriana!"

"The night of his party *he* nailed me, as you put it, and that same night he and Jazz made some type of deal. He paid Jazz, not me," she said between clenched teeth.

Tyler's fists loosened and he let Bhriana's small hands slide through them. His mind raced back to the portrait of Bhriana that Steven drew. He remembered the carbon copy of the check written out to Jazz.

"I'm not taking all the blame and I'm not going down all by myself. If you had been at that party, like Steven said you would be, none of this would have ever happened. I would have spent all my time with you instead of getting drunk with Steven and then him taking advantage of me."

"Take advantage of you?" he asked and eyed her up and down. "You gave it up to Steven because you wanted to and both of you screwed me."

"It didn't mean anything. I don't love Steven. I love you, Tyler."

Every time she opened her mouth, it was like Bhriana sucked the air out of the room. Tyler felt that he was about to suffocate. "I gotta get out of here before I throw up from all of the crap you keep dumping," he told Bhriana as he opened the door.

The sunlight crept through and landed directly on Bhriana. It was as if Tyler saw Bhriana for the first time and he hated what he discovered.

"Don't ever call me, write me, e-mail me, or fax me. Don't even send out a Morse code or a smoke signal. Just forget that I ever existed 'cause trust me, Bhriana, I will forget about you."

* * * *

Tyler blasted an oldie but goodie tune, "Back Stabber," while en route to Steven's home. The lyrics talked about how back stabbers smiled in your face but tried to do you in behind your back. Tyler's rage intensified as he translated that message to his own life. He replaced the words back stabbers with Bhriana and Steven. Supposedly, they were his friends and yet, they could have ruined not only his life, but also Imani's.

Once at Steven's door, Tyler rang the doorbell repeatedly. As soon as Steven's face was in full view, Tyler connected a powerful blow to it. He invited himself in and watched Steven try to regain his balance. When he stood erect, Tyler's fist plowed into Steven's stomach. "That's for Imani."

Steven fell to one knee. "What the hell are you talkin' about?"

"I never thought my boy would play me like that, Man!"

Tyler extended his arms and Steven covered up his already scarred face. Tyler grabbed him by the collar of his polo shirt and yanked Steven up to his feet. He wanted to punch him again but decided that by the way Steven looked, he had suffered enough. Tyler pushed him away and watched as Steven limped to the nearest chair.

"You better have a good reason for going ballistic on me, T-Man," Steven said and then coughed.

"Don't sit there and act like you don't know the deal," Tyler began. "But why, Man?" Tyler asked with outstretched arms. "How could you do that to me?" Tyler didn't wait for Steven to answer. Instead, he proceeded to tell Steven what he had found out from Bhriana. Steven's light complexion became even paler when Tyler got to the part that he got Bhriana pregnant.

"I don't remember having sex with your girl."

"Don't play that amnesia crap with me, Steven. Whether you remember or not, it happened. You were even stupid enough to draw the portrait as proof you did it to her. You want me to go to your room and get it?" Tyler asked as he pointed upstairs.

Steven shook his head.

"I can get that duplicate check you wrote out to Jazz while I'm at it."

Steven looked down at the carpet and shook his head again. "I can't deny the portrait or the check but I just don't remember doing those things."

"And because of that, I can't pounce on you the way I really want to. But don't ever let me find out that your memory is back 100% because I might be tempted to visit you one more time."

"Even if I did have sex with Bhriana-"

"If nothing Steven, you did!"

"Okay..." Steven said and grabbed his stomach as if in pain. "Even so, she's just one girl. You got what it takes to get any female you want. Don't let Bhriana bust us up."

"You broke our bond, Steven. You were like a brother to me," Tyler spat out and watched Steven's eyes glaze over. Tyler's throat tighten. He knew that he too was on the verge of a breakdown.

"It wasn't my fault, T. You see it was the alcohol and Bhriana was all over me, and..."

Tyler listened to Steven blame everybody and everything but himself. His anger diminished and he felt sorry for Steven. "Go get help, Steven," Tyler suggested and rose to his feet.

"What you gonna do? Hit me again? Will that even the score?"

Tyler looked down at Steven and then the door and knew that once he walked out, it would be the last time he'd ever see Steven.

"Naw," he answered as he headed towards the door. "But, Bhriana's gonna put a serious hurting on you. And, wait until that baby's born. Maaan, you're gonna get your butt kicked for the next eighteen years or more."

With all of his burdens transferred over to Steven, Tyler felt light and free, yet, drained from the day's bittersweet events. The heat was off him and out of the air. He could breathe again and the cool night air that filled his nostrils smelled great.

When Tyler walked into his home, he yelled out, "Dad, where are you? I need to talk to you."

"In the den," his father hollered back.

Tyler stood in the doorway and his father glanced up at him. He closed the cover on his laptop and asked, "How long have you been driving around by yourself with only a permit? You wanna be like Steven and have your driving privileges taken away? And, how long have you been sneaking out in my car?"

"Dad, I need to talk to you," Tyler repeated and walked into the room.

"And don't lie to me, Boy. I don't know what's gotten into you lately but you better straighten up," Mr. Powers continued and ignored Tyler's plea.

Tyler stood there, speechless. His father's tone and questions stung worst than Bhriana's slaps to his face.

"W-e-l-l-l, I'm waiting," his father said.

"Are you waiting for me to speak or are you waiting for another question or accusation to come to mind? I said that I need to talk to you and for once, can't you be quiet and listen?"

Tyler didn't take his eyes off his father as he stood up and walked around to the front of his cherry wood desk. He leaned against it and crossed his massive arms on his burly chest. "You may be man enough to get a girl pregnant but you'll never be old enough to speak to me that way. Understand?"

Tyler refused to back down from that familiar intimidating glare. He held onto his father's eyes so long that his own eyes burned. Tyler finally blinked and broke the silence.

"I hope you're not saying that I can never challenge your opinions or express my own. I hope you're not saying that we can never have a man-to-man conversation. And, I most definitely hope you're not sayin' that I can never make decisions on my own."

"Hold it," Mr. Powers said and held out his hand. "I know where this is headed but Son, the decision has already been made and you're gonna marry that girl."

"Is that the business deal you made with Mr. DuPree today?"

Mr. Powers stood up and looked down at his son. "What?"

"Oh come on Dad, I know that marriage thing was just as much a business deal as it was a moral call. After college, was I supposed to come back here and work with the two of you?"

"Maybe."

"Maybe? Well, did it ever occur to you that *maybe* I want no part of your business and that *maybe* I'm not the baby's daddy."

Mr. Powers' eyes widened.

"That's right. She admitted it's Steven's baby."

"Your buddy, Steven?"

"Ex-boy," Tyler snapped.

Mr. Powers shook his head from side to side as he mumbled, "Young love and deception." He stared at his son and asked, "What the heck is wrong with you teenagers today?"

Tyler sat down in the chair directly in front of his father. "I can't speak for all of us but I can tell you what's buggin' me."

"Son-"

Tyler held up his hand up. "I'm not finished."

"Okaaay, I won't say another word," Mr. Powers replied and sat in a chair next to his son and for once, listened.

FRIENDS – FOR REAL

It was a typical Saturday afternoon at West Fair Mall. The fast food restaurants, kiddie rides, record and video stores, and arcade were packed. The arcade was the first stop for Imani, Tyler, Fatima, and Hanif. Fatima and Hanif were engrossed in the auto racing video game while Imani and Tyler dueled it out at the "Hoop It Up" basketball game.

"The winner gets treated to lunch," Imani said.

"Including dessert," Tyler added.

"But let me warn you, I don't eat like a rabbit. I can put away some food," Imani said as she inserted her tokens into the machine.

Imani moved quickly as she fired the miniature basketballs at the mobile basketball hoop. She hadn't missed a shot as ball after ball swished through the center of the small hoop. When time expired, Imani had made twenty-one shots.

She turned to face a surprised looking Tyler and teased, "I'll start out with some appetizers before my main meal and then I'll ease into a brownie sundae."

"It ain't over yet," Tyler replied and grinned.

"I like a confident guy."

"And l like a player who talks trash and can back it up."

Imani raised her hand. "That's me."

Tyler landed a kiss on her cheek. "Yes it is."

Imani's eyes caught a hold of Tyler's and didn't let go until a high pitched voice broke her spell. "Can I play now?" asked a pint-sized boy who squeezed his way in between the tall couple. Imani smiled at the little kid whose black and red jersey hung like a gown on him. Tyler got down on one knee next to the boy.

"How would you like to be on my team?"

"Yeah!" the kid exclaimed.

Imani watched in amazement as Tyler hoisted the kid up onto his shoulders. The two did work as a team. Tyler fed the balls to the little guy and he tried his best to score. On the rare occasion when the ball went through, the kid screamed and Imani cheered him on.

"Hurry up, only 3 seconds left," she yelled.

"Alright!" they all shouted as the last shot beat the buzzer.

"Let's do it again," the kid said as Tyler lowered him to the floor.

"I've been looking all over for you," a woman said and grabbed onto the child's hand.

"But mommy-"

"Don't 'but mommy' me. You scared me to death. In a crowd like this, anybody could snatch you up. Don't you move away from my side again," the short woman warned and marched away.

The kid tried to keep up with his mother's fast pace as he looked over his shoulder at the same time. He waved to Imani and Tyler with his free hand.

"Isn't he cute?" Imani asked.

"I don't think she thinks he's so cute right now."

"That's a full-time job right there," Imani said.

"Yeah, a job that I'm not qualified for right now," Tyler said and waved back. "But, I can handle buying my lady lunch. Let's find Fatima and Hanif."

And ate they did. The foursome's table was covered with mozzarella sticks, onion rings, buffalo wings, chicken fingers and their accompanying sauces. Pitchers of soda, iced tea and water added to the clutter.

"How long you gonna feed that big baby?" Fatima asked Tyler as she watched her friend pig out.

"Until she's full."

"You're gonna burp her, too?" Fatima asked and everyone laughed.

Their waitress came over and removed the empty plates to make room for their main courses. After she walked away Hanif asked, "Speaking of babies, what the heck's goin' on with Bhriana and Steven?"

"Now why you gotta go and mess up everybody's appetite?" Fatima asked.

"I just reckoned that you and Sherlock would wanna know," Hanif said.

"That's your nickname for Imani?" Tyler asked.

"Yup, I wished you could have been there, Man," Hanif said then laughed.

Tyler didn't laugh and his expression was serious as he addressed his friends. "Imani didn't tell me what you guys did until after I confronted Bhriana."

"I didn't want him to slip up in the heat of the moment and tell her how he got that information. I didn't want Shonda to get into trouble," Imani said.

"I understand that part," Tyler began, "but I still can't believe you guys went through all of that trouble just for me."

"We couldn't stand by and watch you go out like that," Fatima said and the others agreed.

"You were like a chicken following feed to a slaughter house," Hanif chimed in.

"What?" the others asked in unison.

"You know, he was probably being set up so we had to get the facts for ourselves," Hanif said.

"Oooh," the trio said.

Tyler shook his head and told Hanif, "But you hardly know me-"

"I was just tryin' to help a brotha out. Plus, somebody had to watch out for Snoop and Sherlock here."

When the laughter subsided, Imani asked, "So what were you gonna tell us about Bhriana and Steven?"

"Y'all won't believe it," he said then placed his red straw into his mouth and sipped on his iced tea.

"Try us," Fatima said.

"Naaay," Tyler replied and went back to his beverage.

"Don't even try it," Fatima said.

All eyes begged Tyler to get on with the story. Finally, he proceeded to tell his friends how he heard that "Bhriana admitted that she had sex with both Steven and Justin in March and either one could be the baby's daddy."

"Steven?" Hanif asked.

"Uh hummm," Fatima began, "Imani already laid that news on me."

"Either way, Hanif, she's decided to give the baby up for adoption. She didn't want her baby to have an alcoholic father, even though Steven is in Alcoholics Anonymous, and she wasn't about to marry a poor boy like Justin."

"Will we ever know who the father is?" Imani asked.

"I heard that Steven is going to take a paternity test after the baby's born sometime in December."

"And this whole adoption thing was out of the question when she tried to pin this on you," Imani said.

"Well, obviously the girl needed help and I heard she's seeing a psychiatrist."

"Forget the shrink, all that demon needs is an exorcist," Fatima said.

"For real," Imani added.

"Maaan, I can't imagine what you went through with everybody siding with her," Hanif said.

"My father and I had a long talk about that and some other stuff." He turned to Imani. "By the way, he wants to invite you over for dinner one night."

"Me? Was that his idea or yours?"

"His because I kept talking about Imani this and Imani that and I guess he realized just how important you are to me."

"Oooh, don't make my mascara run," Fatima said as she dabbed at the corners of her eyes with a white paper napkin.

Imani sniffled.

"What did I say?" Tyler asked as he hunched up shoulders.

"Man, you know how women get all emotional."

Fatima punched Hanif on his upper arm and told Tyler to continue.

"Well, to make a long story short, he learned some things about me and I found out that parents try so hard to do what they think is best for you that they forget whose life it really is. When my father finally heard me, he realized that I thought about my own future and wasn't just sitting back waiting for him to tell me what to do next."

"Did you talk about black colleges?" Imani asked.

"Yeah, and instead of a flat out no, he put the ball in my court. He told me to present him with information about the ones that I was interested in attending and why and then we'll take it from there."

"While y'all in college, I'll be in beauty school," Fatima began. "Imani and Hanif keep braggin' about my skillz and they right. That's what I love to do and one day I want my own salon." Fatima looked at Tyler then Hanif and added, "No offense brothas but I can't be countin' on y'all to support my diva lifestyle."

"Hey now," Imani said and exchanged high fives with Fatima.

"That's great but I think you should take some business courses so you'll be ready to run your own company," Hanif suggested.

"He's right, Fatima. You could take a class or two at night at the community college," Imani added and everyone nodded.

"Alright y'all, stop ridin' me like Grandma Rose and gimme some time to think about that."

The waitress came with her arms and hands full of plates. She memorized who ordered what and sat the entrees before the guests. Different aromas of burgers, pizza, fish fillets, and fries mingled before them.

"I wanted to wait but now's a great time to tell you guys that-"

"That what?" Fatima asked.

"Well, Tyler already knows."

"I can't believe you haven't told them, yet," Tyler said to Imani.

"I was waiting for the right moment and-"

"And what?" Fatima and Hanif yelled in unison.

"That I'll be graduating from Westmoore next year. I got the scholarship!"

"I know you ain't been holding out on me, Girrrl," Fatima said before she stood up and hugged her friend.

"I just found out today," Imani managed to say in between the congratulatory hugs and kisses from her friends.

"I'm proud of you, Girrrl," Fatima said then sucked her teeth. "But, I knew you had it wrapped up all along."

"And I know that you know how relieved I am. My mother's probably told the whole congregation by now."

"Yeah...Mrs. Jackson's out there tootin' your horn," Fatima replied and the girls laughed while the guys looked puzzled.

"Seriously though, thanks for believing in me, Fatima, even when I didn't."

"I don't need no raccoon eyes so don't get me started."

It was a while before everyone settled down and got back to their food. Well, everyone except Tyler who still had not touched his plate. "Hanif," he called out and got his attention. "Not every body was against me, Man. My beautiful lady here stood by me," Tyler said and kissed Imani. When their lips separated Tyler said, "I call this one, 'Thank You'

> Thanks for being there
> and showing me just how much
> a for real friend cares."

"Oooh, I know he ain't just whip a poem on my girl like that," Fatima said and then watched her best friend blush. "I ain't no poet so I'm just gonna keep it plain and simple. Thank you too, Girl 'cause you've kept me from blowin' up a couple of times."

"How many times?"

Fatima rolled her eyes. "Oh alright, most of the time but being for real, I couldn't have made it through that whole Money and Mad D. thing without you."

"I can't take all the credit. Hanif helped too," Imani replied. She caught hold of Hanif's eyes and told him, "You're a really cool brotha and good lookin' out for my girl." Imani took a deep breath and added, "'Cause Lord knows I need help keepin' her out of trouble-"

"I ain't no trouble."

"It was nothing. I would do it all over again if I had to but I hope I don't because I hope someone put a call into the police like she said she would," Hanif spat out in a single breath.

"I ain't down with all that drama. Of course, I gave them the 4-1-1 on the down low, though."

Hanif's greasy lips met her shiny ones. "Thanks, Baby."

"Plueeeze, let's not even breathe the word 'baby' again," Tyler said.

"I don't wanna hear that word until I'm thirty-something," Imani said.

"Dang skippy," Fatima chimed in and raised her glass of soda.

Imani stood and raised her glass and the others followed. "Here's to my old friend and my new ones. Let's keep it real."

ABOUT THE AUTHOR

Born and raised in Newark, New Jersey, Jackie Hardrick is still a Jersey girl. She attended Newark's public elementary and high schools. Jackie, an alumna of Seton Hall University, is dedicated to giving back to society by writing "what's happening now" novels & poetry for teenagers that are inspiring, entertaining, and enlightening.

The author is hard at work on a new novel and a collection of poetry...just for all of you.

3 Easy Ways to Order Imani in Young Love & Deception
(Book & Discussion Guide)

1. Call Toll-Free 24 hours/day, 7 days/week: **866-862-8626**
2. E-mail: jackie.hardrick@enlightenpublications.com
3. Regular Mail: Fill out order form, place in envelope with money order or credit card info, affix postage stamp, & send to:
    Enlighten Publications, PO Box 525, Vauxhall, NJ 07088

Whichever method you use, please provide the following information: Your name, Address, Phone # include area code, Method of payment, if charging, Account # & Expiration date, & sign if by mail. Make Money Orders payable to Enlighten Publications, state item quantities. *(Sorry, we cannot deliver to P.O. Boxes)*

*10% Discount on 10+ Book order - *Guide not counted as a Book*

Name *(Please Print):*

Address:

City:

State: Zip Code:_____

Day Phone: (   )_____

E-Mail Address:

   Circle Method of Payment: Money Order, Visa, Mastercard, American Express or Discover Card   (No Checks or Cash)

Charge Acct. #__ __ __ __ __ __ __ __ __ __ __ __ __ __ __ __

Expiration Date: __ __ /__ __

Signature as it appears on card _____

(IYLD5/01)

ITEM	QTY.	UNIT PRICE	TOTAL PRICE
*Book	_____	$14 each	_____.____
Discussion Guide	_____	$ 4 each	_____.____
		SUBTOTAL	_____.____
*If Book Qty.=10 or more Deduct 10%			(_____.____)
		ADJUSTED SUBTOTAL	_____.____
(see chart below) **SHIPPING CHARGE**			_____.____
6% SALES TAX (NJ RESIDENTS ONLY)			_____.____
Allow 1 - 2 weeks for delivery		**TOTAL $**	._

Shipping Charge: Adjusted or Subtotal   (Outside of U.S. call for shipping info.)

Up to … $16 ….. Add $2.00	$90.01 - $120 ….. Add $5.50
$16.01 - $30 ….. Add $2.50	$120.01 - $160 ….. Add $6.50
$30.01 - $60 ….. Add $3.50	$160.01 - $300 ….. Add $9.00
$60.01 - $90 ….. Add $4.50	Orders over $300 call for shipping info.